SILENCE

ALSO BY ANTHONY QUINN

The Blood Dimmed Tide
Blind Arrows

The Celcius Daly Mysteries

Disappeared
Border Angels

SILENCE

ANTHONY QUINN

MYSTERIOUSPRESS.COM

Cover design by Mauricio Díaz

ISBN 978-1-4976-6587-3

Published in 2016 by MysteriousPress.com/Open Road Integrated Media, Inc.
180 Maiden Lane
New York, NY 10038
www.mysteriouspress.com
www.openroadmedia.com

To Monsignor Denis Faul, my former headmaster and teacher, whose dogged search for the truth inspired this book

SILENCE

PROLOGUE

South Armagh, 1974

The afternoon light shuddered and all the black treachery of the winter sky, the rain clouds hurrying from west to east, condensed into the shape of a perfect downpour, a vertical altar of water cascading over the figures of the policemen bent to their grim task in the river. Dressed in waterproof blue overalls, the four officers had settled into such a rhythm of immersion and interrogation that they barely noticed the fizz of the raindrops on the river's surface, the rods of water drilling upon their backs.

Like brethren performing a difficult baptism, they heaved together once again, and hauled the body from the water. It was a young man with lank black hair sticking to his face. The greyness of his skin, the defeated grimace on his face and the way in which his arms hung limply at his sides suggested he had already drowned; however, when one of the policemen yanked back the youth's hair, the grimace writhed into life, spattering water from his mouth and nostrils.

'The river's much deeper today, Daniel,' said the officer gripping him by the hair. 'We almost lost hold of you there.'

Gulping for air, Daniel twisted his head round and peered into the driving rain.

'Get to the point,' he said thickly. Water gleamed everywhere, churning his vision of the river and their overalls into splinters.

'Headquarters want you to work for us now.'

'Yesterday I was a murder suspect. Things change very quickly with you people.'

'Oh, things have changed. That's definitely the case.'

The policeman plunged Daniel's head back into the river so quickly that bubbles streamed from his nostrils and the water boiled around him. The first immersion had been the longest. A way to get the interrogation going, to ensure he listened to their questions. With each dunking, he had felt his body grow heavier and colder. The policemen tightened their hold and his face slid back to the surface.

'Have you read today's newspapers?' The officer's eyes blinked white in the rain.

'Not this morning. Missed them.' The face Daniel wore was a blank, borrowed from the stones at the bottom of the river. 'What did they say?'

'A van of workmen were killed yesterday evening by a bomb. The paramilitaries are on a war footing. Things are getting out of hand.'

With weary tenacity, they pushed Daniel's head underwater, and this time he welcomed the immersion. His thoughts descended into secret chambers of coldness, guided by the hands of his interrogators. Normally when he lied, some facial tic betrayed him, but now the freezing temperature of the river jarred his body, overwhelming the delicate signals even a trained liar could not control.

When he re-emerged, he felt detached and disorientated. The rain chipped the surface of the river, filling his low vision with flint-like drops. Along the banks, the shapes of blackthorn trees seemed to float as light as bubbles against the darkness. In keeping with his blurred view, the voices of the policemen sounded garbled, broken into echoes by the roar of the river.

'We have questions.'

'Fire ahead.' He was unable to control his shivering.

'How many more innocent people have to die?'

'Why should it matter to you?'

'Trust us on this. It matters.'

Daniel knew that more killings were going to happen, tit for tat, an eye for an eye. Mass killings will happen, he wanted to tell his interrogators. Great numbers of dead will mount up, he wanted to blurt out through his trembling lips. It was only a question of time. Ruthless men were waiting in the wings, the shootings so far just the tentative rehearsals for widespread terror. It was the only way out of this stalemate, all this political weakness and confusion.

'We have a message from Major Hannon.' The officer's eyes were empty but his voice was intense. 'He wants your secrets, Daniel. The things that run through your mind before you fall asleep.'

'You can tell him I haven't slept in weeks.'

He shut his eyes and held his breath as they pushed him under. He was getting used to their rhythm. This time they dipped him so close to the riverbed he could feel the sharp edges of its rocks against his face.

When he returned to the surface, the human wall huddled closer.

'Tell us what you know while you can still speak. Who are the IRA targeting next? Where are they hiding their weapons?'

'Don't know.' His panting chest lifted his body up and down in their arms. He was so numb he could barely spit out the words.

'Then tell us their names.'

'Can't.'

'Shane Mulligan, who owns the fertilizer business on the border. We know he's a key operator.'

'Don't know who you're talking about.'

He almost passed out so long was the subsequent immersion. The river was flowing at full tilt and his shoulders buckled under the weight of its current.

He was frantic for air when he re-emerged. He gulped and retched, but before he could fill his lungs, they forced him under again. When he resurfaced, he spluttered with anger and desperation.

'You made a mistake,' he told them when he had recovered. 'You didn't ask me a question. You pushed me in again. You're meant to ask a question first.'

They shrugged and laughed. He could hear them whispering

together, and then a gun prodded him, nuzzling the back of his neck. He tried not to register its presence. They had stopped speaking. The press of the gun was their new form of communication, the solitary signal that they were still deliberating what to do with him. The gun nudged against his sodden hair and swung into view. He stared up at its point-blank eye. He felt weightless, held up by their arms in the rushing water. He was out of his depth completely, he realized.

'We're asking you now, Daniel. It's time to talk. This is your last chance.'

The gun gaped before him, and his heart almost stopped. Everything slowed down with the clarity of approaching death: the toiling of the river, the jolts of raindrops crashing on its surface, the bulging eyes of his interrogators, their bodies anchored against the buckling currents, and beyond, the unfathomable darkness of the blackthorn trees.

Slowly, the hand pulled the trigger. Daniel clenched his teeth, but the mechanism did not fire. The only thing still afflicting him was the fierceness of the rain. Even their eyes had turned away. The rush of fear slowly passed. He stared at the fast-flowing river, feeling a sudden appreciation for its chastening beauty.

The policemen retreated, dragging his body on to the muddy bank. They left him there and stepped back, resting a while under the shelter of the overhanging trees. Their shadowy figures quivered in the downpour and then they were gone. Daniel listened above the gasping of his chest and the drumming of the rain. He heard the sound of their Land Rover starting up, the whine of its engine, the swish of its tyres along a flooded road.

He felt stronger when he realized he had survived their interrogation. Soaking wet and triumphant, he pushed his way through the thicket towards the road.

He wheeled around when he heard a voice call him through the thorns. A clamour of caws broke from the overhead branches and then all was quiet. He waited, listening intently. The rain had stopped but the ground still sizzled with drops falling from the canopy of branches. Several moments passed. The cold was setting in and he felt dazed. He stumbled on, clearing a path with his arms.

A branch cracked nearby and the voice spoke again.

'You were lucky today, Daniel Hegarty.'

The voice seemed to emanate from deep within the thorns.

'Who are you?'

The voice did not answer. He pushed towards it on groggy legs, feeling a secret force tugging him. The voice had a power, an edge to it. A man's body drifted alongside him through a screen of branches and disappeared.

The voice sank deeper into the thicket.

'The policemen will be here for you tomorrow and the day after that,' it warned. 'They're taking their time to practise their aim, their choice of questions, their interrogation skills. Some day, they'll shoot you out of impatience, if they don't drown you first.'

The blackthorn tips seemed to ooze a deeper coldness than the river, leaving him dizzied and frozen to the spot. Instinctively, his hands clawed at the branches, searching for a way out, but then he stopped. Somehow, he found room in his head for the thought that the voice wanted to help him out of his predicament. He held his breath, waiting for it to continue.

'You have to tell me who you are.'

A gust of wind shook a silver pattern of raindrops from the branches. Daniel stood still, his ear hunting the trail of the voice, waiting for it to begin talking again in its secret way. Waiting was part of its game, he realized. It wanted him to dangle in its silence.

'I'm the recruiting agent for a special intelligence service.'

This time the voice spoke from behind him. Daniel had the impression that it had been circling him, trying to make him lose his bearings. He scanned his surroundings, the river coiling in its shadows, the trees tossing darkly, the patches of sky full of travelling cloud.

'My name is Major George Hannon.'

'What do you want from me?'

'I want to give you the opportunity to remedy your failures.'

'What do you mean my failures?'

'Your failure to stop your brother's murder. Your failure to die alongside him. Your failure to heal your parents' grief.'

A wave of pain and anger welled within him. The immersion in the river had felt like a numbing relief to his grief, but this was something else. His mind was stunned and sharpened by the major's words. He hadn't realized his appetite for revenge was so strong.

'You are in great danger, Daniel. There's nowhere else for you to go. The police are arresting all your friends, throwing them in jail, without trial. And they're the lucky ones. Have you visited the local cemetery recently?'

'I was there on Sunday. If the grave is good enough for my brother it's good enough for me.'

'What about your poor mother and father? Who will look after them?'

'If that's the way it is, so be it.'

'It doesn't have to be like that.'

'What other choice do I have?'

A pair of eyes appeared through the web of thorns and raindrops. A pair of eyes that gave nothing away. The rest of the man's face was camouflaged in shadow.

'You're freezing,' he said.

Daniel nodded, and an upright military-looking man stepped out of the undergrowth. Removing his leather gloves, the man took a cigarette from a packet in his pocket. He handed it to Daniel, stilling his shaking hand so that he might light it.

The young man's mind slowly recovered from the cold, the deep drowsiness of the river. He took several drags.

'Listen to me,' said the man. 'This country of ours is all about gangs. Everyone belongs to one. Some join gangs that do bad things. Steal cars, smuggle weapons, plant bombs, terrify the wits out of innocent people. But some of us manage to drag ourselves up to the light and join a different sort of gang.' His voice altered. 'I want to make you, Daniel Hegarty, a member of the most effective, well-resourced gang this fucked-up country has ever seen.'

Daniel felt as though he had been plunged into a more suffocating pool, immersed in the man's warmth and charm, his aura of power, the sweetness of the tobacco smoke. He clasped his hand as it held the cigarette to his chest, trying to stop his arm from shaking. He felt the intensity of a pinpoint gaze, the man's eyes adjusting to all his little movements, steady as the magnetic needle of a compass, centring in on the flaw, the tic he had managed to conceal from his riverside interrogators.

'I'm not for sale.' He raised the cigarette to his lips, fingers clenched tight. 'All I need is this smoke.'

The voice sighed.

'Everyone has a price, Daniel. That's a fundamental truth.'

Water collected on the tips of thorns, glinting like tiny claws. The wind picked up and the thorns swiped at it.

'Why are you interested in me?'

'We've nobody on the ground in border country. We want you to work for us. You'll be operating alongside people just like you. People who have lost family members. People who feel compelled to action, who want to stop terrorism in all its forms, all these senseless murders.'

'"Stop terrorism in all its forms." Is that your way of convincing me I won't be a traitor?' However, something tight swelled in Daniel's throat – not fear, but a dark hope, the thought that he might have his revenge for his brother's murder after all.

'We'll pay you well, look after your parents. You won't have to worry about their security.'

The mention of money sparked his interest further. He knew he couldn't go on living the way he had been, sleepless, jobless, practically penniless, relying on the small income his parents made from their farm. A twilight existence, dominated by fear and humiliation.

'I sense you're interested in my offer.'

'I'll think about it.'

'That's good, Daniel. We all have to do our bit. Get this country back to law and order.'

Daniel snorted.

'Some law and order. Your policemen almost drowned me.'

'They took the wrong approach entirely. I can see that now.'

'No more fucking around with water, then?'

'You have my word.'

'And will you leave me alone?'

'I can't promise you that.' The major smiled. 'Go home and think about what I have said. I promise you that our training is first-class. We've been running this unit for decades in far more dangerous parts of the world. We'll train you in man-to-man surveillance techniques and how to shake off paramilitary scrutiny of your movements. Remember, our war is directed at Loyalists as well as Republicans.'

He handed Daniel the rest of the packet of cigarettes.

'A boom is on its way, Daniel. A boom in killing. Tons of illegal weapons are coming into the country. From South Africa, Libya, the Lebanon. The intelligence services are predicting a surge in violence.'

Daniel nodded. It was the solemn truth. He flicked open the packet of cigarettes. Inside was a calling card with a number and a contact name and next to it a wad of ten-pound notes. He looked up, but the major had gone.

He scrambled back to the road feeling tired and cold. His car was parked next to where the police officers had set up their checkpoint. He turned on the heater and the windscreen wipers. The empty road seemed more unreal than the thicket of thorns and the fast-flowing river. He started up the engine, and drove his usual route home. That was the thing about living in border country, he told himself, you had to acclimatize yourself to intimidation, develop a regular routine, get used to the uncertainty of living each day suspended between fear and suspicion, life and death, somehow surviving these impromptu checkpoints and interrogations.

He drove on, delving deeper into the maze of introverted little lanes that criss-crossed the border. He wasn't ready to go home, not yet. The roads had the dull, soothing quality of loneliness, their broken white lines glimmering in the rain. Dripping trees slashed backward and forwards. He listened to the hiss of water sliding along the wipers, coiling from the tyres. He drove as if still caught in a whirling current, trees flickering by, the windscreen a river of ghostly reflections, the twisting lines of the border roads luring him deeper into their darkness.

He already felt like an outcast in this country. A condemned man. The landscape and weather hated him. The freezing rivers, the blinding rain, the tattered hole of the sky through which the sun infrequently shone, the roads that threatened to empty him every time he pressed his foot to the accelerator pedal. No wonder his neighbours and friends were leaving in their droves, those who weren't dead or in prison, emigrating to England and America, never to return. They left in silence, without uttering a word or fighting with anyone. Many of them had been in the middle of building new homes, like his brother. Their half-finished houses dotted the countryside, building sites overgrown with briars and nettles, wastes of muddy puddles. He did not want to go to England or America but he did not want to be left behind either, amid their abandoned dreams.

He knew with certainty that in the weeks ahead, there would be more interrogations at checkpoints, more smiling men like Major Hannon, more pestering, more harassment and insinuation, more whispering about failure and revenge, and the dire consequences of his inaction. He began to think there must be some other way to leave behind these hills and their sprawling thickets of thorns, this warren of roads disappearing into tunnels in the dark.

The rain intensified. He switched off the wipers. It was cosy in the driver's seat as he moved up through the gears. He peered through the web of raindrops densely crowding the windscreen. He came quickly upon a blind corner and pressed the accelerator pedal as hard as he could. The car skidded as he took the bend. He had the impression of blurred branches sailing close to the car, a few seconds of flight, and then the crunch of gravel as the wheels bit into the verge, and the car corrected itself.

He drove off again, foot pressed flat against the accelerator. He took the next corner at even greater speed. Again, the car teetered. The engine whined and the wheels locked into a spin. He was no longer in control, the speed of the car dragging him on. He shut his eyes, waiting for the brute force of the impact, but instead of noise, everything went silent. He felt the darkness beyond the thin shield of the windscreen erupt in upon him, and then an overwhelming force lifted him out of his seat. For a moment, fragments of broken glass and thorns rose with him. He felt so pure and free that he grinned with delight. He forgot about the cold business of the river and its trees dripping darkness and betrayal. He willed himself up towards the tranquillity of the night sky, up and up, but then he butted against the stubbornness of his flesh and blood. He felt himself dragged back to the crashed car and the lonely black mass of anger that was his heart.

When he came to, he lay slumped over the steering wheel. The car had slid down a gully and crashed into a tree. He gaped at the hole where a branch had smashed through the windscreen. Inside he felt disappointed. It was not as easy as he thought to escape border country. A few lights flashed on the dashboard but his head felt too light to understand their instructions. Perhaps they were warning signals. He swung open the door and staggered out. His thoughts felt mangled. He climbed back up the slope and sat hunched by the roadside, trying to quell his giddiness.

He set off, head bowed, unsure of which direction he was going, until a passing car slowed down. In the twilight, he could just make out the car registration – AIB 726. He recognized the young woman behind the wheel, a neighbour who had recently lost her brother in an IRA attack. Her name was Dorothy Agnew. He looked at her, wondering if she would recognize him. She smiled at him and instinctively he waved back. She held her chin up bravely, but her eyes were downcast, her smile still carrying the shadow of her grief. To his surprise, she stopped and gave him a lift home.

After she had dropped him off at his gate, he felt confused. He had been close to ending his life, but somehow her smile and act of kindness had filled his mind with new confidence, new conviction. In the course of their short conversation, he had told her about his brother's murder at the hands of Loyalists and she had responded with sympathy and curiosity. They were both survivors from different sides of the community, they realized, falling through border country with their anger and grief. Why should either of them shoulder this darkness alone? His mind began to burn with the new plan he was formulating. The business with the major seemed more urgent now. He would give Hannon a phone call and outline his requirements. He was going to cross invisible boundaries into a new mental landscape, one where he would roam with killers and psychopaths. His thoughts grew luminous, purposeful, contemplating the dark path that lay ahead.

1

February 2013

Thoreau's line – the question is not what you look at, but what you see – was a favourite of Inspector Celcius Daly's, not just because it said something about detective work, but also because it described the way in which he and his fellow citizens were dealing with their country's conflicted past. Daly lived between two views of the Troubles, the one he saw with his eyes wide open and the one he saw with his eyes firmly shut. He had trusted the former over the latter ever since childhood, but every now and again the unruly brew of his subconscious, imagination or his dreaming threw up a suppressed memory or an old secret that threatened to disrupt the carefully edited view.

It had not taken much to set him off that wintry night at the start of February. He was preparing to go to bed when the call came through. He listened to the details: a single-vehicle car crash, a line of misplaced traffic cones and a dead motorist. A freak accident, he thought, the result of too much speed, alcohol or the driver falling asleep at the wheel.

He drove through Maghery and headed towards Dungannon. Soon he was on the new motorway. He took a deep breath and eased the car into top gear. There was a full moon and the empty carriageway stretched westwards towards the border, a vaulted path of tar and concrete bridges shining in the moonlight.

For decades, the Irish and British governments had neglected the border roads, allowing them to fall into ruin, but ever since the ceasefire, they had been at pains to reverse the decline. Gone were the checkpoints, the military fortifications, the sabotaged roads and blown-up bridges. New carriageways were replacing the meandering roads that had once made even a short trip along the disputed frontier feel like a trek through a labyrinth.

Inexorably, he thought, *the crooked little lanes of my troubled country are disappearing. Soon there will be none of them left. Soon there will be no more getting lost on by-roads, no more skulking in shadowy places; soon there will be nothing left but straight roads with no hiding places.*

He flicked his headlights on to full beam and accelerated, the lamps scouring the darkness ahead. Perhaps this was the freedom everyone had been fighting for during the Troubles, he thought, the freedom to drive all night, free and fearless, on wide roads without ever coming to the end of one's tether.

The motorway cut through a narrow valley, and Daly crossed a bridge. He glanced through his side window, and saw the old country below, felt its dark gravity, its mesh of forgotten roads, its interlocking parishes of grief and murder. He had spent the last seven years policing this part of Northern Ireland, and it was a relief to be carried on so many tonnes of concrete and steel above its shadows; everything below was crime and violence, age and death, loose bits of the past squirming their way through the darkness.

He had relaxed into a state approaching drowsiness when his car swayed a little, buffeted by crosswinds. The central reservation loomed closer. He was surprised to see how much his car had drifted across the lanes. He tapped his brakes and gripped the steering wheel. That was the problem with feeling afloat on such an elevated road, he thought: it made you forget your precariousness in this world.

The motorway cut deeper through the countryside as he approached the border, and the terrain grew rockier, bleaker. He slowed on reaching the final uncompleted section. Roadwork diversion signs redirected traffic on to side roads, but Daly ignored them. He held firm. Ahead, his headlights picked out the broad tract where diggers had been tearing a hole through the hills that formed the border with the Republic. His tyres rumbled over the uneven surface. He eased his car up the last hundred yards or so to where the tape of the police cordon fluttered amid the warning lights.

He stared through the windscreen, taking his measure of the scene. At first, all he could pick out beyond the signs and flickering lights were heaps of soil, denuded rock and digging machines, which, perched on the dark mounds of earth, seemed to float over the chaos. Then he saw the moving figures. Men and women in uniforms, walking about with flashlights.

He was back in border country.

'What happened?' Daly asked the young officer in charge of the crash site. It took him several moments to work out the sequence of events. The officer and his colleagues had arrived at the roadworks shortly before 10 p.m. to investigate a report of criminal damage to the diggers. They discovered that the vandals had also removed the diversion signs and rearranged the traffic cones into a lane that would have guided unsuspecting motorists straight over a precipice. Immediately, they had set up a cordon and checkpoint.

It was a dangerous prank, explained the officer, especially in the dark. He and his colleagues had been removing the cones when an elderly driver pulled up. For some inexplicable reason, he had ignored the police cordon and driven off at speed, almost knocking over one of the officers.

That was his first error, said the policeman. His second and fatal mistake had been to steer a path through the rearranged cones without once tapping his brakes.

'The poor bastard went over the edge into a thicket of thorns thirty feet below,' he added. 'He seemed to drive off in some sort of panic.'

Daly stared at the road swimming in a trickery of light and reflective signs. He saw the line of shining cones, and at their end the pool of darkness into which a car and a life had vanished. A fatal diversion masquerading as an escape route. Road accidents were usually a combination of bad luck and stupidity, but what had made the elderly man disdain the advice of law and order?

'I wonder what frightened him so badly?' he asked the officer, scrutinizing his young face.

'I don't know. A guilty conscience?' The officer shrugged. 'Did I mention he was a priest? A Roman Catholic priest. He was wearing a dog collar. According to our records, his name was Father Aloysius Walsh.'

Daly raised an eyebrow. The worst, the blackest reading of the driver's actions was that he had a secret to hide and feared arrest. It was the simplest explanation for his behaviour, but Daly suspected that given the history of this part of the country, and the fact that the dead man had been a cleric, the truth might turn out to be a little more complicated.

Daly took the officer through his conversation with Walsh. Perhaps he had let slip a word that had agitated him. Doubtless a priest of his age had seen and witnessed a lot, especially during the Troubles. In addition, the media were hounding many elderly priests over their handling of clerical child-abuse cases. God only knew what was going through his mind when he saw the police cordon in the darkness.

The officer stitched together the sequence of events, and the words he had spoken, but Daly failed to detect any hint of menace in them.

'I just warned him the road was blocked and a diversion in place,' he said.

'What were you doing while you spoke?'

'Warming my hands. It was a cold night.' There was something appealing about his honesty and the patience with which he answered Daly's questions. 'He gave me a strange look. As though he recognized me. But I'd never seen him before.'

'And your colleagues. What were they doing?'

'They were repositioning the traffic cones.'

Daly glanced at the men, who were dressed in blue overalls and standing by the side of the road, more like a huddle of suspects than investigating officers.

'Why aren't they in uniform?' he asked.

'We'd just come from an illegal fuel plant. They hadn't time to change out of their protective gear.'

Daly nagged him with more questions. Was there a car following the priest? Did he seem anxious from the start or only after the officer started speaking? Was he in a hurry, anxious to be on his way? Did he seem a stranger to the area, unsure of his surroundings?

The officer answered the questions as best he could.

'Are you going to check the car itself, sir?' he asked helpfully.

Daly, however, was unwilling to let the subject drop.

'Did you smell any alcohol on his breath? Any sign of drugs? Was his car the first you stopped? What about the vandals, any leads there?'

However, none of the policeman's answers provided a satisfactory explanation for his priest's actions. Daly could detect nothing that might have made Walsh feel pressured or threatened, frightened or worried, certainly not desperate enough to break a police cordon.

'Perhaps he was depressed,' suggested the officer.

'Depressed people don't behave that rashly,' said Daly. 'Their illness makes them averse to risk or spur-of-the-moment behaviour. If they commit suicide it's usually planned meticulously.'

Daly bent under the cordon and walked towards the traffic cones. The flash of a camera lit up the scene. A police photographer stood to the side, attempting to capture the confusion with his lens. Daly frowned. He turned back to the group of officers in blue overalls. He thought he detected a look of wariness in their faces. He strode on. The warning lights thronged the sides of his vision, hemming him in. The police officers emitted their signals, too, their defensive stance, their eyes shadowed, another set of potential pitfalls to be ignored by motorists at their peril.

For a moment, Daly felt as though he was standing outside of time, in a zone without road markings or warning lights, a no man's land, with only dim memories of the past to guide him. He felt a change in his body chemistry. His heart rate increased to a painfully fast tempo, and a line of sweat formed on his forehead. Teetering on the edge of panic, he glanced at his watch, more in an effort to ground himself than to check the time. The police officers stared at him, their faces watchful, curious. He saw himself through their eyes. A middle-aged detective, greying, haunted by the darkness of an unfinished road.

He was at a loss to explain why, but he suddenly found himself running along the route marked by the traffic cones. If he had been in his car, he might have accelerated just as the dead priest had done. But why? What had triggered this feeling of incipient doom? He was forty-three years old, and had spent almost half his life unravelling crime scenes more confused and gruesome than the one he now found himself in, but something about it troubled him deeply. His eyes swivelled as he ran, taking in the innocent-seeming details of the roadblock, the four policemen, three of them in overalls, the row of traffic cones pointing towards death. What was it about them that seemed to speak darkly of a mystery in his country's troubled past? He felt as though he was hurrying towards something that no one had approached for decades. A lost secret. A crashed car at the edge of the Irish border and a dead body.

Daly saw the tyre markings cutting through the grass, and down below the glinting boot lid of the wrecked car, tilted at an unnatural angle. He fastened on to it with the intensity of someone who'd witnessed this before, in circumstances that had been both unexpected and emotionally overwhelming. Relief flooded through him when he made out the rest of the car in the beam of the flashlight – a silver Audi with long scrape marks along its sides – as if he had been anticipating another car, another body. The panic subsided completely by the time he had scrambled down the bank and peered in through the driver's broken window. He saw pieces of broken glass on the leather upholstery, but no sign of the priest's body. The force of the impact must have propelled him through the smashed windscreen.

He plunged further into the thicket, head bowed, arms fending off branches, and came across the body in a small clearing padded with moss and old leaves. Daly leaned closer with his torch, the thorns bristling around his face. The rain had webbed the dead man's hair to his scalp, the pattern of slick strands resembling roads criss-crossing a map. Apart from scratches and grazes, there was very little sign of blood on his downturned face, which wore a tired expression, or on the rest of his body, sprawled and helpless-looking, his legs sticking out like crooked piping. He looked unhappy to have ended up like this, a grisly spectacle of motoring misdirection.

However, the most poignant element of the scene lay in the strange object the dead man gripped in his right hand. Daly narrowed the beam on to the stiffened fingers, which were wrapped around an untidy braid of children's rosary beads and holy medals, strands of charms tied up with wisps of broken string. He stared at this twisted pigtail of religious effects and wondered what significance they had held for the dead priest. Did they represent a cry for spiritual assistance, or something more sinister? Some of the beads had rusted over, suggesting their original owners had long ago abandoned them. Did they hold the clue to the mental flux that had set the priest on his final journey?

The more Daly looked at the strange bundle, the more it spoke to him of something more personal: his own religion. Although he was an infrequent Mass-goer, the rituals and imagery of Catholicism were still firmly planted in his memory, lodged there like an entangled obstruction, resistant to all the turmoil he had undergone in the intervening years. He didn't like to think of himself as a lapsed Catholic, rather that the course of his life had taken him to the margins of his faith. He still felt the soothing power of the Church's symbols, the rosary beads and the miraculous medals, and he worried that if he removed them completely from his life, he might find himself pulled down a tapering funnel into a deeper darkness. Worse than that, he feared the horrors that might emerge from the depths of his subconscious if he were to clear away the obstruction.

He wondered what the priest had seen amid those dishevelled strings and beads. He knew enough of the human condition to understand that for a priest, the life of selfless dedication to God could prove a very troubled sea. Even the holiest of men might find themselves occasionally flung upon a strange shore, battered and lost.

A branch cracked nearby. Daly pulled himself away from the corpse. Perhaps the bundle meant nothing to the investigation. Perhaps it had more relevance to his own spiritual life, or lack of one. He made his way back to the crash site and saw the figure of a man in plain clothes standing to the side of the car.

At first, Daly could not see who it was, since he kept his head turned away. An unmoving shadow concentrating on something in the darkness. Daly shone his torch on to the back of his head and the man turned round. His eyes blinked in the light. It was Detective Derek Irwin from Special Branch.

'Lost in thought?' asked Daly, his voice sounding more annoyed than he intended.

'No, just checking my messages.' Irwin flashed his mobile phone. He ignored Daly and stared at the device, his thumb stroking the screen in an obstinate way, as though he were trying to get rid of an annoying wrinkle. Ever since he'd been recruited by Special Branch, Irwin had developed the unpleasant habit of hovering at the edge of Daly's investigations, and behaving in wilful ignorance of correct police procedures. It constantly perplexed Daly how Irwin managed to maintain, let alone advance, his career in the special investigations unit.

'Special Branch quiet these days?' asked Daly.

'Not really.' As Irwin spoke his phone peep-peeped and died. He juggled the device and slid it back into his pocket.

'Then why are you attending a road fatality? Did Fealty send you here?' Fealty was Head of Special Branch, and a different animal entirely from Irwin, leaner and more professional with a razor-blade smile and an icy stare. Daly's career had survived several run-ins with him.

'I heard the call come through from switchboard.' Irwin yawned. 'I thought it might be worth a look.'

'Hell of an evening to come out for just a look.'

Daly glanced grimly at the thorn trees, the river coiling below, and began to fear that there might be an element of design in the way the priest had met his end.

'I've an interest in practical jokes.' Irwin smirked. He kicked the door of the car, sending a shower of glass fragments to the ground. 'Given the state of the Catholic Church these days, who knows what sort of pervert we're dealing with?'

Irwin's discourtesy to the dead man indicated a presumption about his past that Daly felt was unprofessional, if not a little bigoted.

When Daly did not speak, Irwin looked up at him.

'No offence, Celcius,' he said, the easy smile never leaving his face. 'But the Catholic Church looks more like a rogues' gallery these days.'

Religious honour was indeed at stake, and Daly feared the priest was going to let him down badly.

'Find anything unusual?' asked Daly.

'No evidence of criminal activity – if that's what you mean?'

'Anything else seem out of place?'

'What are you suggesting?' Irwin's phone might have blacked out but judging by the watchful look on his face, his inner receptors were still showing vital signs.

'I've no idea. What about the bundle of rosary beads? What does that say?'

'Does it have to say anything?'

'Holding on to it was probably the priest's last act before he crashed the car. His final communication with the world. Otherwise, why bother?'

'The priest was the victim of a dangerous prank. His guilty conscience made him ignore the police warning. What clues could he tell us even if he did leave a message?'

Irwin was right. It shouldn't have mattered, but Daly was intrigued by the beads and medals. It triggered a dim memory from his youth, from a more innocent time.

'I think I've seen bundles like that somewhere before. All twisted up and left to rust in the rain.'

He stared at the corpse for several more moments. He was convinced that the priest had not planned to end his journey this way. That the trick of the traffic cones had come as a surprise. That the path he found himself on had been ordained not by God or even chance but by darker forces.

When he turned back to Irwin, the detective had located another phone and was stabbing in a number with his thumbs. A busy signal made him mutter under his breath. He glanced at Daly with an impatient look.

'Waiting for a call?' asked Daly.

Irwin put away the phone and asserted himself.

'I'll be heading off now, Daly. Time to leave this place to the scene-of-crime officers.'

'Before you leave, tell me: what are the ramifications of this man's death for Special Branch?'

'Ramifications? It's not political or intelligence-related, if that's what you mean?'

'But the crash site is unusual.'

'In what way?'

'You're here for a start, and that puzzles me. I find it hard to believe that you came here in the middle of the night out of curiosity. And I find it strange that you keep trying to make contact with someone on your phone as though you have an important message to relay. What do you think? Am I being overly suspicious?'

'My presence or absence here should be of no concern to you.'

Daly stepped closer to him.

'This is more than a road accident,' he persisted. 'You haven't come here just to look at a practical joke that went wrong. You came here to search for something or do something. You can't expect me to write up the usual accident report and file it away without addressing these concerns.'

Irwin clambered up the slope and stood at the top looking down at Daly and the crashed car. His expression was a blank.

'Write up the accident report how you like, Daly. That is your job. Write it up with all your opinions and suspicions. Remember to include all your paranoid thoughts. Wait and see, you'll end up a laughing stock with your fellow officers.'

Daly hurried up the slope after him.

'Is that it? You're offering me no proper explanation as to why you're here?'

'I'm a Special Branch detective. I have the right to come and go as I please at crime scenes within this jurisdiction. I have exercised that right. I am also entitled to my silence. If you have any other questions, I suggest you raise them with Inspector Fealty.'

When Irwin had left, Daly began to feel a little chastened by the outburst. Perhaps the younger detective was right and he was being paranoid. Perhaps the accident was nothing more than a freakish curiosity, and by tomorrow morning the cold light of day would reduce it to its correct proportions. All he had to do was write a concise report describing the various lines of investigation into who had rearranged the traffic cones, and omit any mention of the Special Branch detective's presence at the scene. After a few days, his suspicions would lose any significance whatsoever.

He hunched over the crashed car, thinking quietly. It looked unstable, balanced on the edge of time as well as space. He laid a hand on its metal and felt the warmth leave his skin. It might slip further down the slope at any moment, he realized. He got up and retreated to the unfinished road.

He noted the absence of any skid marks on the tarmac or the grass verge. The priest had not even touched his brakes, driving off the road in a perfectly straight line, like an arrow into the dark. He took one final look at the car below. What was it about the scene that left him simultaneously fascinated and repelled?

'The border runs very close,' said the young police officer, joining him on the verge. 'It's just on the other side of the river.' His tone suggested that the border was something vagrant and dangerous, spinning by in the darkness. 'Funny how bad things always seem to happen on this side of it.'

2

Daly decided that nothing encapsulated the edgy desolation of border country better than the empty filling stations sidelined by the new motorway. On his way home, the petrol warning light had flashed up on his dashboard, and he had been grateful to find one that was still open.

He sat in the car after the elderly attendant insisted on dispensing the petrol himself. Rust wept from the signs, and the coiled fuel hoses trembled with the vibrations of lorries thundering by on the nearby motorway. Everything seemed to speak of impending ruin: the outbuildings permanently shuttered, the battered fuel stands looking all at sea on the forecourt muddled with diesel stains, the frail attendant glaring at him through the side mirror. As well as the new road, the vagaries of price differences and currency exchanges between the North and South had gradually decimated the passing trade on this side of the border.

'How's business?' asked Daly, by way of conversation.

'Are you fucking joking?' was the reply.

After paying, Daly asked was there a Mass-rock or holy well in the vicinity. The priest's bundle of old rosary beads had given him the idea that he might have come from such a place.

'Why do you want to know?'

He seemed immediately on guard. Daly could hardly tell him the truth, which was that he wanted to probe the life of a dead priest.

'When I was young I was brought to a holy place near here,' he said. 'There was some sort of religious procession. I'd like to see the place again.'

'That used to happen years ago at a little glen on the other side of the mountain.' He gave Daly directions. They were convoluted and involved skirting a stony hill and looking out for a hole in the hedge through which a path led into the glen. The lines on his face deepened. 'Mind, with all the rain you'll have to crawl through muck to get there.'

'I don't mind.'

The attendant's face twisted further.

'The farmers there don't like people trespassing.'

'I thought it was a holy place.'

'Holy?' The attendant grimaced. 'It was until they murdered the little girl there.'

'Who did?'

'Your people,' said the attendant. He hawked up phlegm with the sound of a shovel scraping, and spat on the ground. 'I have a job to do here,' he added.

Daly drove off, staring at the attendant's contorted face in the rear-view mirror as the man mumbled something. The detective's window was still down and he could just about hear the words: 'You should keep your fucking police nose out of that place.'

Daly drove off, wondering how he had leaked the fact that he was a policeman. Deciding that it was too late to visit the glen, he made a mental note of the directions and headed for home. He switched on the radio, but the closeness of the border hills meant there was no signal. He felt uneasy until he found his way back on to the motorway. After an hour, he reached the exit for the final trek home. It was past midnight and he was tired.

He reminded himself to be on the lookout for potholes, as his headlights picked out the familiar countryside. By the time he reached the shores of Lough Neagh, a ground mist had covered the sunken fields, making his neighbours' cottages look remote, embedded in the past, as if they were melting back into bottomless darkness.

He pulled up at his own cottage and switched off the headlights. He let the engine idle to keep the heater working. He wasn't ready to go to bed. He waited for his eyes to grow accustomed to whatever light was in the night sky. A full moon appeared from behind a cloud. He stared at his smallholding of fields, which was part-islanded by the shore of the lough, and felt a twinge of guilt at its air of ruin: the jutting trees, the front garden gone to weeds, the hummocky fields lapsing back to their natural state, sprouting thorns and swathes of gruesome-looking nettles and thistles.

However, in the night sky there was order and peace. The constellation of the Plough had swung into its familiar winter alignment over the cottage roof, and the moon was in the south, lighting up the little road on its way to the lough. He switched off the engine and sighed. This was as close as he got to a feeling of peace these days.

Over the past seven years, he had reconciled himself to living within the cottage's warren of damp rooms. The untended farm was his protective barrier of solitude, its wildness obscuring his neighbours' cottages. His fondness for the old house had set him in direct opposition to the social trend of building bigger, brighter homes with almost unpayable mortgages. Not that there was anything wrong with trying to move up in the world; it was just the pace of change and the size of the debt that he had found objectionable. His ex-wife and colleagues had repeatedly encouraged him to move into town, to a new development of turnkey houses, with all the modern comforts, but he had resisted their advice. Somehow, the unruliness of the surrounding fields always settled his mind and helped him sleep better. After all, where else could he dare to lead such a simple domestic life than in his father's dishevelled cottage; where else could his mind, saturated with the grisly impressions of detective work, be wrung through such an apparatus of emptiness and silence?

When he entered the front porch, he spied the glossy feathers of his black hen roosting on the windowsill. He smiled to himself. He was ignorant about fowl keeping but had taken an interest in the hen's welfare after the foxes had slunk out of the thickets one brutal moonless night and destroyed the rest of the flock. To his shame, he had forgotten to close and bolt the coop door before going to bed. Ever since, the black hen had kept close to Daly's heels, always trying to follow him indoors, head dipping and wings flapping against her sides in her anxious hurrying. There was something tenacious in her attachment to him. She had stopped laying eggs since the fox attack, and was economically worthless, but Daly found in her constant presence something old-maidenly and reassuring.

Now she had fallen into this nightly habit of roosting on the windowsill, and waiting for him to carry her back to the coop, which he always made sure to bolt firmly. He lifted her into the air, holding her as lightly as he could. She was compact and still, her plump body tensing slightly at his touch. He followed the worn path to the coop, thinking that it was a little like putting a baby to bed. He felt glad that her comforting presence had entered his life. In the vacancy of the neglected farm, it was the only intimate ritual he had left with another living thing.

He stood for a few minutes in the moonlight, holding her close to his chest. A lough breeze fanned his face. He stared at the dimly lit landscape. In this arena, he was a spectator, nothing more. The sprawling bog, the lapping lough, the stars and moon slowly revolving in the sky knew nothing about his thoughts and cares. True country living began with such moments of strangeness and quiet, he thought.

He carried the hen to the coop and nudged her into its darkness. She was reluctant to leave him. He gave her a little push and bolted the door. He wondered was he finally attaining the simple communion with nature that his father had always enjoyed? The goal was possible, as long as he kept the complications out of his life, the thoughts of work and worries about the future. But did this mean becoming more like his father? The thought would once have terrified him, but now with the approach of middle age he began to think that the old man might not make such a bad role model after all.

He made his way back to the porch. His thoughts drifted to the crash scene, the police cordon and the flashing lights. His fingers jittered with the keys as a flood of darker memories welled within him. A restless impulse took hold of him again. He turned back into the night, striding off through the overgrown garden and into the adjoining bogland. It wasn't the perfect time or weather for a ramble across such treacherous terrain, but in the moonlight he was just about able to follow the wriggling geography of grassy lumps and bog trenches, an interweave of life and death that had to be negotiated carefully, even in broad daylight. The lough wind flexed itself along a ridge of thorn trees: an easterly streaming bundle of spines that whined against the starlit sky. He paused for breath, watching in the distance the silvery waves sidling along the shore. Then he turned to view his father's cottage, nestling within a dell of ash and elder trees. Gradually, the peacefulness of the scene diluted the adrenalin flooding his veins.

It was the last time he would look at the cottage with innocent eyes, before its secrets and the revolting curse of its past darkened his vision and revealed the real reason why he had never been able to sell up and leave its gloomy confines – there was more truth to be discovered in a crumbling old house than a brand-new one.

3

Awakening earlier than usual the next morning, Daly trailed through the darkened rooms of his cottage, and pottered about in the kitchen. The whistle of the boiling kettle helped anchor his thoughts. This was his favourite time of the day; his small cottage never felt more expansive than in the half-light of a winter morning, its cramped furniture and sharp corners seeming to melt away into the darkness. By the time he had showered and dressed in a shirt and tie, his porridge had come to the boil on the gas hob. He stood at the window with a steaming bowl in his hand, a vantage point that pitted the domestic against the elemental: the tiny window frame, a slow-working dawn, the bogland leading down to the lough, and flocks of migrating whooper swans – deep silences that were just beyond his reach, but which touched him profoundly.

He washed his bowl and put it away, feeling soothed and refreshed.

By the time he drove to the new police headquarters, it was almost 9 a.m. He got himself a cup of coffee in the canteen and walked through the almost-empty corridors. From the flat atmosphere of the place, Daly surmised that most of the uniformed officers were out on patrol or on a training course.

For several months, Daly had stayed away from the sprawling new headquarters, preferring his old office at Derrylee station, with its reassuring smell of damp plaster and old paper files. The new building daunted him, as did the lines of fresh police recruits milling through its corridors, labouring towards the bright future of policing in Northern Ireland.

In the aftermath of the ceasefire, the government had decided that what the country needed to transcend all the bitter history of the Troubles was this grandiose new base, coupled with the closure of most of the fortified border police stations. It was a commanding state-of-the-art building with a gym, student accommodation, and even a diving pool to train the scuba unit. Society was struggling to deal with the violence of its past and the economic woes of the present, so the thinking went, and what the country needed was a new building for a new police force, a totally professional and trustworthy police force, bringing peace and order to a society splintered by forty years of violence.

Consequently, the police service had spent over seventy million pounds on the building, which overlooked Lough Neagh like a gleaming new ark, built to rescue a people and its law keepers from a troubled history. Unfortunately, the dream was not entirely an innocent one. For many former police officers, it carried an ugly little secret: not everyone was worthy of rescue. A swathe of senior detectives and uniformed officers had been encouraged to take early retirement, or pensioned off on the sick, to make way for the new recruits, well-groomed university-educated men and women, who had been born at the tail-end of the Troubles.

Gone were the grizzled, red-faced policemen of Daly's youth, who looked as though they could handle themselves in any bar-room brawl. Gone were the cabals formed in smoke-filled incident rooms; gone, too, was the latent sectarianism, the bigotry. As a Catholic detective, Daly had once been in the minority, but thanks to positive discrimination, the numbers of his co-religionists had swelled, and Catholic graduates flocked to this shiny new building in the deep sticks of Tyrone. This was why he had put off his move for as long as he could. He was reluctant to seal himself away in a building that might become an expensive monument to doomed expectations.

'Daly, I wonder if I might have a word with you,' he said.

The detective sidestepped him.

'Not this morning. I don't have much time.'

'Hold on, I've even less than you.'

Daly noticed that Donaldson was perspiring. Before he could object, his former commander frowned and posed a question that put him immediately on the defensive.

'Why do you maintain this childish feud with Detective Irwin?'

'What business is it of yours?'

Donaldson sighed.

'Personal grudges don't lead to successful police work. They're bad for investigations, and good for criminals.'

'Has he made a complaint?'

'No, not at all. But he has asked me to mediate. To help bring the two of you closer together. So you can work as a team.'

'What has the investigation got to do with you? You're no longer my commanding officer, or Irwin's. Why should you care if we cooperate or not?'

'Of course, you're right.' Donaldson's eyelids lowered, and his demeanour relaxed.

Daly edged away but the former commander reached out to grab him by the arm. If the corridors had been busier, it would have been much easier to escape.

'Wait, Celcius, hear me out,' he said. 'Have you taken a good look at this bloody building?' Donaldson glanced around him like an old beast surrounded by hunters. 'The force has changed beyond recognition,' he complained. 'You can see it in the faces of the new recruits. They're always laughing. In my day, the spirit was more serious. More vehement.' He bared his teeth in a grimace. 'Their lack of loyalty is where the key to the change lies. And their new uniforms. These T-shirts and open-necked shirts, and the new emblem, make them look like laughing stocks. Look at the footwear they've been given, for God's sake. I still remember my first pair of boots. Handmade, they were, and so waxed and buffed you could see your face in the polish.'

Daly frowned, wondering where Donaldson was taking him with this digression.

‘Pulling those boots on you felt sure of your place in the world. We belonged to a force dressed in the best-polished boots in the United Kingdom. In those days, Daly, you looked after your colleagues like you looked after your boots. You took care to make them last. You watched out for each other, covered each other’s backs. None of this jostling for precedence and fighting over how to handle investigations.’

‘Is that it? Is that all you have to say?’

‘I just want you to remember the spirit that once held this police force together.’

‘What spirit was that?’ All Daly could think of was the sectarianism of the old days.

Donaldson did not hesitate.

‘The spirit of loyalty.’

‘Loyalty is neither here nor there. The loyalty you talk about belongs to the past, to another world completely.’

‘I’m just asking you to cooperate with Irwin and not make this investigation difficult for him.’

‘Sorry, I can’t promise you that. I have to follow my own lines of inquiry. You are asking me to ignore my instincts, and that is asking too much.’

‘You misunderstand me. I’m not asking you to ignore what goes on in the darkness of your mind. That’s your own business. All I’m asking is that you conduct yourself in a professional manner and share your information with Irwin.’

‘My suspicions shape my detective work, and right now they’re telling me that both you and Irwin want to muddy the waters of this investigation. That’s all you need to hear from me.’ Daly moved off down the corridor.

‘I have to warn you that unless you rethink your attitude you’ll be hearing from Inspector Fealty.’

‘So be it,’ replied Daly.

4

Clutching his empty briefcase, Daniel Hegarty sat in a corner of the hotel bar, waiting for the arrival of the priest. He had been waiting since the previous evening and was rattled by the delay. He had concentrated his mind on meeting the priest. Thwarted, he could not bring himself to leave, even though a wedding party had overrun the hotel, spilling from the lounge and function room into the foyer, blocking his view of the hotel entrance doors. He hoped that if he stayed quietly in the background, the truth might reveal itself, that he might work out the reason for Walsh's worrying absence.

The arrival of the wedding crowds had been not so much a distraction as a comfort. Somehow, it was less humiliating to be surrounded by people who did not know how long he had been waiting. He limped back to the bar, firmly gripping his case, which felt uncomfortably light, ordered another whiskey and returned to his seat. He mulled over his drink as the noise in the room intensified. The priest had him dangling on a hook. The realization left him feeling helpless, angry with Walsh for his secretive manner and reluctance to discuss his schemes on the phone, and now this prolonged delay.

A fresh wave of relatives swelled into the room, compacting the several generations already squeezed there. He scanned their faces and their clothes, laughing men and women who looked as though they only saw each other at weddings and funerals. He observed the way they shook hands and bought drinks for each other, flashing their new suits and dresses. He did not know what to think of such gatherings, these rituals of family life, which represented everything he had left behind and never experienced because of his long career as an IRA informer. Was it a blessing or a curse to have been spared these gaudy events, the freshly made in-laws burdening the family tree, the troops of unruly children pushing their parents onward into middle age? He stared at the newly married couple steering through the room, shaking hands and receiving embraces. Nearby a woman picked up a baby and made gabbling noises at it. Soft-headed from the whiskeys and the suffocating cloud of goodwill in the air, he almost slipped into a daydream of what his life might have been.

He returned sharply to reality with the appearance of a young woman in a dark coat and grey trousers. He only had to glance at her to know she was not part of the wedding party. She walked into the bar with a measured pace, and then stood, rooted to the spot. A pretty woman with a striking face and black hair, letting her eyes roam over the crowd. He recognized her as the journalist who had been working with Father Walsh. For a moment, he felt rescued from the noise and happy confusion. He waited, expecting Walsh to appear behind her, but there was no sign of him. He realized that she was alone and searching the room for company. He leaned back into the shadows.

Her eyes briefly met his, but then flicked away. He noticed the subtle change in her face, the slippage in her blank expression. She tipped back her head and ran her hand through her dark hair. She looked interested. For the next ten minutes, she followed him with her gaze, seating herself at the bar to get a better view of him. He moved into the lobby, through the throng of people, and she trailed after him. He felt like a fugitive, chased from corner to corner of the hotel by this young woman with the eyes of a hunter following its prey.

Eventually he gave up the game they were playing and walked right up to her. He was impatient for everything now, another drink, the priest, their secret deal, the betrayal of his former employees in British

Intelligence, the setting up of his enemies, but he knew that he had to hide his restlessness.

'I'm here to see the priest,' he said.

'He told me he was expecting someone.'

'You know my name?'

'No.'

'Why has he kept me waiting?'

'I'm as much in the dark as you are. I haven't seen him since yesterday morning. He's stopped answering his mobile phone.' She looked genuinely worried. 'Father Walsh said you had some important documents to offer.'

'That's correct.'

She glanced at his briefcase sceptically. He wanted her to know he was someone important, a stranger with a secret to tell, but she kept looking at him as though she didn't quite believe him, this lonely old man with a limp and an empty-looking briefcase.

'I'm his assistant. Why not let me handle it?' She glanced at his briefcase again. 'You've wasted enough time hanging around the hotel.'

'I made a commitment to deal only with the priest,' he replied. 'These documents require the utmost delicacy. The risks are considerable if they fall into the wrong hands.' He flinched a little, thinking of his empty briefcase. Had she guessed his deception?

'If the documents are as important as you suggest, then the risks are considerable to Father Walsh, too.' She sighed as though she was tired with the preamble. 'That's the problem with trying to dig up the past. Everyone has his or her pet conspiracy theories. It takes a while to work out which ones are the liars and fantasists and which are telling the truth.'

Her probing look disarmed him.

'What about you?' he asked. 'You're a strange assistant for an elderly priest.'

'I'm a writer. A journalist. Father Walsh and I are working on a book about murder. Mass murder, in fact. A series of killings organized by a secret committee of police officers, judges and politicians during the Troubles. The exposé of the century, you might say.'

There was something childish about the excited look in her eyes.

'You know what I'm talking about, don't you?'

'Yes.'

'The only problem is we've hit a dead spot.'

'Writer's block?'

'You could call it that. We need someone to fill in the blanks. Provide some fresh leads. Someone with access to old Special Branch files from the 1970s.'

Hegarty tightened his grip on the briefcase, shifting it slowly, anything to disguise its emptiness.

'First I need to find out what has happened to the priest.'

'Why is it so important to see him?'

Her question made him wary. He wondered whether her talk about being a writer was a lie. She behaved more like an investigator or an intelligence agent with her probing questions.

'I need to talk to him before I work out my next step. In the meantime, no one else apart from you and the priest know I'm here. So I'm going to stick tight until he shows up. Right now, this is the safest place in the country for me.'

In truth, however, he knew there were no completely safe places for him any longer.

She leaned towards him.

'Who are you hiding from?'

'People who ask questions like that.'

She smiled. She offered to buy him a drink but he refused.

'I'm glad you came over.'

'Why?' If her behaviour was meant to reassure him, it wasn't working.

She shrugged and finished her drink. She glanced at her watch, and a stillness settled over her features. She was waiting for something to happen, thought Hegarty, but what exactly? A fear rose in him that he was not safe at all, and that he was trapped in a strange hotel with a dangerous woman. It had been a mistake, he realized, striking up the conversation in the first place.

Her phone rang and she answered it briefly. She slipped it back into her handbag with a smile.

'Good news. Father Walsh has returned.' She stared unblinkingly into his eyes. 'He's in his room right now. You can come up with me if you want.'

'What was the reason for the delay?'

'He didn't say.'

'But surely he owes us some sort of explanation.'

'No, he does not,' she said curtly. Before he could protest, she stood up and waited for him to follow.

'You must excuse me for a moment. I need to visit the bathroom.' He grabbed his briefcase, its lightness reminding him of his vulnerability.

She flashed him a look of impatience.

'You have to hurry.'

'I've waited for him since last night. I'm sure he can hold on for a few more minutes.'

He limped into the toilets, locked himself in a cubicle and stared at the creases in his trousers and his shoes. He took out his phone and tried Walsh's number. It went straight to a recorded message. Why didn't he answer if he was ready to see him? His sense of anxiety increased. He removed his handgun from his jacket pocket and rubbed its cold metal along his sweating temples. He inspected the firing mechanism, and fingered the shiny litter of bullets. He lifted the safety catch and peered down the barrel as if it was a keyhole into a hushed, dark little hiding place. The mouth of the weapon exhaled the reassuring smell of metal and grease, the sweetness of death. He pressed the barrel to his forehead and caressed the trigger. His forehead dripped like a wet cloth and his hand shook slightly.

He had held the weapon this way countless times before, whenever he felt trapped. Somehow, the pressure of the gun against his temple always returned his self-control, easing his sense of empty panic. His heart flooded with an appalling pleasure, the contemplation of how much power and destruction the gun wielded, this little black idol nestled in his hand. His finger tightened on the trigger, but before he could pull it his craving to live returned, his will to keep on seeking revenge in a world full of violence and stupidity. His breathing relaxed but he still held the gun firmly to his forehead.

Someone shook the handle of the cubicle violently. Hegarty was rattled. Instinctively, he pressed the gun to the door lock. An elderly sounding man complained bitterly at the other side. He took out the silencer and screwed it on to the muzzle. The weapon felt forceful and whole. He slipped it into his briefcase, and unlocked the door.

5

The lane to the abbey looked old and seldom used, overshadowed by a tunnel of oak and beech trees. Daly half expected to encounter fences and closed gates but there was nothing to impede his approach to the weathered-looking entry doors. It took him a while to find the button for the bell. It was rusted and almost covered in ivy. When no one answered, he ignored the feeling of trespass, pushed open the door and walked inside.

The abbot, Father Graves, had been informed of his visit. Daly found him peeking out from a room full of leather-backed books.

'Ah, there you are, Inspector,' he said, slowly nodding, as though he had been searching for him. He set off at a brisk pace down a corridor, and Daly, succumbing to the childhood rules of obedience, fell into pace behind. They passed into a side room with a large desk and chairs, which must have been the abbot's private office.

'You've come to tell me how poor Aloysius died?' said the abbot.

It wasn't the only reason, but Daly followed his lead and began summarizing the details of the car crash. Graves stared at him with a gaze that lacked focus. When Daly finished his account, he told the abbot he had some important questions to ask.

'Questions? What sort of questions?'

'What exactly were Father Walsh's priestly duties, and how long had he been living here?'

The abbot stared at him uncomprehendingly. 'A priest is a priest. I would think the job description is fairly well known. Like every other member of the religious orders, he performed a daily Mass, held confessions. He was always diligent in his religious observances.'

Daly wanted to ask was he a good priest, but his sense of deference prevented him. However, he was unable to suppress any longer the question that most consumed his thoughts.

'Yet before he crashed, he broke through a police roadblock and almost knocked over an officer. What made him do that?'

The abbot shrugged and looked perplexed.

'How should I know what was going through his mind?'

'I'm interested in hearing your opinion.'

'Are you indeed?' Graves held his tongue for a moment but then seemed to relent. 'Well, if you think it's relevant to the investigation. All I can say is that Aloysius was certainly not the type to ignore a police checkpoint. As far as I know, he never broke a motoring law in his life. Didn't even have a parking ticket to his name. And if he had committed some misdemeanour, he would have owned up and accepted his punishment. He certainly wouldn't have tried to evade the police.'

'You're suggesting he wasn't acting under his free will when he drove through the police cordon?'

Again, Graves looked a little confused.

'Oh no, I can't comment on his state of mind. I've told you that already.'

'We're trying to trace his mobile phone. Do you have his number?'

The abbot's eyes shrank to pinpoint glints.

'Why are you interested in finding his phone? Is Father Walsh under suspicion of committing some crime?'

'Not that we're aware of.'

'Then I'm relieved.' The abbot relayed the number from a leather address book. 'Well,' he added, rising from his seat. 'Thank you for your visit but you must excuse me, I have things to do.'

'Wait a moment,' said Daly. 'I'd like to ask you some more questions.'

The abbot sighed and sat down heavily. He removed a pair of glasses from a case and put them on. He stared closely at Daly, blinking.

'Tell me, Inspector, why exactly have you come?'

'I'm trying to piece together Father Walsh's final days.'

The abbot scrutinized him through his glasses, as if for the first time registering the true nature of his visit.

'You must understand that I cannot reveal any details of his private life.'

'Of course you can – you were his superior. Unless you're trying to spare the order some sort of embarrassment?'

'Inspector Daly, my work here is usually very simple. There are half a dozen priests and monks, and they live right under my eyes. We are one of the best-run religious communities in the country. It is because we have a philosophy of not seeking contact with the secular world. Unfortunately, Father Walsh found it impossible to adhere to that precept.'

The abbot took off his glasses and put them back in the case. His shoulders slumped slightly and he lowered the tone of his voice, as though from now on he was going to tell Daly a different type of story.

'Do you remember much about the late 1970s, Inspector? You were probably only a boy then.'

Daly flinched. Of course he remembered. When he peered into that portion of his childhood, he saw the darkness surrounding the death of his mother. She had been killed in crossfire between IRA gunmen and police officers at a checkpoint. The experience had marked him deeply, leaving him haunted throughout his adult life with the dread of losing another loved one, the fear cramping him in his relationships as effectively as a prisoner's shackles.

'For the past year, Aloysius had been spending very little time in the monastery. He wandered a lot. Restless is how I would describe his behaviour.' He stared at Daly with a look that resembled fear. 'He was always talking about the past. Frankly it was becoming an unhealthy obsession.'

'We all have memories we treasure,' said Daly. 'They are our refuge in times of trouble or uncertainty.'

'I'm not talking about his childhood past. I'm talking about the historical past. Aloysius was trying to verify the dates and locations of certain events during the Troubles. They were the kind of memories no one treasures. He was gathering up the details of unsolved murders in Tyrone and Armagh during one particularly dark year and charting them on a map. It was the most macabre piece of cartography I ever saw. He was trying to prove the murders were part of a conspiracy involving some very powerful institutions.' The abbot shrugged. 'How can you discover something that happened in a cloud of secrecy and fear all those years ago? The truth about those terrible killings is locked away in people's hearts. He must have known there would be so little left to find now, a few hazy memories, the dregs of evil filtered through failing minds.'

Daly's curiosity was strongly aroused. Maps were a way of taking on an unknown landscape, seizing it and making it one's own through detailed observations and connections. But why would an elderly priest want to chart such grim territory?

The abbot spotted the glint of interest in his eyes.

'If you feel you must, you have permission to visit his room and examine his maps. The door's unlocked. I'm sure to Father Walsh the room had its own order, and he knew where everything lay, but to the rest of us it was an abysmal mess.'

The curtains were drawn in the cell-like space of Walsh's room. Daly pulled them aside to reveal an elderly scholar's room, stacks of paper everywhere, folders of newspaper clippings, legal notebooks, and old-fashioned cassette tapes. The priest had glued several sheets of paper on to the largest wall in order to accommodate a sprawling map of the border areas of Tyrone and Armagh. Across the top, he'd written in block capitals 'THE TRIANGLE OF DEATH'. From a distance, the map resembled a medieval cartographer's life's work, overgrown by a forest of names, dates and arrows, and pockmarked by red pins. On closer inspection, Daly was able to make out the macabre details: the pins representing the locations of murders, mostly perpetrated by Loyalist paramilitaries within a triangle of about thirty townlands and parishes.

Daly scanned the map and pages of handwritten notes. Father Walsh had been a curate in a number of border parishes during the

1970s, and the memories of tending to grief-stricken families had stayed with him. He knew he had witnessed a pivotal point in Irish history. After moving to the monastery in the early 1990s he had begun carefully writing down what he'd seen and heard, corroborating the details with eyewitnesses, and then later with disgruntled former police officers and ex-informers.

To Daly's eyes, there was an amateurish air to the research – the efforts of an ordinary man to record history rather than a professional historian or a well-connected journalist. The notes were strewn everywhere, bringing back memories of twisting lanes, checkpoints in the dark, the blood-spattered porches of isolated farms, and men with hoods roaming the darkness of border country. The names and dates flickered by without offering him any clues. He was confronted by a feeling of helplessness. Father Walsh's investigations focused on the year 1979. A year of unparalleled savagery. In total, 121 sectarian murders. It was also the year his mother had been killed, and he felt an instinctive recoil. The priest had spent his final days slowly dissecting the events of a brutal year and staring into its bloody blackness. Somehow, he had discerned a pattern. Daly could see that much. He had listed the same names and weapons repeatedly, the movements of a paramilitary gang linked to some of the murders, their vehicles, a Luger 47 and the surnames Mitchell, Browne, Agnew and McClintock. Each murder was somehow rooted in the details of the others.

Daly was so absorbed by the map he didn't hear the abbot approaching. Suddenly Graves was there in the room standing alongside him. He looked more diminutive than when he had been sitting at his desk, and his face had grown paler. He waved at the map in a disheartened way.

'How did it get so bad?' His voice was that of a tired confessor contemplating an overwhelming abundance of sin. 'I remember the start of the seventies and the civil rights marches, the campaigns for better housing and fair employment. It all seemed to herald a new dawn for Northern Ireland.' The words tumbled from the abbot's lips. 'How did we end up with murder gangs and medieval justice, vigilantes pursuing revenge with guns and bombs? Where were the warning signs that we were harbouring such murderers in our midst?' He stared up at Daly, as if expecting him to shed light on the puzzle.

'What drew Walsh to this particular set of murders?' asked Daly.

'Evil.'

'What do you mean?'

'He was a different sort of priest to the one you're familiar with. He believed not in miracles and goodness but in the power of evil. Most of us have a blind spot in that regard. We are sane and solid and we place our trust in society and the power of law and order. But Father Walsh didn't accept the conclusions of others, and there was a danger in that. He wanted the details of these murders cleared up. He wanted everyone he believed guilty held to account.'

'And who was everyone?'

'The murderers, the intelligence services, the men who pulled the strings in the background, the politicians. Even the police and the judiciary.'

Daly raised an eyebrow.

'And did you believe his murder conspiracy theories?'

'No,' he said. 'I'm a monk and everything I believe in is shut up inside a golden box on an altar. I tried to ignore the facts of evil he was at such pains to reveal. Many of his fellow priests thought he was a crank, out of step with the politics of peace and moving on.'

The abbot made to leave. He bowed politely but Daly could see the unease working its way though his mind.

'There was one other thing,' he said. 'It struck me as odd that he had taken to wearing a watch. It added to the sense that he was in a hurry. In all the years he'd been here, I'd never seen him wearing one before.'

The abbot waited for a response from Daly but there was none. The detective was thinking about the priest speeding off from the checkpoint. He had certainly seemed in a hurry on the night of his death. He was reminded of his meeting with Donaldson and his new watch. Another old man anxious about time. Did the former RUC commander also have a ticking deadline?

'You see, the days here are structured, and the church bells are always ringing out the hour. I couldn't understand why he was always glancing at this new watch of his.'

Daly tried to analyse the detail as simply as possible. What did it mean for an old man, living in an institution like an abbey, to start wearing a watch? He needed to measure time. Not the time inside the abbey, which appeared to stand still, but time in the outside world. It signalled a new relationship with life outside the abbey walls, the possibility that he was synchronizing his life to some other beat, another person or a series of events.

'Did he have any unexpected visitors? Someone you hadn't seen before?'

The abbot drummed his fingers on the table.

'Yes.' He hesitated. 'There was a woman. A journalist. Her name was Jacqueline Pryce.'

'Why did she want to see him?'

'She was helping him piece together the details of the murder map. I believe she was going to write a book about it.'

The revelation troubled Daly. Walsh's research looked disordered and unfinished, but the idea that a journalist was writing a book on it suggested a measure of order and completeness. Journalists were in the business of making a name for themselves, especially when they undertook to write books about the Troubles, and they seldom stopped until they were published, no matter the consequences. Walsh's research was beginning to look less and less like the secret obsession of a harmless old priest.

'Do you know her?' asked the abbot.

'I've never heard of her.' Daly made a mental note of the name. 'Something about this map must have whetted her interest.'

The abbot had decided he'd said enough. He nodded and left Daly to peruse the room on his own.

The detective stood for a while, contemplating the priest's handiwork. A wall full of secrets in a silent room in a silent monastery. He blinked at the map. He could see that it had been in a constant state of flux. Walsh had rearranged the intricate facts of each murder, drawing new connections between them. Daly scanned over the details. The names of the weapons, the size and number of the bullets fired, the description of the strike marks, the entry points on the victims' bodies, the getaway cars, and the statements of eyewitnesses, some of whom reported seeing police checkpoints near the murders. The priest had also compiled the names of men charged with minor roles in the killings, some of whom were listed as ex-police officers. Daly stood so still he almost didn't breathe. He began to understand why Irwin and Special Branch might be so interested in Walsh and his crashed car.

He stepped back, trying to absorb the web of facts and conjecture in its entirety. To his tired mind, the map seemed to be alive, wriggling with the details of evil. He stared at the northeast corner of it more closely. Blinked again. The jarring detail did not fade. He stared at the red pin placed at a corner of Lough Neagh, directly over the location of his cottage. The name beside it was Angela Daly; his mother's. His face was motionless. His hands hung limply by his side. He saw her blue nurse's shoes lying on her bedroom floor. He rubbed his eyes and glanced at the map again.

Was it his imagination or did the network of roads seem to coil under and through each other like serpents? He leaned closer, looking deeper and harder in an effort to fix the details in his mind. He was unwilling to phrase what floated through his mind at that moment, but the dark question that struggled towards expression was in the nature of: What was his mother's name doing in the company of so many people he had never heard of, in the context of such cold-blooded murder? He asked himself more questions: How had Walsh decided that his mother was another victim of the Loyalist gang, and, if it was true, what had she done to bring herself to their murderous attention?

'Mum.' He half mouthed, half whispered the word. The dryness of his voice disturbed him, and the hollowness of the childish monosyllable he had not uttered in a long time. He stepped back towards the door, thinking he had to call his father, tell him what he'd seen, but then he realized his father was dead. He was forty-three years old, divorced, childless, and his first instinct had been to call on his deceased dad for support. How ill-starred his life had been.

'Mother,' he said to himself again. 'Who would have thought your death and my work would cross all these years later?'

He had few clear memories of his childhood but he remembered the details of that spring evening in 1979, the police detective standing directly in front of his father, almost whispering in his ear, relaying how his mother had died in the crossfire between an anti-terrorist police unit and an IRA gang. His father's face was deathly white and his eyes were staring directly at Celcius, who listened to every word. The quietness of their voices made everything seem far away, as if he did not belong to the tragedy that was unfolding, as if it was a play or some sort of lie that was being told for his benefit.

'She was in the wrong place at the wrong time,' said the detective softly.

He remembered how the veins had stood out on his father's forehead, thin and shiny like nylon string, and his eyes had bulged. He couldn't see the detective's face, his back was to him, standing so still he might have been a spectator at the event. His father's eyes were fixed on Daly, but he didn't seem to see him any more. His father said in a thick voice, 'She wasn't.'

The detective didn't move.

'What do you mean, she wasn't?'

'She wasn't in the wrong place at the wrong time,' his father said, still staring at Celcius. 'She was in the right place at the right time. She was coming home from her work. She was driving down the same road she took every evening.'

After a lengthy pause, the detective said, 'I'm very sorry for your loss, Mr Daly.' He glanced over his shoulder at Celcius before leaving the room.

His next memory was of his parents' darkened bedroom, his mother's blue nurse's shoes lying on the floor and his father's shadowy figure, clumsy and fumbling, rummaging through the drawers of her cupboards. He remembered his father's determination, mumbling to himself as he searched through her things. He kept lifting out and rereading old letters. Daly had never seen him look so agitated.

In the weeks after her funeral, Daly's father had been haunted by the nagging suspicion that the police detectives were failing her, that there was unfinished business to the investigation. Both the IRA gang and the police unit had melted mysteriously away. No charges were ever brought against the person who had fired the weapon, or the IRA men responsible for the attack.

Daly's father was given barely half an hour's notice by the police when the inquest was called. He had managed to get to the courthouse in Portadown just in time, but had been forced to sit at the back of the room, unable to fully hear the proceedings. All he heard was the coroner's conclusion: that his wife's death had been a tragic accident, one of many that blighted those years.

Time had reduced the pain for Daly and his father. If not healing the loss, then permitting them to forget it gently, growing scar tissue around those months, sealing them off. Gradually, they'd been able to reconcile themselves to the coroner's findings, and the lack of any charges or arrests.

What did Walsh's red pin change? Everything. It suggested that his mother had been the intended target of a murder gang, one of dozens marked within the triangle, her death not an accident but a cold-blooded assassination. He felt a sense of outrage. Walsh had obtained a confidential police report showing that the gun used to kill her had been a Spanish-made Star pistol, the same weapon used in several of the other attacks marked out on his map. It was impossible not to agree with Walsh's line of investigation. When a weapon was used in a similar type of attack, in a similar area and at around the same time, it suggested the attackers were at least linked, if not the same people. But why the cover-up and why his mother? She was a God-fearing Catholic, completely innocent, unconnected to any political party or paramilitary organization. Why concoct a story that she had died in the crossfire between an IRA gang and a police unit, when it should have been clear that her death was linked to a sequence of sectarian murders?

Daly tried to sort through the legal papers and newspaper reports that Walsh had accumulated on his desk. According to Walsh's research, the Star pistol bore the serial number 59488. It had been the personal-protection firearm issued to a man called Ivor McClintock. He had been charged in 1983 with membership of a Loyalist paramilitary organization. Daly read further, eager to find out why McClintock had been issued with the weapon in the first place, but he struggled to concentrate on the facts. His eyes kept flicking back to the map, to the red pin and his mother's name, the memory of her shoes on the bedroom floor.

To restore some order to his teeming thoughts he took out his mobile phone, fiddled with it, pointed it at the map and took several photographs, zooming in so he could capture all the details. His eyes were steely and blank, staring at the image on the phone's video screen. It was the latest model, thinner and more expensive than the last. He disliked its heft; somehow its lightness disappointed him. He belonged to the generation for whom solidity and weight were allied with dependability, and the phone's slimness made it seem an unreliable wedge between him and brutal reality.

When he put the phone away, the chaos began to flow. He had a vision of the map and its criss-crossing lines shifting together, the dozens of deaths entangled, as if they were leaves and thorns whipped up in a wind. They surged towards him, helter-skelter, the names and locations flashing before his eyes. What had happened to their grieving families, all those disrupted lives, and what about his own? What had happened to him after that memory of his mother's blue shoes lying on the floor and his father rummaging through the drawers? He found it impossible to take the image forward and remember what happened next.

He stepped back and sat on Walsh's bed. His mind shot back to another memory, before his mother's death. He was standing with his schoolbag surveying his tidy bedroom as though it were a zone of anger and humiliation. His mother had found a secret list he'd been hiding in his room, and destroyed it. The memory left him stumbling out of the priest's room, down the long corridor. The abbot saw him as he made to leave the building.

'Is anything wrong?' he asked. He must have seen the look on Daly's face.

'Nothing at all,' said the detective. However, everything was wrong.

He drove out of the monastery grounds and stopped at the first bridge straddling the new motorway. His mind was not yet willing to accept what his eyes had perceived. He needed to investigate Walsh's findings further and verify the facts listed on the map. He tried to plan a course of action while staring at the streaming traffic. For a while, he thought about passing the case over to Irwin, and allowing Special Branch to get their teeth into it. *I don't have to get involved in this*, he told himself. *I will not be pulled into the mire of the past.* However, something about Irwin's presence at the car crash warned him that he could not leave it to Special Branch to deliver justice and the truth. He had the nagging feeling that Irwin had been shielding some sort of secret. The younger detective wasn't in the business of straightforward law and order, especially when it came to handling unsolved crimes in the past.

He got out of the car and looked at the dual carriageway spreading before him, the lorries speeding by in their hollow thunder. He stared at the verge of sodden grass directly below, the stew of litter and overgrown weeds raked by the wind of passing vehicles. The murk of the evening made him feel like a stranger. He climbed back into his car and switched on the engine.

His pain was so solitary that there was no relief to be granted by watching other people's lives. This was not his road, he thought. He could see the truth now. If your past harboured a dark secret, you could travel nowhere peacefully, because home would always exert its dark gravity no matter where you went. Home for him would always be a gloomy cottage enmeshed by thorn trees and winding lanes, brooding over a lough of restless water.

6

The journalist was waiting for Daniel Hegarty in the corridor outside the hotel toilets. A glint of ruthlessness shone in her eyes. The spy began to think that she was not as attractive as he had first thought. With a stab of awareness, he saw she was hiding an ugly secret. Her prettiness was as hollow as her story, which he had been eager to believe in, as an antidote to his rising impatience. Something had happened to the priest; he could see that now in her cold face, the clenched teeth behind her smile, and the defiant tilt of her chin. She scrutinized his briefcase, and for a moment he feared he had betrayed his secret by allowing her to guess its emptiness. A man bringing an empty briefcase to such an important meeting was not to be trusted. However, she turned and led him up the stairs and along a windowless corridor, her dark hair bouncing on her tense shoulders.

When they reached the hotel room, he lifted up his briefcase as if to take out the documents. He slipped his hand in, felt the gun and waited as she knocked on the door. He stared at the back of her head, her motionless neck. He admired her calm. She knew what she was doing, leading him into this dark little trap. She glanced back at him, her face expressionless, and then down at his briefcase, as if she were weighing it all in her mind, balancing the briefcase and its contents with his life, her blue eyes unblinking, as if both were worth nothing. He let the case hang a little lower.

She walked into the room and he edged in behind her. A disco had started on the floor below and the heavy music reverberated in the room.

The old man sitting on the bed had been flicking through a travel magazine. Hegarty entered the room, and the man looked up, his eyes glittering with a dangerous light.

'Hello, Daniel,' he said. He sounded happy to have company.

'Where's Walsh?' asked Hegarty.

'He couldn't make it. What's in your briefcase?'

'It's empty. You can see for yourself.'

Hegarty tossed the briefcase towards him. It splayed open in mid-air. The man grabbed at it, when he should have recoiled backwards for cover. Quick and deft, Hegarty pointed the gun. The weapon flared twice, the bullets striking the man in the neck and the top of his chest. The briefcase clasped shut and fell on his body.

Hegarty walked stiffly towards him. The dying man's eyes fastened on him with an intensity that suggested they had once known each other, the muscles of his jaw convulsing while blood poured from a wound in his neck. His throat lengthened and grew rigid, as though he were trying desperately to say something.

'I thought you had retired,' said Hegarty, finally recognizing him. He was one of the shadows who'd been watching him for years. A man who had assassinated many innocent victims.

'Yes,' hissed the man through a mouth frothing with blood, but his eyes were already clouding with forgetfulness. His body fell to the side.

Hegarty delivered a final bullet to his head, and turned his attention to the journalist, whose entire body had frozen to the spot.

'This will do wonders for my writer's block,' she said hysterically, her eyes signalling some strange sort of relief. And then she laughed, but it was a silent laugh, more a ghost of a laugh. Her reaction made him pause for thought. By the time he raised the gun to shoot she had slipped out of the room and into the corridor. He followed her and fired. Her run faltered and she glanced back at him with a pained look.

To his surprise, she started running again, this time limping heavily. The bullet must have grazed her leg. He was about to raise the gun and take aim again, when a family with young children emerged from a room into the corridor.

He ducked back into the room. In the mirror, he caught a glimpse of his face spattered with blood. By the time he had washed and re-emerged, the woman had gone.

A mess of blood filled the bed. He checked the dead man's body, careful not to get any more blood on himself. The black wedge of a gun jutted from an underarm holster. He searched the room for any evidence that might link him to the killing. Already there was too much blood on the carpet. He was careful where he walked, what he touched. For the first time that day, he felt relaxed, transposed into another more vital existence. He picked up his briefcase and left the room. He was no longer contemplating his own death.

7

After leaving the abbey, Daly felt too troubled to return home. He decided to phone ahead to the hotel Walsh had been staying in and arrange a search of the deceased's room. As he drove back into border country he tried to think of a series of events that would have led to his mother becoming a target for Loyalist paramilitaries. He arrived at the hotel without having made any progress.

Clary Lodge Hotel was situated at the bottom of a black mountain, half-hidden behind an enclosure of laurel and rhododendron bushes. It had once been the mansion of a grandly delusive English landlord, who'd wanted to turn the emptiness of the surrounding bogland into a visual spectacle. When Daly pulled up in his car, he thought that in winter few landscapes could have presented a gloomier prospect to travellers.

However, the hotel seemed busy with the aftermath of what must have been a wedding party, parked cars festooned in white ribbon, young children colliding with each other, and groups of well-dressed men and women standing at the doors, grabbing a smoke between drinks. They steered clear of Daly as he approached, as if they knew exactly what he was, a portent from the outside world, a carrier of bad news.

The receptionist at the front desk was not facing the entrance; he was turned towards a computer screen and speaking into a telephone. Daylight flickered against the wall. From the corner of his eye, Daly caught the silhouettes of children bolting past the windows. The front doors banged open and shut. A man appeared out of the shadows, kneading his forehead. After several minutes, Daly cleared his throat to get the receptionist's attention.

'My name is Inspector Celcius Daly,' he said.

The receptionist turned to regard him, placing a hand over the receiver.

'They warned me you were coming.'

'I need to search a room. It was booked by a priest called Walsh.'

'You'll have to wait a moment.' A frown shadowed the receptionist's face. He continued talking on the phone. The coolness of his manner irritated Daly.

'Father Walsh died last night in unusual circumstances,' he said, leaning over the counter in anger. 'I can arrange for the details of the hotel to be circulated to the media as a key to the mystery of his death. You'll have the press here taking pictures and interviewing guests within the hour. If that's what you prefer?'

'Absolutely not.' He looked aghast. 'That's not the type of publicity we want.' He replaced the phone. 'I was wondering why Father Walsh seemed to be hiding from everyone.'

'Who's everyone?'

'There was a woman and a man enquiring about him. He missed some sort of meeting. What was your name again?'

'Inspector Daly. When did you last see him?'

'Yesterday morning at breakfast time.'

'How did he seem?'

'Fine. Like any other guest at that time of the morning.'

'What room had he booked?'

'Follow me and I'll show you.' He led Daly up a wide staircase to the second floor. 'His room has the best views of the nearby mountain,' he said.

A fine prospect for a dead man's last day, thought Daly. A drove of children had converged upon the top of the staircase. They pointed down at Daly and the receptionist as though they were figures of fun. It must have been difficult finding something worth giggling at in such dismal surroundings.

The receptionist swiped the door lock with a card.

'That's odd,' he said, pushing open the door. 'It's unlocked.'

They walked into a darkened room. Daly sensed something throbbing within, a swarming presence. When his eyes adjusted to the dim light, he made out a tired-looking carpet patterned with dark congealments. For a long moment, they listened to themselves breathe. Whatever it was that Daly had expected to find, it was not this. Someone had turned the room into a pit of red. He turned on the lights and saw that it was blood staining the walls and the blankets on the bed. Only the light shade dangling from the centre of the ceiling had escaped the spattering.

Outstretched by the bed lay the body of a man, the source of all the blood. Daly walked with small steps, careful not to disturb any evidence. He approached the bed and saw that the bloodletting had been arterial and catastrophic. He stared at the body, an elderly man with sunken features, the blankets around him swamped in blood. Methodically, he scanned the bedclothes and floor for anything the murderer might have dropped. He glanced at the victim; his mouth contorted in a grimace and his head tipped forward, blue shadows forming around his drained features. The window hung slightly open. Laughter and squeals of children playing on the lawns rose against the curtains. A car pulling away spat on the gravel drive.

Inside the room, the eddies of silence deepened. The dead man's blood had dripped from the corners of the duvet and pooled on the carpet. Daly felt a slight weakness in his knees. The silence was broken by the sound of a mother and her two young children walking along the corridor, the happy babble of girls' voices ringing clear as a bell. The mother flashed Daly an inquisitive look as she passed the doorway, and then, glimpsing the room, her attention swiftly withdrew. Daly turned and saw the receptionist bent in two, retching into the tiny sink.

Daly returned to his search. He found a driving licence lying half under the bed. He could make out part of the surname without touching it. 'McClintock', it appeared to read. On the bedside locker sat a copy of the bible and the priest's breviary. Father Walsh's presence lurked in the room like a ghost with gruesome secrets.

Daly told the receptionist the name of the dead man.

'Was he a guest?' he asked.

'I'll have to check the register. He might have come for the wedding.'

Daly grimaced at the idea of questioning the bridal party. He hoped for their sakes that the bride and groom had already escaped on their honeymoon.

The receptionist had left the sink and was watching him from the door, his face inclined in an attitude of enquiry, as though he believed Daly had already worked out what had caused the violent events that had unfolded in the room.

What had he worked out? Very little. He tried to gather information, make some sense of the grisly scene. The pathologist's report would pinpoint the time of the victim's death and reveal if it had occurred before or after Walsh's car crash. With the help of the scene-of-crime officers he would analyse the body and the room, place them in some sort of stable context, but for now, his detective skill of selecting relevant details was overwhelmed by the proximity of so much blood, the rawness and violence of it all. He heard the sound of a lift opening echo along the corridor.

He was standing in a hotel room about ten miles from the Irish border, submerged in a reddish haze.

The receptionist tried to slip away.

'Strictly speaking, my shift ended about ten minutes ago,' he said hoarsely.

Daly glanced at his watch.

'You can stay a little longer. I should have clocked off an hour ago.'

8

Back at headquarters the following morning, Daly and Detective Irwin walked up a flight of stairs and down another long corridor. The polished floor gave way to carpet, and a hush descended. Special Branch Inspector Ian Fealty greeted them with a frozen smile and led them into his office, which was spacious, but filled with a heavy, cold light, the walls bare of anything that might soothe a troubled mind. Behind Fealty, a set of windows gave bleak views of the lough shore's flooded hinterland. Rain drummed lightly against the glass, adding to the sombre mood in the room.

Daly worked out he was in a north-facing wing on the third floor, a section he'd never visited before. The architecture of the building seemed to have the ability to sprout a new wing or two, then mysteriously disappear, and on more than one occasion he had found himself lost amid its avenues of corridors. He surveyed the room and the views from the window, thinking that this was the little summit the Special Branch chief had managed to clamber up, his new lair from which he could overlook all the entanglements of the past.

Fealty seemed at home in his new surroundings. He dipped his head and indicated Daly a seat, while Irwin stood to the side. Daly was surprised to see Donaldson standing there, too, his eyes fixed on him, unblinking and severe, like the portrait of a family ancestor.

'Coffee?' asked Fealty.

'No, thank you.'

'This will not take much of your time, Inspector,' said Fealty. 'Irwin has explained to me your interest in Father Walsh's death. On this occasion, let me be very clear about how this investigation will proceed. Fortunately for you, it is very straightforward. With McClintock's death, the case has reached a new level. Any further discoveries or leads are a matter for Special Branch and the intelligence services. Your intervention has been invaluable and we convey our thanks to you. Of course, you will undertake not to disclose any of the information you have discovered to anyone else.'

Fealty regarded Daly with a measure of anticipation. His eyes met his, alert to every nuance of physical communication. Daly stared back. That icy gaze of Fealty's. Always calculating the precise degree of professionalism in its targeted object. Daly took care not to blink.

'So,' said Fealty, picking up a pen, allowing his words to fall as matter-of-factly as the rain against the window. 'We have your agreement on this?'

'I'm sorry. I can't agree to that.'

'Why not?' asked Fealty.

'You haven't explained why the investigation should be handed entirely to Special Branch.'

Daly had encountered Fealty's strong-arm tactics before, while investigating the disappearance of a former Special Branch agent with Alzheimer's. He and Fealty often shared the same investigative territory, but carried out their police duties in parallel, only overlapping in cases of political sensitivity. He had doubted from the start that the hastily arranged meeting would be one of mutually beneficial revelations.

Fealty sighed.

'Very well, I shall explain to you the rationale behind our decision. We've identified the body in Walsh's hotel room. Ivor McClintock was a former police officer, a member of the Royal Ulster Constabulary. In 1984, he was convicted of supplying weapons to a Loyalist paramitary group and served a one-year jail sentence. At the time, he was not a serving police officer, I hasten to add.'

'What was he doing in Walsh's bedroom?'

'It appears that Walsh had an unhealthy obsession with the past. He was working on a conspiracy theory, and had been interviewing McClintock about his links with Loyalists and the police.'

Fealty swallowed as if trying to overcome a deep-seated reservation. Was he about to break the taboo of Special Branch family history and mention the dreaded word 'collusion'? Daly stayed silent, allowing a strategic pause to develop.

'Walsh had come up with new allegations of a cover-up at the highest levels with regards to a series of murders in the late 1970s,' added Fealty. 'He levelled accusations at MI5 and the higher echelons of Special Branch.' He smiled thinly. 'If there was such a cover-up I don't think it could have escaped the attention of the media and the legal profession for over thirty years.'

It was revealing in itself that Fealty hadn't been able to say the word 'collusion' aloud, even within the confines of his own office, thought Daly. Only the guilty or ashamed relied on euphemism rather than the blunt truth.

'But many people in this country suspect there was collusion between the police and Loyalist terrorists,' said Daly.

'Yes, and until we tidy up this little mess, they'll keep believing the conspiracy theories of fantasists like Walsh. The worry is these rumours and lies will become entrenched in the public imagination and destroy the reputation of the Royal Ulster Constabulary.'

'And what's so terrible about that? The RUC no longer exists; most of its officers have been pensioned off.' Daly glanced over at Donaldson. The former commander ignored the comment. He stood upright, unflinching in his own stolid way, a monolith from the past.

'We are still a force in transition, Inspector Daly. Never forget that. And we are advancing by trial and error. It's in no one's interest to have unfounded allegations hanging over our officers, past or present.'

Donaldson cleared his throat, and Fealty glanced at him, nodding as if to confirm he could speak.

'The past is a dangerous place,' said Donaldson. 'Fragmented. Murky.

That's why the Police Service of Northern Ireland is trying to move on. Look to the future.' His face carried the strain, the rigor of someone bent on concealment.

'What exactly is your point?' asked Daly.

'Walsh was living in the past, Daly,' replied Donaldson. 'Don't let him drag you back there, too. It's true that back in the early days some mistakes were made by commanding officers. However, it was because they wanted to believe their men's statements. They were caught up in the fear of the time, the sense of a country unravelling. Walsh got it wrong. There was no definite plan to cover up or condone these Loyalist attacks and certainly not any direct police involvement in them. We discovered a few rotten officers in the force, but these men were disciplined and expelled as soon as their links with Loyalists became clear.'

Fealty eyed Daly sharply.

'You seem nonplussed by your former commander's explanation.'

'Believe me, I am anything but nonplussed. Every cell of my body is gripped.'

'But not so gripped you'll rush out and interfere with this investigation. Right?'

Daly felt his blood churn like a suppressed spring.

'You should know that I made a personal discovery in Walsh's research. I came across my mother's name.'

'Was she a confidante of his?' Fealty looked puzzled.

Daly scraped his chair on the floor as he leaned forward.

'Her name was not on any list of friends or contacts. It was next to a red pin on his murder map. His triangle of death.'

Fealty's eyes bulged with genuine surprise.

'Your mother was one of the murder victims?'

'Correct.'

Fealty risked another question.

'How did she die?'

'Her name was Angela Daly. She died on the second of April 1979. According to the official line, she got caught in crossfire between a police unit and the IRA. However, Walsh discovered that the weapon used in the shooting was the same one used by the Loyalist gang.'

Fealty paused and thought. He seemed to lose some of his confidence.

'I am sorry for your loss, Inspector. However, if this claim of Walsh's is the reason you insist on investigating his death then you are misguided.'

'Misguided? I've discovered that my mother was quite possibly a murder victim. I want to verify Walsh's research, and have my mother's killers brought to justice. Am I misguided to want that?' Daly leaned closer to Fealty, his physical bulk crowding Fealty's desk. He was prepared to drag an answer from the Special Branch detective with his bare hands.

'No. You are not misguided. But your personal loss will interfere with the investigation. You will see everything through its distorting mirror.'

Fealty's cool reasoning only heightened Daly's anger.

'If these twisted cowards had taken your mother and not mine, you wouldn't be sitting here trying to divert my search for the truth.'

'You can't let her death skew your approach to the investigation,' said Fealty.

Murder was the word Daly wanted Fealty to say, not death, but the Special Branch detective had already moved on.

'Detective Irwin has raised concerns about your reliability in handling such a sensitive case. He claims that Walsh's mobile phone was removed from the accident site.' Something about Fealty's tone suggested he doubted Irwin's ability to conduct a thorough search of the scene. 'I have to remind you that this is an important piece of evidence,' he added.

'Why is it so important?' asked Daly.

'It wasn't important until a murder victim turned up in Walsh's hotel room. We don't yet know what clues it will yield, if any.'

'Clues that might prove Walsh was murdered?'

'That's overstating the case. All I mean is that information on the phone might reveal why McClintock was in the hotel room and who else knew he was there.'

'All I can tell you is that I haven't got the phone.'

'A pity,' said Fealty. 'For a moment I thought you were going to provide us with a valuable lead.'

'But I do have an idea where Walsh might have hid it.'

As Daly said this, all three men exchanged glances.

'Catholic clergy are used to communicating through symbols,' explained Daly. 'Walsh left behind a clue that points straight to where he hid the phone, assuming you know where to look.'

'Which is where?'

He was not being entirely truthful with Fealty. He believed he did have a clue about Walsh's phone, but it was a flimsy clue, a single, almost invisible thread that was in danger of slipping through his fingers. It was less a clue and more an inkling, one that might yet guide him closer to the heart of the mystery

'If you're so anxious to find the phone, let me follow my hunch.'

Fealty stared at Daly, sizing up his resistance.

'Very well, Inspector. How do you plan to proceed with your hunch?' His voice was smooth but hard.

'Do you think if I knew I would tell you?'

'Then let me warn you against getting too immersed in this case and forgetting the realities of modern-day policing. I want you to update Detective Irwin with whatever leads you develop. And don't get so personal that you forget what's what. Be careful of jeopardizing your career and the reputation of this police force.'

'My job is to seek out the truth and bring justice to those who break the law.'

'Just remember, Daly, you're a police officer, first and foremost.'

After the meeting, Irwin followed Daly into the corridor.

'A good performance in there,' said the younger detective. 'That ought to buy you a few more days on the case, but nothing more.'

Irwin's eyes looked angry, but calm had settled over Daly.

'Rest assured,' continued Irwin, 'this is my show, my circus, and the whole thing will be packed up and gone within a week – less, if I can manage it. And what will you do then?'

'Wait for the next circus?'

'If this were the old police force, they'd have booted you out long ago.'

'The same police force that colluded with the enemy, I presume?'

'Here's a short history lesson for you, Daly. We weren't at war with

Loyalists. We were fighting the IRA. Given the provocation, I think the RUC carried out their duties with great composure.'

Daly could have said more, but Irwin's intensity repelled him, and he no longer felt like goading him. His mind had settled on a different target and he walked away. In hindsight, it was easy to see the truth in what Irwin had said. Daly understood the corrosive effect of repeated IRA attacks and bombs, how they might paralyse not only the security forces but also the individual lives of many police officers, souring ambition, darkening minds, sapping the will to uphold law and order to the most rigorous standards. Moreover, if there had been a secret committee operating through the RUC it had undoubtedly betrayed many honest, hard-working police officers.

9

After the meeting was over, Fealty reached his hand up to his collar, loosened his top button and pulled off his tie. He slipped it into a drawer and leaned back in his seat. He listened to the distant siren of a police car speeding off to an emergency and, closer by, the sounds of muffled steps in the corridor and someone coughing. He sighed and lifted a thin file from his desk. He held it in his hands without opening it. For a long time, he sat there staring at the windows in an unfocused way, dimly aware of the raindrops pattering against the glass. It had been a bleak, strange day made doubly odd by Daly's revelation about his mother. The conversation had tired him, but it had also stimulated his memory, dredging up old images from the past.

As his mind turned over almost-forgotten incidents, the emptiness of the room began to daunt him: the blankness of the white walls, the lack of any filing cabinets or shelves, the absence of any mementoes or souvenirs from his long career, as though his office was nothing more than a hollow container for the light from the windows and his lonely figure. Not for the first time since moving to the new headquarters, he felt like an invisible guest in an anonymous hotel.

The paleness of the walls added to his tiredness. Perhaps it was the smell of fresh paint. He gripped the file as though it was all he had managed to salvage from his old office at Armagh police station, a building that had once been at the centre of Walsh's murder triangle.

He understood that the new headquarters had been erected to lead the police force into the future, rather than carry the burden of the past. All those branching corridors and clean, ordered rooms, which he hated, as if architecture might offer an elaborate means of forgetting where you came from, the mistakes you made, the unfinished business of unresolved crimes.

Unfortunately, in spite of the best efforts of the police chiefs, the past still loomed. It was undeniably powerful and close. He had felt its force in Daly's revelation, and he held it in the slim file. It demanded attention and loyalty, but loyalty to the past meant betraying the present and the principles upon which the politicians had founded the new Northern Ireland. This was the difficult choice he now faced.

He sighed heavily and stared at the photograph of the elderly spy on the cover. Daniel Hegarty. He was surprised that the informer had returned to border country, like an old dog marking the territory of his youth. History moved in strange ways. Northern Ireland had gone through a peace process, decommissioning, elections for an Assembly, the country slowly evolving towards a brighter, more peaceful future, but every now and again there were setbacks. Something came along that threatened to dismantle all the years of progress.

For most of the 1980s and 90s, Daniel Hegarty had been a pivotal agent working for British Intelligence within the IRA. He had probably saved dozens of lives, but also been implicated in just as many murders. For informers like Hegarty, there was no such thing as courage without some form of betrayal, and it was inevitable that they became entangled in criminality. Fealty reasoned that if Hegarty was about to blow the lid on all his terrorist crimes as an agent of the state, it could be argued that the future peace of Northern Ireland was at stake.

I am doing the right thing, he reassured himself as he leafed slowly through the pages. *How could I behave any differently?* The scale of priorities outweighed the plight of one lonely detective like Daly. Special Branch had lost one round to Hegarty, but the game as a whole would be theirs. They would come out of this with something more important, a smokescreen to hide the most unsavoury deeds of the past. All he had to do was stage-manage the hunt for Hegarty and his eventual capture. To do so would mean breaking some of the most fundamental codes governing intelligence work. However, Hegarty had left them with no other practical solution to the problems he posed and the power he wielded. The changing political realities of the country dictated that the spy should be sacrificed for the greater good of society. Sometimes betrayal required more courage than loyalty.

He removed a flash drive from the file and attached it to his computer. He opened the video file he had been watching that morning. It was the footage from the hotel CCTV cameras taken the day before.

Fealty had developed a fascination with the grainy images of Hegarty's lonely figure – the way he sat slumped in the hotel chairs, his balding head as he walked through the foyer, clutching a glass of whiskey at the bar, his face always lowered, carrying the same briefcase wherever he went. Fealty followed his limping figure, watching him wander seemingly invisible in the wedding hubbub. At times, it was like tracing the movements of a little boy weaving his way among grown-ups, or an old man lost among children. Fealty tracked his movements again through the sequence of cameras. The spy seemed to follow the secret path of a sleepwalker's dream, picking his way through the throng, from the bar to the reception rooms and into the foyer, the crowds forming and dissolving around him, oblivious to his presence.

Fealty froze the video at the point the young woman entered the bar. Her face was only ever in profile and half-covered by her hair, but her pose was unmistakable, her shoulders straight, and her head held high and haughty. That bloody reporter, he thought. What was she doing there? What leads to a story was she sniffing out? Journalists like Jacqueline Pryce were dangerous because they tended to follow the most poisonous of secrets, the ones that had the potential to become the scoop of the year. He watched her as the crowds milled past the bar. He would have liked to see more of her facial expression, to determine what was going through her mind, but her features were always averted, her head tilted slightly as though she was watching someone.

Several times, he replayed the moment Pryce and Hegarty made contact. He crouched over the screen hunting for a telltale clue, a chance to lip-read what they were saying, a glimpse of her face. His tension increased, a helpless, deep-seated anxiety. He watched the briefcase; the two of them clearly meeting as strangers; the confident flick of her hair; Hegarty's limp and look of consternation. They were messages that he interpreted as a summons from the dangerous shadows of the past. He would have liked to ignore them, but to do so now would be to condemn himself to inaction.

He stilled the images at the point where Hegarty was about to follow Pryce up to Walsh's room. The close-up shot revealed his bulging eyes and tightened mouth. Fealty watched the rest of the footage. The look of surprise remained etched on Hegarty's face. It was, Fealty realized, something more than an expression of surprise. It was the face of a man inhabiting a dream that was going from bad to worse. Recognizing that look heightened Fealty's uneasiness. Men like Hegarty had the gift of dragging others into their personal nightmares. In many respects, his life was a tiny, insignificant nightmare in the long dark night of the Troubles, but with Pryce's involvement, it had the potential to become one of the most decisive stories of the last forty years of Irish history.

Unfortunately, there was no guidebook to help him control the consequences of Hegarty spilling his secrets. It was inevitable that over the passage of time, some of his story would come to light. The hope was that society would have undergone many transformations in the meantime, so that eventually the protagonists and their motives might appear outdated and ambiguous. If that was not the case, it was Fealty's job to control the succession of secrets as they unravelled and somehow direct public opinion, the hovering of suspicion and anger that still haunted the country, so that it reached a safe target, an expendable target.

He closed the video file and returned to contemplating the last of the evening light shining through the windows. Diluted through the screen of raindrops, it cast a vague luminosity on the walls, and on the white paper on his desk. It was the type of light that could be more oppressive than any darkness. He brooded over the file, waiting for the light to fade completely. He tried to think of another course of action that would resolve his difficulties, but he drew a blank. He flicked on his desk lamp, picked up his telephone and summoned Irwin and Donaldson.

'The man we are looking for is called Daniel Hegarty,' Fealty told the pair when they returned. 'He used to be a spy.'

'What sort of spy?' asked Irwin.

'An informer within the ranks of the IRA,' replied Donaldson.

'We know there's a full file on him held by the Ministry of Defence, but it's highly classified.' Fealty drummed his hands on the desk. 'It will take months to obtain it.'

'Fortunately, the RUC held files on all the MOD's informers,' said Donaldson. 'At least the ones we knew about.'

'You mean you didn't share intelligence?' said Irwin.

'Not a chance. We were fierce rivals.'

'The information we hold on Hegarty is scant.' Fealty handed Irwin the file. 'We know that he was recruited in 1974 by a Major George Hannon, and that he has been implicated in several murders.'

Irwin flicked through the information.

'In the circumstances, it's highly regrettable to have involved Daly,' remarked Donaldson.

'But then again, he is involved.' Fealty bared his teeth in what might have been a smile but looked more like a grimace. 'His mother's death is unfinished business for him.'

'I'm concerned, too,' said Irwin. 'He's out of control. He'll take risks other detectives would avoid.'

'Your judgement is correct,' said Fealty. 'In fact, I can't think of anyone better suited to serve our purposes.'

'Which are what?'

'To have someone act as human bait and draw Hegarty out of his hiding place. Let Daly chase his mother's ghost in border country. He'll go in deeper than any other police officer would care to.'

'I thought you wanted the investigation brushed aside as quickly as possible,' said Irwin. 'Rather than stir up the past.'

'We are in a more delicate position than we first thought,' said Fealty. 'I'd rather the investigation end now but that's no longer my major problem.'

Donaldson's thinking was more organized than Irwin's.

'You're getting pressure from above. They don't want the investigation to end here.'

'In a few more days, they might come round to our way of thinking. But first, we have to find Hegarty. Or rather we have to guide Daly towards him.'

'Give Daly a fugitive to chase and he'll go for it,' said Donaldson. 'Remember that tight spot he got into with the Croatian prostitute?'

A smirk crept across Irwin's face.

'I think Daly will find Hegarty much too fascinating to ignore. The shame of his betrayals. His secret life as a spy.'

Donaldson nodded.

'He tends to fall under the spell of people like Hegarty, outlaws who live in the shadows.'

Fealty agreed. Daly approached dangerous runaways as though he were a thwarted social worker, using them so soak up his own loneliness and loss. Fealty showed them the footage from the hotel.

'What's Hegarty carrying in the briefcase?' asked Irwin.

'From what we understand, he has a number of confidential intelligence files. Information that was destined for Walsh, which risked compromising the security of former agents. We presume that Hegarty had been feeding Walsh information about the weapons used in his so-called murder triangle and the gunmen's links to the RUC.'

'Do we know his next move? What will he do with the files now that Walsh is dead?'

'We have no idea.'

'The MOD must be shitting bricks.'

'We all are.'

'But our only worry is Hegarty, at least for now.' Fealty paused and eyed up the Special Branch detective. 'Listen, Irwin, I want you to find out the full history of Hegarty's involvement with paramilitaries, starting with when he was first recruited by the British Army, and ending today. I want a complete list of his betrayals and double-dealings. We'll have to move fast against him. Establish him as someone not to be trusted. Someone tainted by the darkest shadows of the Troubles.'

'What if we can't find anything?' asked Irwin.

'Then we'll have to invent a past for him.' Fealty thought of the journalist Pryce. 'One with enough links to the truth to make the story credible to our friends in the media.'

After they had left the room, Fealty worked his way through the footage one more time. As he followed the flickering images, he remembered a point that had occurred to him during the meeting with Donaldson and Irwin. He zoomed in on the briefcase Hegarty was carrying. It was hard to make out its shape, a crooked little shadow. He worked backwards through the footage. His mind felt bright and alert. The tension in his body increased.

At one point, he saw that Hegarty was holding the briefcase slightly higher than usual, as though it had grown lighter. In the next scene, it had dropped again, but the informer's arm looked rigid, forced. He realized that he had observed an important change, one that Hegarty had tried to disguise. At some time during the morning, he must have emptied the briefcase of its contents. Perhaps he had suspected he was falling into a trap and had jettisoned the secret documents as a safety precaution. But where had he hidden them?

He ran through the entire morning in the hotel. He saw that apart from Pryce, Hegarty had not approached anyone else. He had not even conversed with the waiting staff or bartenders. Several times, he stared at a member of the wedding party, as if building up the courage to break his isolation, but at the last moment he always turned away.

Fealty scrutinized the footage again: Hegarty sitting shadowed in his seat while the wedding crowd flowed around him. The informer always seemed to occupy the edge of the frame, gravitating towards something beyond the scope of the camera. Fealty managed to narrow the mystery of the briefcase to the half-hour or so before the informer met Pryce. Hegarty had briefly placed the briefcase on the windowsill next to his seat. He sat motionless with his back to the window. There was no one beside him but he seemed to be talking to someone. Why had he left the case on the sill? Was it some sort of signal?

Fealty leaned forward, slowed the video frame by frame, and spotted the key to the puzzle. A small pale hand appeared through the window, slipped into the briefcase and removed something. Hegarty had stopped talking. His shoulders were slumped. He reached round and removed the briefcase from the sill. His face appeared soothed. He waited for a moment, and then got up and walked away.

Fealty scrolled through the footage captured outside the hotel. He wasn't sure what he was expecting to see. It was difficult to match the sequence of events outside the hotel to that within, but he persevered. He focused on the footage of a group of boys playing with a ball on the hotel's front lawn. They ran in and out of the frame. He mulled over the scene. At one point, the game was interrupted for about a minute when the ball rolled close to a wall beneath a half-opened window.

A small boy with ginger hair ran to collect the ball but froze before the window. He stood there for almost a full minute. Several times, he wavered and looked back at his playing companions. The other children remained at a distance, like an audience watching an unfolding drama. The boy stepped closer to the window. He nodded his head and adjusted his stance. His hand reached through the open window and removed a yellow folder. Then he ran back to the other boys. Fealty allowed himself a small grin of satisfaction. He had spotted the informer's trick. The point at which he had transformed a passing child into a courier, a secret messenger.

After another hour of scrutinizing the footage, Fealty worked out the room number the boy had been staying in with his family. He noted it down and rang the hotel. After he had finished speaking to the receptionist, he put down the phone and rocked back and forth in his chair for a while. He had made a breakthrough, and no longer felt the helpless tension that had haunted him since the afternoon and clouded his thinking. The way forward was quite simple. Hegarty had broken the rules of engagement and now so would he.

10

Daly descended into border country again, switching from the motorway to the side roads. He wasn't really driving; the narrow twisting roads were dragging him along. He sat hunched over the steering wheel, the engine humming and whining with the strain of shifting gears.

The meeting with Special Branch had made him more determined to uncover the truth behind Walsh's death and the murder of McClintock. *Why were Special Branch so keen to take over the case?* It seemed to Daly that Walsh's rooting around in the past must have thrown up something unpleasant and potentially devastating for someone still alive and in a position of power within the security forces. It was the only rational explanation. Those terrible events in the 1970s must be linked to something that was happening right now.

He pulled up at a crossroads close to where Walsh had crashed his car. It was quiet, almost dusk. He hadn't a clue which road to take. He watched the cows in the fields returning to their byres. A dark anonymous-looking house sat nearby. It was a public house, as obscure as they made them in South Armagh, the beer kegs piled at the side of the building the only evidence of its true function.

It seemed a logical place to ask for directions to the holy glen that the petrol attendant had described to him on the night of Walsh's crash. Inside, he encountered the old-fashioned layout of a country bar and lounge, more like a front room and back scullery, the kind of bar that was all obstacles and tight corners, an unforgiving place for a lost stranger. The faint smell of urine and bleach lingered in the air, and a sweeter odour, that of poteen, illicit booze, the stuff of which truly great hangovers are made. He bruised his shin against a low table and cursed.

Laden bottles clinked from a room within. Eventually a middle-aged barman appeared from the blackness at the end of the bar. For a moment, it felt liberating to be an anonymous passer-by asking directions to a site of ancient pilgrimage. It was so far removed from his normal work as a police detective. However, the resistance from the bartender surprised him.

'Why have you come here?' the barman replied with undisguised coldness.

The question confused him and he took a moment to answer. A few old men sitting in a snug glared at him. They gave each other a knowing look. Daly noticed a picture of the Virgin Mary and a set of rosary beads dangling beside the whiskey optics. He knew that it would be to his advantage to play the religious card rather than disclose the fact he was a police detective. It was the most expedient tactic he could think of.

'My father used to bring me to the glen as a child. But I've forgotten where it is.' His voice lowered. 'I've a special intention to pray for.'

The barman had a round face with beefy jowls. He looked the type of person that would usually be easy to get on with. He frowned.

'Are you a reporter?'

'No. Not at all,' said Daly, smiling in an attempt to lessen the mystery.

Yet he had failed to allay the barman's suspicions. Daly could sense he thought he was a fraud or something worse.

'There are men and women who drive up there after dark and flash their headlights at each other.' The barman regarded Daly warily. 'Their cars come down from the motorway. Are you one of them?'

As a police officer, Daly was all too aware of cases where couples sought out wild beauty spots for sexual adventures with like-minded people. *Maybe the glen is plagued with people seeking sexual thrills and he thinks I'm one of them*, he thought with an inner smile.

'No. As I said, I have a special intention to pray for.'

The bartender seemed unconvinced.

'The path to the well is covered in mud at this time of year.'

'I don't mind.'

'Hardly any ceremonies take place there now. Ever since the cops shot little Tara Grimes.' He looked sharply at Daly, his hostility increasing.

Daly nodded. He remembered the details of the case. The girl had been playing with a stick in a roadside hedgerow when a police patrol shot her believing she was a gunman preparing an ambush. The barman placed his heavy hands on the other side of the bar. They looked used to wielding larger, blunter objects than beer taps and glasses. Daly was glad he was not here in an official capacity. More locals drifted in behind him, waiting to place their orders. Their impatience was more compelling than anything Daly could say or do.

'It's a mile further up the back road,' said the barman eventually. 'There's a little lay-by on the left-hand side and opposite is a hole in the blackthorn hedge. That's the entrance – blink and you'll miss it. Just follow the steps down.'

'Thanks.'

'It'll be dark soon. I wouldn't hang around there if I were you.'

Daly parked the car in the lay-by. He opened the door and heard the panicky flight of unseen birds. He stood at the gap in the hedge. It was a bleak threshold. He spotted a lacy bra hanging from a bush, and wondered what sort of people made love amid cramped thorns and shadows. His feet sank in mud lined with the tracks of cars. Several centuries ago, persecuted Catholics filed to lonely glens like this to hear Mass in secret and to drink from the holy wells. Now their descendants came stumbling in the dark, clumsy as bullocks. It felt like a final unravelling of a God-fearing society, a trampling of sex and secrecy, the careless tyre tracks, the beer cans and cigarette stubs embedded in the mud. He felt a sharp need to push through the thorns and seek out somewhere more remote and wild, where there was no longer any evidence of human intrusion.

In the months after the separation from Anna, his wife of ten years, Daly had taken to visiting the glens and holy wells around Tyrone. He had returned to the sites of childhood pilgrimages in the hope they might sharpen his faith and help him through that difficult time. No doubt he was searching for some sort of refuge or key to enlightenment up and down the wild glens that riddled the border countryside. As if it was as easy as entering the right landscape to return to childhood and resurrect the memories of faith and moral certainty.

He had not been receptive enough, or perhaps he had lacked the mental detachment from his day-to-day problems, or the correct blend of the two, for he had found nothing. Just the same black pools of spring water, the same thorny twigs stirring against a dark sky, the same rain-soaked petitions hanging from the trees. No burning bushes or oracles. Not so much treasure chests of spirituality as spoil heaps of frustrated prayers.

This particular glen was no different. Daly stared into the depths of the reputedly miraculous pool but all he saw was an unnerving stillness, a darkness distilled moment by moment from the surrounding rocks. Along the sides of the well, he found evidence of recent prayer: a collection of burnt-out candles, snippets of paper, rusting rosary beads and holy medals tied to the thorns, as well as fresh boot-marks in the squelchy terrain.

It was the practice of the devout to hang a religious ornament or a piece of string to the overhanging tree as part of their pilgrimage, hence the collection of ornaments dangling from the twigs. They were the clue that led Daly to believe Walsh had been coming from a holy well on the night of the crash. He had deduced that the priest had visited the well and removed a bunch of the tangled artefacts because he was looking for a key too. Something to resolve his predicament, or reduce the burden of the past.

Daly examined the offerings hanging from the tree as though they were evidence to be analysed and dissected. Visitors had left behind their written petitions, some of them in plastic envelopes. He gazed at the handwriting, the mishmash of prayer, scripture and heartfelt pleas. He could almost hear their words whispering in his ear. Every twig held a burden; more than the tree's spiny branches could bear, it seemed to him. He stepped back, overwhelmed, the tree writhing over him like a black sinuous altar.

Out of instinct, he mouthed a few Hail Marys. It was not his most convinced praying, but nor was it simply a lonely detective speaking to himself. It was something else entirely different. A spell to bring evil out of its hiding place. Perhaps that was why people still flocked to half-pagan sites like the holy well, he thought, whispering prayers that were more like magical incantations, seeking deliverance from darkness. As a detective, it was his job to track down the murderous forces that lurked within the minds of ordinary people, the urge to kill and destroy. He was engaged in the human war against evil. He didn't need to invoke prayers. He would discover his own way to lay siege to the people responsible for Walsh's death and drive them from their hiding places.

He approached the tree again. He reached up with his hand and felt amid the crevices of its branches. He groped with his fingers until he found the object he was looking for. Something thin and metallic. Not a holy offering, more a profane stowaway. A mobile phone. Its screen glowed as soon as he touched its keys. He smiled at it. He lifted it into the air, and walked around with it, holding it as high as he could, trying to get a signal but failing. He walked back up to his car. He took out his own phone; hunted out the number the abbot had given him, and called it. The other one buzzed into life.

It made sense as soon as Daly had worked out that Walsh had come from the glen. He had hidden the phone in a safe place – and where was safer to a Catholic priest than a holy well? No one in Special Branch with all their years of expertise would have understood that as well as he did. It was a question of geography. Holy glens were always secret places, more like tunnels through the labyrinth of hills surrounding the border. Their remoteness and steep hillsides made them impervious to mobile phone technology. Walsh had hidden the phone in the closest place he could find to an inaccessible dimension.

But why? The priest must have felt hunted or followed in some way, and fearing that the phone contained incriminating information, had ditched it. Daly searched in the phone's files but they were all empty. He scrolled through the call history. There were numerous missed calls from the same number on the night of Walsh's death and the following morning. The caller's name had been saved under Hegarty. Out of curiosity, he rang the number. He counted ten rings and then it went to a recorded message. He hung up and tried another number saved under the name Jacqueline. To his surprise, a woman's voice answered almost immediately.

'Who is this?' Her voice seemed to contract as she spoke.

He answered without thinking.

'It's me.'

There was silence on the phone.

'Aloysius?'

'Yes.'

Again a silence, as if the woman wasn't breathing.

'Where can we meet?' asked Daly.

He regretted the carelessness of the question, but she replied immediately, 'Where are you now?'

He didn't answer.

The signal faded a little. She was travelling somewhere.

'I'll be outside the hotel in twenty minutes.' She spoke carefully, as if spelling out a set of instructions to a child. 'I'll see you at the far end of the car park.'

'OK,' he said and hung up.

11

There was only one hotel the woman could have meant. Half an hour later, Daly swung his vehicle into the grounds of Clary Lodge. He drove to the end of the car park, his headlamps lighting up a blue car. A woman stood next to it, dressed in a dark suit, skirt and red-heeled shoes.

She was immediately hostile when Daly approached her with Walsh's phone.

'You're not Father Walsh.'

'He couldn't come. I'm here in his place.'

'It wasn't him on the phone.' Her voice was edged with grief. 'It was you. Aloysius is dead.'

Daly nodded a little sheepishly.

'Who are you?'

'Inspector Celcius Daly. I'm investigating his death.'

She relaxed visibly and looked at him with curiosity.

'We should chat in the hotel bar.'

She turned and walked away. Daly stared at her back, which was stiff and strained-looking. The click-clack of her heels sounded out of beat, the muscles of her bare calves tightening with each step. He realized that she was limping slightly. He followed her up to the hotel entrance, staring at her red heels and deft calves.

Inside the hotel, she nudged beside him as they sat down, her figure composed and neat in her skirt and suit. She swiftly ordered two coffees and smiled at him. He realized that whereas he had explained his connection to Father Walsh, she had not introduced herself at all.

'Coffee is the last thing I need right now,' she said. 'I've barely slept. I've gone through all the usual police contacts to find out what theories you guys are working on but I'm having no success at all. I don't even know if my life is in danger or not. Should I have a protection officer assigned to me, do you think, Inspector?'

She stared at his uncertain gaze.

'Forgive me for not introducing myself,' she said. 'My name is Jacqueline Pryce.' She extended a slim, pointed hand that to Daly felt as neat as a digging tool. 'I'm a journalist.'

'Which newspaper do you work for?'

'The one that pays the most,' she said with a smile.

She passed him an NUJ card, which he examined. However, it didn't contain the information he wanted, which was how this sleek, pretty journalist had got her life entangled with the unhappy business of Walsh's death.

'Ever since the night of Aloysius's crash I've had this feeling that I'm being watched. I keep thinking I'm being followed while driving. Tell me, Inspector, are Special Branch watching me?'

'Why would Special Branch want to do that?'

'It was something that Aloysius said to me before he died. That I should keep looking over my shoulders to check for shadows.'

'What made him say that?'

'Because he believed we were getting too close to the truth. That we had wandered into forbidden territory.'

'What you mean by the truth?'

She told him about Father Walsh's theory of a murder triangle – that a large number of apparently random sectarian killings in Tyrone and Armagh were all connected. He had needed someone to help write up his research into some sort of a book, thus he had given her copies of all his maps and findings. At first, they had seemed rambling and chaotic, she explained, but she kept dipping in and out of them over the space of several months.

'What intrigued me most were his claims about collusion between Loyalists and police officers,' she said. 'I spent a couple of weeks in the newspaper archives, reading as many reports as I could on those murders. I contacted the national archive of government papers and followed his lines of inquiry. Eventually my research began to bear fruit, and I came away with the feeling that Aloysius was correct.'

'How?'

'That there was a pattern. A web of connections between the killings. And something else: it struck me as odd that this gang was able to go undetected for so long. The killings should have rung alarm bells all the way to the top of government. However, nothing was done. The murderous cycle continued month after month. Even when some of the gang members were charged and convicted, they received only the lightest possible sentences.'

Daly decided not to press her on what she meant by the web of connections. He wasn't interested in hearing that kind of detail, at least not yet.

She leaned a little closer to him.

'Now tell me, Inspector, am I being followed? I need to know.'

'I wouldn't know, to tell you the truth. They might be following me as well.'

It was her turn to express surprise.

'Why would they do that?'

There was something exquisite and finely honed about her curiosity. Her eyes flashed at him. Daly's mouth felt dry but he decided to plunge right in.

'My interest in Walsh's murder triangle is more personal than you think.'

Daly was surprised at how easy it was to talk to this strange woman. She had access to brutal facts about his mother's death, and this made him more wary and respectful than he had been of any other journalist, or woman for that matter. She might reveal things about his mother that he had never known. Journalism was a fickle business, with rapid deadlines and a superficial attachment to the truth, but something in her manner struck him as oddly trustworthy.

'One of the pins on his map had my mother's name next to it.'

'She was one of the victims?'

'That's correct.'

She stared at him and waited.

'And you were…' She paused to scrutinize his face. '… surprised to see her name there?'

He paused.

'Yes.'

Amid her concern, he detected a trace of satisfaction – excitement, almost. She was eager to get inside his feelings.

He stumbled on with his story.

'I was only a boy, nine years old, at the time. They told me a different version of events. That she died during crossfire in an IRA attack on a police unit.'

Her interest doubled.

'Who were "they"?'

'The police at the time. My father, too.' He hesitated. 'I was a lonely child, unworldly in many ways. I never thought he kept anything from me. Now I'm confused.'

She leaned forward again, gazing at him intently. He reminded himself that he barely knew her. He viewed her slender face, the outline of her lips, and below, her exposed neck leading to the top of her chest. Was this a form of encouragement, he wondered, a token of her appreciation that he was opening up? Daly was unsure, but he could tell she was a subtle interrogator, and observant, too. She knew he was intensely aware of the proximity of her body.

'I would like to have it sorted out,' he told her. 'The truth, I mean.'

He wondered how much of the story he had invented himself based on the meagre details relayed to him. Perhaps that was the nature of childhood memories, a hazy narrative created by immature minds to deal with loss and pain.

'Somehow, I always believed in the back of my mind that the explanation of her death was inadequate.' His voice cracked slightly.

She appeared to bask in his discomfort, the inner conflict between his reticence and his need to spill the truth. He grew shy, worried that an excess of grief might leap from his heart and overwhelm him. However, she had a journalist's knack of showing no discomfort or surprise at the most intimate of revelations.

'What do you remember of that time?'

'I remember countless checkpoints. Soldiers and policemen searching my father's car.' He stared at his hands. 'I never saw the scene itself. You know, the place where she was killed. But somehow I remember it clearly. I wasn't an eyewitness, but I've invented all the details in my imagination. Do you know what I mean?' He stared at her. 'I wasn't there that morning but I can recall it as though I was. Am I making sense?'

'Yes.'

'And now that I've learned the story was a lie, and I try to remember what actually happened that morning, where I was and what I was doing, there's nothing there any more. Just a blank.'

He glanced at her. She was deeply engaged with what he was saying. Motionless, she waited for him to continue, but he had nothing more to say. With a neat shuffle, she moved her body closer to his.

'Father Walsh was committed to the truth,' she said, examining his face for a reaction. 'To exposing cover-ups and lies and filling in the blanks that remained amid all the grief. His search was leading him to some shocking conclusions.'

'Like what?'

'That the murders weren't political assassinations. None of the victims were in any way involved in politics, let alone the IRA. Including, I presume, your mother.'

Such was the arbitrary nature of sectarian murder, thought Daly.

'It's clear they were killed because they were Catholics,' he said. 'Surely, that's all there was to it.'

'Aloysius believed there was another reason.' She leaned closer and almost touched his hand.

'Where are you going with this?'

'Aloysius believed there was logic behind the apparent randomness of the attacks. The geographical pattern and the dates. For a start, the majority of the murders happened on the first Monday of the month.'

Daly shook his head. He was in no mood to follow her reasoning.

'What are you suggesting? That my mother was deliberately targeted for some reason other than her religion?'

'Yes.'

'But there was no sense behind the killings. They were the work of psychopathic gunmen and you know it.'

'Think about it for a moment. The gang must have studied their targets, followed their movements. They didn't just pile into a car and drive off looking for a Catholic to murder. They were specific.'

She made the suggestion as gently as possible, but she might as well have been probing a painful wound with a razor. He tried to seal himself off from the source of grief so that he might understand the outrageous thing she was suggesting.

'Why are you taking sectarianism out of the frame? What other motive could there have been?'

She held back from going any further.

'That's the puzzle. Poor Aloysius spent years trying to solve it.'

She ordered another set of coffees.

'Where did your mother work?'

'She was a nurse at the local hospital.'

'Did she have any Protestant friends?'

'What are you implying? That a colleague marked her down as a target?'

'We'll have to dig up staff lists for the wards she worked on. Find out if anyone had links with the paramilitaries or the police.'

She kept questioning him as he sipped the coffee, trying to pin down his memories of that dark year. However, they were slipping from his grasp. All he had left was the image of his mother's blue shoes on the bedroom floor and his father rummaging through the drawers.

'I've already told you how flawed my memory is,' he said. 'There's no point asking any more questions.'

Suddenly he felt tired. He reminded himself that Pryce was a journalist, not a therapist or confidante. She was interested only in proving controversial conspiracy theories and stirring up the past. Perhaps the theory was nothing more than a journalist's ploy to gain the greatest possible publicity for her book.

He was completely sure of one thing, however. A stray event had robbed him of his mother, the wanton behaviour of a gang of lunatics who did not know what they were doing from one moment to the next. That was what gave terrorists their edge, after all. Murder on a whim, their target constantly changing.

'Are you a practising Catholic, Inspector?' she asked.

He glanced at her, and then looked at his empty cup of coffee. He wanted desperately to walk away from this impetuous woman and her oddly intimate manner. He did not believe that the obsessive research of a lonely priest could dispel the murkiness of the past. The truth had disappeared more than thirty years ago down a labyrinth of twisted country lanes along with his mother's incognito killers. It was gone forever, he told himself. Like his mother's body. What was the point in following it into the labyrinth?

'I asked are you a practising Catholic?'

'Sorry, I was distracted.' Had he imagined a judgemental tone in her voice? 'What do you mean?' He felt challenged and a little disorientated by the question.

'I mean, if you were, it might be a form of consolation that the man who shed light on your mother's death was a priest.'

'How?'

'I don't know. In the sense that his research was a way of sanctifying evil.' She spoke with a measure of reverence.

'I don't think anyone can sanctify evil. Not even the holiest of priests.'

'Perhaps you're right.'

Daly said nothing. He considered there might be a measure of truth in what she had said – in that the priest's meticulous charting of the murder triangle had exalted the deaths of its victims. Walsh had wanted to make the secret of their murder so large and all-encompassing it could no longer be buried in the past.

She leaned in closer.

'I think we recognize something in each other, Inspector. Sometimes fate brings people together.'

He blinked.

'You will find out what happened to Father Walsh. I can see that in your eyes.'

'What do you see?'

'A mother's only son who wants to know as much as I do about what happened that night. Why and how Walsh died. That's the reason you rang me in the first place.'

It jarred him a little that she knew he was an only son. How had she discovered that piece of information?

She removed her mobile phone.

'If you give me your mobile number I'll ring you if anything fresh comes up.'

He felt uncomfortable with where she was leading him. She was drawing him down a road into the past, but not the past he knew. It was a sinister place, stranger than any wilderness. He should walk away right now, he thought. He should just leave, and turn away from this road; yet knowing this, and still resenting the intimate draw of her voice and her smile, he acquiesced and gave her his mobile number.

She stood up, smoothed her skirt and held out her hand for him to shake. It felt slender and pointed. He was reminded again of a cold little digging tool.

12

When night fell, Daly was so tired he almost forgot to carry the black hen to its coop. The urgent peck-peck of its beak against the glass woke him as he drifted into sleep. He got dressed and lifted her from the porch window. He stumbled alarmingly in the darkness, holding the hen close to his chest. A fox barked a few fields away. He could feel her trembling. The track to the coop had never seemed so uneven and overgrown, and he was glad to slip the hen into its hay-filled darkness. He could almost have fallen into that cosy little hiding place, too.

He crawled into bed and fell into a fitful sleep. Episodes from his childhood percolated through his mind, memories of his father mumbling to himself, his mother's shoes, the two of them standing together in one of the back fields staring at the ground. His subconscious was trying to isolate clues from the things his father had done and said, dragging him up out of sleep to remember. A pattern in the fields. His father digging energetically. Something inexplicable, hovering at the edge of his awareness. What had the old man buried there? He forced himself back down into sleep, hoping that by morning time he might begin to understand.

He dreamed that he saw the back of his mother walking slowly down a dark lane. She was wandering in a maze of little roads, partially dazed. She turned to smile at him absent-mindedly, beckoning him to follow, but something warned him that her journey was botched, that they would never discover the roads that would lead her back home.

Afterwards, he lay awake thinking that the lough-shore terrain of entangled lanes might be the landscape of the past itself. He needed instructions on how to untangle this inner geography for he felt as dazed as his mother had looked in his dream. He needed more clues than those provided by Walsh's murder map. It did not bode well, beginning this journey into the past feeling so confused, but he had no other choice.

In another dream, he imagined that his cottage had grown a set of spindly legs and was strutting about the fields. Every time he stepped close to the front door, the building became agitated, whirling and spinning in the air with a mind of its own. The more he watched the cottage, the more it resembled an old hen looking for a place to roost. Finally, it settled in one of the back fields of the farm.

Yet when Daly went looking for the cottage, it had disappeared without a trace. In its place stood his father with a spade gripped in his hands. It was raining heavily and the earth around the old man was disturbed.

'You're going to get drenched,' said Daly.

'I'm on guard,' replied his father.

'What are you guarding?'

Daly's father gestured at the blackness of the upturned soil.

'The secrets of the past.'

At his father's words, the earth began to boil like tar, lumpy and full of craters. It piled up behind his the old man in the shape of a rising wave.

'What secrets are you and the cottage hiding from me?' Daly demanded.

But before his father could reply, the earth heaved into a steep slope, and swept over his thin frame. Daly looked up just before the wave slammed into him, and woke up with a start.

The next morning, he made his way gingerly through the rooms of the cottage. He hunkered down at the breakfast table and ate some lumpy porridge. It was ironic, but he had never felt so stranded, so far away from home. He recalled his strange dreams and tried to interpret their imagery. He wondered what message his unconscious was trying to communicate to him.

He peered through the small kitchen window, and for the first time in his life contemplated the humps and folds in the field behind the cottage. Had they always been there, or was his memory correct in believing they dated from around the time of his mother's death? From what he could remember his father had abandoned grazing that particular field and never tried to farm it in any way.

He forced his feet into an old pair of Wellington boots and scrambled over a little iron gate. At first the folds of the field felt familiar, the hiding places of his childhood, but the terrain soon changed. He spent half an hour trailing through hummocky grass and peering into thickets of blackthorn; his trouser bottoms grew soaking wet. His thoughts kept wandering off into his solitude, his mind a blank. He had no inkling as to what he was searching for. He kept returning to one corner of the field, more bramble than grass, with an odd conjunction of raised banks and old stones peeping through the weeds. However, the undergrowth of briars and nettles had welded itself together, blocking any further investigation. Badly scratched by thorns and stung by nettles, he stepped back and tried to survey the scene. Nothing about the field and its contours seemed logical. Why had his father left it all those years ago, squeezing his hungry cattle into the marshier, outlying fields of the farm?

He stared at the raised banks. He realized that they were too long and high to have been the result of even his father's most Herculean digging. Something mechanical had been at work here, piling the earth and stones into these irregular mounds. However, he had no recollection of ever seeing diggers working in the field. Perhaps his father had attempted to clear the field of its stones and bushes to make it more arable. Perhaps the abandonment of the project had more to do with grief or infirmity, or the descent into old age, than anything mysterious or sinister.

A cold chill rose from the insides of his boots. A misty rain filled the air, shrouding everything with a nullifying greyness. He was wasting his time here, he realized. He had been mistaken in believing the humps and folds of that strangely uneven field might reveal the secrets of the past. He left the puzzle behind and returned to the warmth of the kitchen.

From the mantelpiece in the living room, he took down a framed photograph of his father in his later years. He scrutinized the familiar face. It surprised him to realize he had only ever glanced at the picture in a superficial way. He had always thought the photographer had caught his father's charming, slightly downturned smile and the warmth of his eyes, but now, examining the smile at the corners of the eyes, he thought he saw something strange and subdued, a sadness, perhaps even a trace of bitterness. Another detail that disturbed him was the clock on the shelf behind his father. It still sat in the same sun-faded position against the scullery wall, showing the same time as it did in the photograph: a quarter past eleven. He had thought the clock had stopped working some time after his father's death, but from the evidence of the picture it had stopped years previously and never been fixed.

Gripping the picture, Daly had the sensation that he was teetering at the edge of a void, and that he might fall without a place to land. He replaced the picture on the mantelpiece. Now that Walsh's map had questioned the past, he feared that all his memories in the years following his mother's death had been nothing more than an illusion created to hide a dark secret.

That night, Daly sat by the turf fire with his nightly glass of whiskey and the radio on, but he was unable to relax. As a detective, he was perpetually searching for clues, uncovering secrets, solving mysteries and bringing them to public attention, but what did it matter whether one secret more or one secret less was exposed? Hadn't enough secrets been revealed already? Did his country need so much examination of its past? Could any society bear so much truth-telling? And moreover, whose truth was it anyway? He could only investigate and interrogate his own truth, his own experience of the Troubles, which in the grand scale of things was as small and insignificant as the grains of sand churning in a boundless desert storm. Perhaps he should unravel the mystery of his mother's death but keep the findings to himself, like a writer penning a book that he never intends to publish. He would discover the secret and then become part of it himself.

He stared at the flames but all he could see was a tangled mass of memories floating before his eyes. He got up from his armchair and walked around the cottage, turning at every sound: the creaking of the floorboards; the shifting of the glass panes as the wind picked up. He needed someone to talk to but could think of no one to phone. He tried to do some housework, put away the dishes, empty the laundry basket and sort out the rubbish, but anxiety gradually consumed him. He knocked back another whiskey, too soon after the first. He raised his hand to the flickering light of the fire and stared at his outstretched fingers and their shadows, almost disbelieving they were his own. This was more than loneliness, he realized; this was something more primitive and unsettling. His ears were crammed with a ringing silence. He felt a sudden need to verify his existence by saying something, but he was more afraid of the silence that would follow his words.

He folded his hands. The thought of praying to God crossed his mind, but what deeper void would his half-remembered prayers plumb? he wondered. He needed a point of focus, a guide, something to hold in his hands and anchor him to reality. He went out to the porch windowsill and lifted the black hen that was roosting there. He cradled her in his hands and took her inside to the fire. He stuffed the turf box with loose bits of paper and let the hen nest there. He sat in his armchair for a long while, listening to her ruffle her feathers and cluck as she settled to sleep. By the time the last glowing ember had gone out and the ashes were turning cold, he had fallen asleep.

13

Daly didn't speak to anyone the next morning at police headquarters. He had the strange feeling that he was out of kilter with the rest of his colleagues, ahead even of himself, thinking thoughts and planning actions that did not correspond to any rational or familiar model of detective work. Why had he gone to the hotel with Pryce and why had he told her so much about his past? Was she an escape route through the invisible barricades he felt were hemming in his normal detective's life?

A younger female colleague told him he looked worn out and chided him for his late nights. She brought him a coffee and a bun, but the gesture failed to lift his mood or give him any satisfaction. He was frustrated to see that there were no significant updates on the crash-scene investigation. He flicked through the reports, pausing at the photographs of Walsh's awkwardly positioned body. What he knew about the dead priest's research hinted at a deeper set of facts beyond the surface layer: the police checkpoint in the dark, the rearranged traffic cones, the collision of metal and wood, the braid of religious effects in a dying man's grip.

His mother's death had been covered up, so why not Walsh's, too?

He remembered the smugness of Irwin's expression as he stood over the corpse. Once you began to suspect a police conspiracy, all the details eventually collapsed into a jumble of paranoia and doubt.

He dug deeper into the paperwork, the careful ordering of the facts surrounding a man's last moments, trying to define the shape of what lay beyond them. He tried to reason with his suspicions and accept Irwin's clear-cut explanation. However, it was impossible to halt the march of his black doubts. He worked backwards through the sequence of events from the moment of collision to the point where Walsh had pulled up at the checkpoint. He was surrounded by fragments rather than a coherent whole: the winking light of the policeman's torch, the blue overalls of his colleagues, the snub noses of their guns, Walsh's frightened response, the lure of the traffic cones and the vortex ahead. What lay concealed beneath the report that might link Walsh's death with his mother's and the other murder triangle victims?

He fetched himself another cup of coffee and went back to his desk. He flicked through his emails and was surprised to see several from the Human Resources Department outlining how much time he was entitled to take off for bereavements. How odd, he thought. He hadn't lost anyone since his father had died four years previously. Were they referring to his mother's murder? He wondered what garbled message had come through from his police chiefs.

The truth was he had too much to do, too many pressing questions to answer before he could even consider taking some time off work. He needed more information to illuminate the past, the deaths in Walsh's murder triangle. It was time he investigated the links that Walsh had claimed existed, and the best place to do that was in the new archive building, where he hoped to find details of all the police investigations from the 1970s.

It was his first time visiting the archive section, and what he found there angered him. The officer in charge of the files told him he needed written permission from Special Branch for any historical enquiries.

'This isn't historical,' replied Daly. 'It's related to a live investigation.'

The officer avoided eye contact. Was it his imagination or did he detect a slight horror mingled with something like a look of pity in his response to Daly's request? Perhaps he had heard the story of Daly's mother from colleagues, and wanted no part in his futile search for the truth, the inverted paranoia of a middle-aged detective investigating his own police force.

'Very well, then.' He removed a set of keys and led Daly down a back stairwell.

He was expecting a state-of-the-art filing and retrieval system, something suited to the new headquarters' grand ambitions, a luminous sanctuary of carefully ordered files, and so was unprepared for the sight that greeted him in the basement rooms. The first thing he noticed was a musty, mildewed smell at odds with the clean, well-ventilated air in the rest of the building. And then the eerie silence. He had the feeling he was entering a world he had ignored his entire adult life. A forgotten world full of shadows. He followed the archive officer into an underground hall filled with aisles of metal shelving that were loaded with untidy stacks of boxes, files spilling haphazardly. He picked up a folder at random. It was an investigation into an illicit alcohol distillery, dated March 1951. The one underneath was about a hit-and-run accident in Dungannon from 1986.

The officer waved a hand at a far corner in the room.

'The ones you're looking for might be over there. That's where all the old files from Armagh went.'

'You can't be serious,' said Daly. 'Surely there must be some way of locating the files I want.'

'Not until the IT people come and digitize them. They were neatly ordered in the old police stations, but the removal company just dumped them here on top of each other.'

'But this is total chaos. How are we meant to find anything?'

The officer shrugged.

'There are files here dating from the 1930s. Even if you sort through them all, there's no guarantee you'll find what you want. Many of them went missing or were never returned by the case detectives when they retired.'

Could the past stay hidden forever? Daly wondered. In a place like this, it might.

'This will have to be fixed,' he said. 'There should be a complete and ordered archive of every investigation going back to the beginning of the Troubles.'

'To do that we'd have to hunt through every attic and garage in the country. This is the past we're talking about. It was a different era of policing altogether. What sort of order do you expect to find in those dark days? The IRA were rampant, blowing up police stations and murdering officers. How do you impose order on mayhem like that?' He handed Daly the keys. 'Drop them back in the office when you're finished,' he said brusquely. 'If you're planning on staying late, you can hold on to them until the morning.'

Daly began working where the officer had suggested. He was furious at the state of the place. Many of the files weren't even typed, which made his search even more difficult. Some of them had the air of discarded schoolbooks, filled with untidy writing. A sense of desperation descended. He searched for several hours like a blind person shuffling on a ledge, with nothing to guide or give him bearings but his hands sorting inch by inch through the dusty boxes. He lost confidence in his method. He needed someone like Donaldson with him, to help light the way.

After a while, he began moving at random through the shelves, opening boxes and appraising their contents. Somewhere, lost amid the shelves, the details of his mother's murder might lie. He moved between countless boxes, placing his hands briefly upon them, as though he might feel the living past squirm within. He carried on for another hour, but failed to locate any of the files linked to Walsh's murder triangle.

At one point, he caught an echo of someone calling his name. He passed back through the aisles of shelves, listening to the near silence. He could hear the faint sounds of footsteps on the floor above, and voices echoing down the stairwell. He felt as though he'd found the dark and hollow core at the heart of the building. He heard the voice call his name again, a woman's voice, sharp and urgent, but somehow muffled.

He wanted to shout back – *I'm here* – but when he looked up the stairwell no one was there. Layers of echoes drifted down, different voices talking, but he couldn't make out any of the words. The voice calling his name had sounded like a summons from the past. He shivered. He was aware that he was surrounded by the records of thousands of crimes, many of them trifling, but a sizable number involving violent and cruel acts. The building was too new to be haunted by the ghosts of the dead and wronged, he thought. Was it his imagination or could he still hear the voice, repeating his name, only plaintive now? The closer he moved towards it, the more it seemed to recede. Perhaps he was overtired and simply hearing things.

He came across a small door that he hadn't seen before. The muffled voice seemed to be emanating from the other side. He hesitated and then opened the door. To his surprise, he walked into an even larger room that was completely empty. A row of ground-level windows filtered light across the floor. The voice stopped calling his name. The emptiness and scale of the room disturbed Daly, the freshly painted walls, and the smooth concrete of the floor. So overwrought were his thoughts that he imagined a black sea of shadows surging towards him from the opposite side of the room. He could see it so clearly, soundless, looming higher and higher, occupying his entire vision, spilling towards him like an inky-black waterfall. The depths of the darkness made him instinctively raise his hands and close his eyes, but when he opened them, the room was empty again.

14

It wasn't until much later in the day that elements of the puzzle began to fall into place for Celcius Daly. A pattern emerged from the chaos of the past. However, the discovery gave him no sense of reassurance or satisfaction. It occurred unexpectedly, in the one place he thought he was safe from the shadows of the Troubles.

He returned to his cottage late that evening, upset that he had made no significant progress in the case, despite his best attempts. He was convinced that the investigation into Walsh's crash should start back in the early months of 1979. That was the key, he thought, the time when both his mother and Walsh were alive. However, the day was almost over, and there was nothing more he could do. He sank into an armchair, exhausted.

In his mind, he tried to step back from all the facts of the case, like a soldier retreating in no man's land, but a sense of restlessness remained. What he needed was a sanctuary for his thoughts. He got out an old portable radio and searched for something classical, a melody to heal the sense of brokenness that haunted him. He tuned into one of Schubert's string quintets. He closed his eyes and nodded his head to the music. For a few minutes, he drifted off. He woke up with a start, his mind clear and alert. It occurred to him that there was still something he could do, a task that he should have completed a long time ago.

He grabbed the radio and hauled himself up a plank stepladder into the attic. It was time he sorted through his father's old chest of drawers and the rest of his boxes. Since his death, Daly had refused to go into the dusty corners of the cottage and rummage through his father's things because of his aversion to nostalgia, but his attitude had grown less sentimental, more curious. Perhaps he might even find a happier glimpse of his childhood, from the time before his mother's death, something to sustain him amid all these revelations of the past.

The drawers of the chest were stiff and unyielding. They were loyal accomplices to his father's secrets, resisting his attempts to open them. He inserted his hand under the bottom drawer and, finding the cavity behind it, forced it open with a grunt. He worked his way through the other drawers in the same manner until he found what he was looking for. An object wrapped in a piece of white muslin. Carefully, he unwound the fabric until he was holding it in his hands. The precious family bible. It had a dead weight, as though its pages contained years of layered sadness.

He carried the bible down the steps and placed it on the kitchen table. He stared at it for a while. He opened the cover and detected the faint scent of lilies and funeral flowers that had lingered from his father's wake. The bible had sat next to the coffin for three days, accompanied by a candle, a crucifix and a bottle of holy water. Daly remembered the nocturnal rosaries and the paralysing wait for dawn, slipping outside to smoke in the dark of the porch, the slow ordeal of wringing out one's grief in the company of neighbours and his father's friends, while glancing surreptitiously at the kitchen clock and wondering had all the timepieces in the house come to a standstill. In all that time, he had not once opened the bible, refusing to seek consolation in any of its passages.

He flicked through the first pages. In the fading light from the cottage window, they had a luminous quality. The first leaf contained a family history of the Dalys, starting in the mid 1800s and ending with the date of his mother's death: 2 April 1979. It occurred to him that he should have added his father's death to the list. He sighed. He was only just beginning to realize that a substantial part of his father had died with his mother. The old man had been restless and depressed during the later years of his life.

Looking back, he understood that time had stopped for his father on the day of his mother's killing. Only a premature death could do that: bring the clocks to a perfect standstill. It was the sacrifice the living felt they should make for those who go before their ordained time.

His father had so cautiously closed the door on his mother's death that Daly had not dared open it. He remembered the uneasy feeling that descended upon the cottage on her anniversary, his father's silences, his agitation, his starting and abandoning of odd jobs around the farm, digging drills in the vegetable patch and then raking them over, rounding the cattle into a new pasture and then chasing them back, sitting by the turf fire chewing his fingernails or going through old bills and burning them one by one, all the time giving the impression that he was struggling with something secret and tormenting.

Daly felt a pang of sadness mingled with admiration. By comparison, his grief seemed limited and simple. God only knew what had been going through his father's head at the time. His greatest wish now was to hear his father speak his mind about his mother's death.

He turned another leaf in the bible and found an A4-sized envelope with his name written on it in his father's spidery handwriting. He handled it as carefully as a wafer of ice. Inside were several documents, a letter addressed to him, a map of the lough shore, some legal correspondence and a newspaper clipping. Daly opened the letter and read its contents.

Dear Celcius,
I have penned this letter and hidden it within the family bible not knowing if you will ever read it. Perhaps it will only come to light years after my death, when our country will have undergone many changes, and the secrets I write of will seem ir-

relevant and harmless. However, that is a risk I am willing to take because I want this outpouring of suspicions to reach you not in an unguarded or accidental moment, but at a time of reflection and solitude, when you are perhaps searching for an expression of the truth, when you might feel susceptible to this summons from the past.

Most of all, I hope that you are still a detective, or at least that your skills of detection remain sharp enough to help you read between the lines and discern the truth that awaits you.

For the past thirty years, I have been reluctant to awaken you to the true story of your mother's life and death. I have found it impossible to speak about the depths of evil our neighbours sank to in the weeks leading up to her murder, but now, I owe it to you, after allowing you to live through your teenage years and adulthood without guessing what I suspected to be the truth. I even accepted your choice of profession without ever hinting at my suspicions.

My dearest son, your mother's death was a crime, not an accident. A gang of Loyalists with connections to serving police officers murdered her in cold blood. I stress that she did not choose to be the victim. She was the innocent party. Her murderers chose her, or rather us, and I believe the gang had been targeting us in the months prior to the attack.

I must warn you that the ghosts of her murderers still haunt the police force to which you belong. They should be driven out and not allowed to take it over as their sanctuary. I want you to read the documents I have enclosed with this letter, and use them to solve the mystery of why we were targeted. I want you to clear the confusion that surrounds her murder. For too long, I have kept the trail of evidence a private matter, my business and no one else's. After my death, I want you to make the details public, and hold her killers to account. I stress that I do not want vengeance. If that were the case, I would have told you everything when you were a young man, but that is not how I believe justice should work.

I also want you to know that I never meekly accepted her

murder. I kept it secret because I wanted a safe passage for you into the future. I did not want the plague of sectarianism and bloodlust to visit my house and take away my only son, as it has done in so many houses up and down the country.

I hope you will forgive me for trying to reduce the darkness and guilt in your life.

Yours forever with love and affection,
Patrick Joseph Daly

Daly held on to the letter as though it were a handrail along a precipice. He read it again, this time more carefully. What did his father mean by guilt? He examined the map and the solicitor's letters. He tried to clear a path through the wealth of detail, and patch the story together while ignoring the void that loomed below him.

He worked out that about six months before his mother's death, the British Army had raided their cottage and found the registration numbers of several security force personnel in a child's scrapbook. His father had been arrested and released on suspicion of collecting information for the IRA. The charges had been dropped after the intervention of a local politician and the parish priest. The correspondence included a photocopy of a scrapbook page with lists of car registration numbers with several circled in black ink. Daly stared at them in dazed perplexity. He recognized the handwriting; it was his own.

His head swam with confusion. The chasm opened by Walsh's murder map now emptied into a greater chasm, one void flowing into a much darker void. For several moments, he stood frozen to the spot. One summer in his childhood, he had taken to writing down car registration numbers. It had begun on a washed-out holiday in Donegal, listening to the steady beat of rain hammering on the caravan roof. Out of boredom, he had written down sets of car numbers on a piece of paper. For some reason, he'd continued the hobby when he returned home, where it became an introvert's obsession.

He remembered the blue and green scrapbook pages and how they absorbed the numbers he had written down. News of the latest sectarian murder would send him scurrying up a tree with his scrapbook.

From his vantage point, he recorded the number plate of every car that passed the cottage. Vigilance, surveillance, thinking in lists – these were the ways he controlled his childhood fears. He liked having the numbers for the record, to build up his collection. It was a form of acquisition. He even gathered numbers in his sleep. Strange cars driven by shadowy men floated through his dreams giving themselves away in a stream of random numbers.

However, he hadn't grasped the pathology hidden within the lists. It was simply a childhood pastime, albeit one that felt out of control. When he didn't have his scrapbook to hand, he found himself memorizing number plates. It became his automatic response when he spotted a strange car. Every vehicle was worth watching, especially on the crooked roads around their lough-shore home. The number plates were like announcements, premonitions he could not ignore, secret messages that had to be recorded and studied later. On nights when he couldn't sleep, he'd flick through the scrapbook, underlining the recurring numbers, searching for sequences. He found he could lose himself in the lists, turning the pages one by one until he fell asleep.

Staring at those numbers and letters, now a middle-aged man, he felt a surge of sadness. In a way, the hobby was the essence of a childhood overshadowed by the Troubles. Innocence hemmed in by murder and fear. More memories came to him. The rapt way his father stood when a car loitered at the end of their lane, his tall figure motionless by the curtains, transfixed by the shimmer of idling metal through the thorn hedge. Strange cars parked on the roads around the farm always held his father spellbound. He slowed down while passing them, craning his neck to make eye contact with the driver, who would normally avert his or her gaze. 'There's activity,' he'd remark to Daly's mother. But the nature of the activity was always unknown. Daly could feel it, however, an unremitting suspicion hanging in the air, motorists passing each other in coded moments of silence and salute, vehicles brushing the thorn hedges, tyres sinking into the muddy verges.

As a child, he hadn't fully understood the context, the frame of reference. People were fighting in a war, a shadowy underground war, and strange cars usually presaged murder or a bombing. He'd kept the scrapbook under his pillow. For a year, the numbers meant everything to him. So he was devastated one day when he returned home from school to find the book missing. He'd searched everywhere, under his bed, in his cupboards, in the drawers of his bedside locker, only stopping when he saw the silhouette of his mother standing at the bedroom door, arms crossed around her waist.

She'd explained to him that soldiers had searched the house that morning after he left for school. They'd found the scrapbook and taken it away as evidence. She'd given him a hug, her shoulders shivering slightly. He'd wanted to complain bitterly, but something about her stillness made him hesitate. He remembered her whispering the words: 'Don't blame yourself; it's not your fault.' At the time, he hadn't understood what she meant but now he felt such grief that his boyhood pastime had brought stress and fear into their lives. What else had he done in his life that had such appalling consequences? Nothing approached it. If he'd played outdoors more and neglected his scrapbook, would his mother still be alive?

Next, he read the newspaper clipping. It was a notice placed in the *Portadown News* by his father, dated 17 February 1979. In it, his father claimed soldiers at a checkpoint had warned him that his details had been added to a Loyalist hit list, and that his life was in danger. Daly grimaced. Placing such notices in newspapers had been common practice among Catholics harassed by the security forces. According to the solicitor's letters, the Daly family had been repeatedly stopped and searched at police and army checkpoints, and after the raid on their home, one of the soldiers had accidentally dropped a map that pinpointed their address.

He turned to the map. Even though it was a photocopy of the original, he could see that it was incredibly detailed. Every house, field and road was carefully noted, right down to the featureless hummocks and thorny hollows that filled the small fields around the lough shore, as well as the dozens of unidentifiable ruins. He assumed it was a copy of the military map dropped during the raid. The Daly cottage was highlighted with a red circle and the letter P written beside it. Did the P stand for Provisional IRA? he wondered, his hands shaking slightly.

He collected himself and sat down on an old chest. Intervals of darkness opened between one thought and the next. He stared into the void and asked himself the question: Had his harmless hobby led indirectly to his mother's murder? Certainly, it looked less and less like a random killing. It wasn't casual or accidental, but part of a premeditated plan. It hadn't mattered that the car number plates had been collected by an innocent child. They were enough to satisfy the pattern, enough for the murderers to fit together the elements of the design and conclude that his parents were working for the IRA. Now he understood that in all those years after his mother's death his father's silence had been built around protecting him from the guilt of precipitating her murder.

He needed a way out of this guilt and fear. He doubted if he was strong enough to survive the emotional damage this revelation might cause, especially if it lingered unproven in the back of his mind. He wanted the truth now. He feared and yearned for the truth. The letter and documents had opened a trapdoor which could never be closed.

He poured himself a large whiskey and sat in the kitchen. He could still hear the radio playing faintly in the attic. He made out a familiar song from another era that somehow sounded slower and more enigmatic emanating from the darkness of the roof space. Daly rubbed his forehead and tried to reconfigure the events of his childhood.

Long after midnight, musical notes and memories pulsed within that room, throbbing with serene disregard for the listener below.

15

The next day, Daly arrived punctually at work. He picked his way through the incident rooms, past his colleagues sitting and chatting at computer screens. The new recruits all seemed so extroverted and well informed. No one seemed to sense the inner trauma dominating his thoughts. He skulked within his own office, and managed not to talk to anyone for hours on end. He felt a primitive need to avoid the company of his fellow police officers.

In a moment of painful lucidity, he worried that his career as a detective was no more than a fraud and that any future involvement in a major investigation might unmask him as the dull, hesitant, clumsy human being he had always felt he was. He ignored any messages that came through from Special Branch. Fealty wanted to meet him and discuss the investigation into Walsh's death, but Daly kept avoiding him. He no longer cared what his fellow officers and commanders thought of him. This rebellious streak was in part a longing to put an end to the farce of his career.

He read whatever police investigations and reports relating to IRA and Loyalist gunmen he could find, but was unable to glean anything that might shed light on his mother's death. His thinking seemed paralysed. Everything in his head was disconnected from everything else: his memories of his mother, her nurse's shoes lying on the bedroom floor, the manner of her death at a checkpoint, his father's grief, their solitary years in the cottage, as if a magnet inside him had had its polarity reversed, repelling and scattering into chaos the fragments of reality he had been holding on to. He had devoted his entire adult life to catching criminals, and now he feared that the greatest criminals might be the people he had worked alongside.

After a while, when he forced himself to go to the canteen for a coffee and a scone, he spied the lanky figure of the policeman who'd stopped Walsh at the checkpoint. Daly saw him walk down a staircase, deep in conversation with Donaldson. He bounded down the corridor and stairs, but could see no sign of the pair. None of the staff he met knew where they had gone. He searched the offices along the corridor and then all the ones on the floor below. Each door he opened was the wrong one, and he withdrew in doubt and bewilderment. He felt lost in a labyrinth of white corridors and empty stairwells, unsure of his way back.

He bumped into Irwin.

'You're looking for Donaldson,' he said, pointing a warning finger at him.

'How do you know?'

'I can see it in your face.'

'Did Donaldson send you?'

'No.'

Irwin walked away.

'You'll not track him down that easily. He's back to his old tricks, busy finding places to hide.' Irwin's voice echoed along the corridor.

'Hide from what?'

'The past. Don't you know? It's the new front line.'

Daly left and clambered into his car. The headquarters hung at the edge of his vision. He looked across and saw that a team of builders were busy working on a new block of offices. His gall rose at the never-ending construction work. More corridors for people like Donaldson to pad with their unfathomable secrets. It was almost comic, the way the offices sprang up and multiplied like white cells. It was the architecture of evasion and containment. The builders were going to be busier than ever keeping pace with the unravelling of the past.

He sat in the car for a while as it felt the safest place to be. On a whim, he hunted out Father Walsh's mobile phone from the glove compartment. He dialled the number that had tried to contact Walsh on the night he died; the one saved under the name Hegarty. It rang and went to a pre-recorded message. Daly asked for the owner of the phone to contact him urgently.

He stretched back in his seat and stared through the windscreen. He watched the sky. He listened to the sounds of cars parking and driving away, footsteps drawing near and then fading. In his mind, he turned over the facts of the investigation that he could categorize, but his thoughts kept clouding over. He tried to analyse this sense of confusion that had overtaken him.

The historical nature of the investigation made it very different from his usual workload. He was beginning to understand that in this case there was no order or structure, only fragmented effort and a lack of direction. He feared that he might never make any progress that could be measured, nor was there the slightest possibility that all his questions could ever be answered.

He pictured Walsh's murder map in his imagination. Drawing it had been the priest's way of organizing the mess, making a network out of the string of seemingly random murders, a web of connections. Daly could see how the map had given Walsh's obsession with the past a sense of purpose and direction. It was an introvert's consolation, like his secret collection of car number plates, but he saw the inherent flaw in the map, how it might give the illusion that the killing frenzy had a secret design, a controlling intelligence.

Yet in spite of his uncertainty, a strange sense of excitement coursed through his veins as he sped away from the police HQ. On the motorway, he felt much freer than usual, almost out of control, attuned to signals from a more primitive, emotional part of his brain, which pulled him away from the professional habit of carefully deliberated decisions, balanced judgements and impartiality, making it all the more likely that he was going to botch the investigation in spectacular fashion.

Therefore, when the priest's phone rang into life, he braked the car and answered it immediately. The caller was Hegarty. Daly did not want to lose his balance completely. He was unbalanced already, reeling round in circles, without any possibility of advancing towards the truth, or retreating into blissful ignorance. His past had been shattered and he was spinning with it, as if chasing his reflection in a broken mirror while it spiralled into bottomless darkness.

'Who's this?' asked Hegarty.

For a moment, Daly said nothing.

'I'm a detective inspector. I'm investigating the death of Father Walsh.'

Hegarty did not respond.

'I need to talk to you if you knew him, or were in contact with him before he died,' continued Daly. 'You're not suspected of anything.' He paused. 'I just need information.'

Hegarty's voice was barely a whisper, hoarse and irritated-sounding. 'I don't talk to policemen.'

Daly expected the line to go dead but the man hung on. He could sense a deep fatigue in his breathing, and something else – a wariness.

'What leads do you have?' murmured Hegarty.

Daly decided to tell him the truth.

'At the moment, the investigation isn't going anywhere.'

'Where do you want it to go?'

'I want to find out if Walsh's death was orchestrated by someone in a position of power. I want to find out if his death was linked to his research into the murder triangle.'

'Why are you interested in the murder triangle?'

Daly hesitated. Should he reveal the personal link? He had told so many; it hardly mattered that this stranger should hear it also. He lowered his voice and told him about his mother. Hegarty seemed encouraged by the revelation, and began to talk more freely.

'Your hunch is correct,' he said. 'Father Walsh could not be stopped. That's why they had to make him take a wrong turn. That's why they had to kill him.'

'Who are you talking about?'

'Your colleagues in Special Branch.'

'Why would they want to kill him?'

'Walsh was investigating thirty years of concealment and obstruction. He was tracking down the members of a secret gang who were involved in the murders of about twenty innocent Catholics, including your mother. He was making contact with all sorts of disgruntled former police officers and their informers. It was a slow process but he was finally getting there. That's the pity. Another month or two and he would have nailed them.'

'You believe he had enemies?'

'Powerful ones.'

'British Intelligence?'

'Even further.'

'Government?'

'All the way up to the level of Minister of Defence. Under two different Parliaments.'

Daly felt a burst of adrenalin in his veins. A part of him wanted to believe Hegarty. In his gut, he suspected it was true. But something also warned him that it wasn't. Paranoia and distrust had that effect on people; it confirmed every outlandish claim. Thirty years of murder and cover-up had reduced many people to a state of rapturous gullibility, keen to believe in any conspiracy theory floated by fantasists and political opportunists. There was nothing new about what Hegarty was saying; the same rumours and suspicions had been floating in the air since the 1980s. He needed elaboration and hard evidence.

'How do you know this? What proof do you have?'

'It's all there in Walsh's research. Someone needs to pursue the links now that the priest is dead. Before they are wiped away forever.'

'What about you?' asked Daly.

Hegarty wheezed with laughter.

'I haven't the flexibility to do anything right now. I want you to pursue them.'

Daly was quiet.

'A thirty-year-old wrong that is single-handedly brought out into the open. Isn't that better than solving a dozen new murders?'

Daly's breathing stiffened.

'Don't try to contact me again,' said Hegarty. 'This is more conversation than I've had for weeks.'

When Hegarty hung up, Daly drove straight to Walsh's monastery. He had no choice but to go into the mine-field alone.

16

Daly was surprised to see that almost all the parking spaces outside the monastery were taken. People milled around the entrance doors as he slipped inside. For a moment, he feared that a crowd of grieving families had stumbled upon Father Walsh's research and were trampling all over his papers. He hastened past the abbot's office. From the corridors rose the rumbling of many whispering voices, and another sound, low and heavy, that reminded him of weeping reverberating through the walls.

He bumped into a shy, awkward-looking boy in thick glasses, but didn't have time to apologize. He hurried past open doors in sight of people praying in fervent groups. Some sort of religious retreat was in full swing, he realized, the participants churning out a steady stream of Hail Marys.

He knocked on Walsh's door once, twice and then tried the handle. The door was still unlocked. The layout of the room with its stacks of files and map-covered walls looked almost identical to his recollection. Everything was intact and in its place. Sweaty and almost euphoric in his relief, he cleared a seat by the window, and began perusing the files. He leafed through them trying to get an overall sense of their contents.

As a detective this should have been the first place he looked for clues, but the idea of digging for leads in this cluttered room, the place he had learned of his mother's murder, had repelled him.

His mind filled with apprehension as he read Walsh's list of victims. He had to read them several times to absorb the details. He wanted to know them so well he could recite them from heart.

The year 1979 began in horror and blood, the priest had written. Janice Whyte, a married Protestant civil servant, died from her injuries after the IRA detonated a bomb in a Portadown bar. The revenge attack two days later was savage, even by the standards at the time. A fake checkpoint manned by Loyalists on a border road shot dead a carload of young Catholic men returning from a football match. Three brothers and their cousin died instantly in the hail of gunfire. According to a legal document released to the victims' families, police recovered thirty-seven spent 9mm bullet cases from the car with forty-one strike marks at the front and sides of their vehicle. Unaccountably, however, they failed to locate four spent bullet cases, which the family discovered after the forensics team returned the car to them.

The family had passed the bullet cases to Father Walsh, who had them analysed by a ballistics expert within the police force. He found that at least two guns had been used in the attack – a 9mm Parabellum-calibre Sterling SMG and a .455 Webley revolver, the same weapons used in the attack on Daly's mother.

By February 1979, politicians and media commentators thought the violence couldn't get any worse, but it did. A week later, a van of workmen heading home from constructing a new police station in Newry was stopped by an armed checkpoint. The gunmen ordered the two Catholics in the van to lie face down on the road. Their workmates, fearing that they were about to be shot by Loyalists, tried to protect their identities. However, the gunmen opened fire on the defenceless workers, firing more than one hundred bullets in less than a minute. A Republican paramilitary group claimed responsibility for the attack.

A few days later, the murderous cycle continued. Loyalists launched a gun attack on a bar in Armagh. Eyewitnesses reported seeing a gunman push his weapon through a small glass door in the inner door of the bar and open fire, killing six people inside. The gunman had a Mexican moustache and left the bloody scene laughing, according to a witness. It was also noted that his accomplices in the getaway car were wearing blue overalls.

Daly sighed. From his post at the window, he could hear the tolling of the nearby church bells marking out the quarters of the hour. He rubbed his weary eyes. For two more hours, he read on.

A plot gradually emerged from the research, a plot that he was part of, but had never known before. About twenty people lost their lives in attacks that Walsh attributed to a Loyalist gang, aided and abetted by state security forces. The killings had occurred against a backdrop of IRA bombings and shootings, but, according to the priest's research, only a small handful of the victims were linked to Republican paramilitaries. He wrote:

'The evidence is clear in Catholic graveyards across Armagh and Tyrone. The murdered were farmers, publicans, businessmen, young couples renovating derelict homes, trade unionists, tradesmen…'

Walsh had asked the simple question: Why? If the purpose of Loyalist collusion was to eliminate the threat of the IRA, why had the organization escaped virtually unscathed? He warned that the British government had taught a deadly lesson to the people of Northern Ireland, that power came out of the barrel of a gun, that the ballot box was powerless against force, and that the police and army can betray their trust.

Walsh had underlined one particular name in red several times. A Major George Hannon. The name jumped out because Walsh had mostly been unable to unearth the names of intelligence personnel, and was forced to refer to them with letters of the alphabet. Major Hannon was a hook, one of the few definite leads that Daly could follow. However, the more he read about Hannon the more he doubted his relevance to the murder triangle. For a start, he was too old to be implicated in the Troubles.

According to Walsh's research, he was active in Palestine in the late 1940s and had been implicated in the disappearance and murder of a young Jewish boy. Daly read that Hannon had been a member of a special squad within the Palestine Police Force, at a time when the country was still under British mandate. Decorated for his bravery in

World War II, Hannon had been chosen to lead the squad in a fight against the insurgents, which at that time were Zionist militants trying to expel British forces and set up an independent Jewish state.

Along with former Sandhurst graduates and SAS members, Hannon had operated covert patrols in Jewish-type clothing and driven Q-cars, civilian vehicles specifically engineered for intelligence gathering. He'd even used a laundry van to mask their activities when operating in a hostile area. The pattern rang a bell with Daly. It was the same undercover tactics the British Army had used in West Belfast in the early seventies.

Sometime in the late 1940s, Hannon had been forced to flee Palestine after his cover was blown. The civilian authorities discovered a hat of his at the place where the Jewish boy had been abducted. In addition, eyewitness reports described a tall, blond-haired man with a reddish complexion that matched Hannon's description.

Walsh referenced the research of several Jewish military historians, who claimed that the squad had been set up to snatch suspects, provoke gunfights and sow the seeds of internecine strife. It was a tactic designed to inflame sectarian tensions with the local Arab population. Some historians also claimed that the squad deliberately mounted assassinations to add to the sense of confusion and bully the civilian population into acquiescence. Walsh's theory was clear. Hannon had drawn a template of counter-insurgency operations that was developed in places like Aden and Kenya before being launched on the streets of Northern Ireland.

Walsh claimed that Major Hannon had arrived in South Armagh in the late 1970s. His name became known to Republican sources when two IRA men admitted to working as British Intelligence agents with Hannon as their leader. Walsh suggested that Hannon had then been forced to flee the country as he had done thirty years earlier in Palestine.

Daly found it interesting reading, but Walsh had been unable to uncover any direct evidence linking Hannon to the murder triangle. The research relied too heavily on conjecture and rumour; the nuggets of intelligence information were like stepping stones that he was finding harder and harder to negotiate.

Towards the end of the notes, Walsh appeared to have descended into paranoia, hinting at plots and intrigue involving intelligence services from Israel, South Africa and the US. Several times the priest mentioned dark forces still operating within Northern Ireland, and referred to evidence he was expecting from one of his confidential sources. The writing grew difficult to read and Daly had to move the papers closer to the window and squint. He skimmed through the pages. Walsh's chronology became garbled, switching between events scattered across the globe, Palestine in the 1940s, Oman in the 1950s and Northern Ireland in the 1970s, rambling on with an irrational fervour that began to depress Daly. He felt that Walsh had dug up too much history, too many facts, to be able to draw up a clear and logical set of connections.

Daly stopped and rubbed his eyes. He began to fear that the priest's meticulous research had fallen into a final madness, which had ended with his car swerving off a darkened border road. Whatever secrets he had tried to reveal to the world were lost in this bunker-like cell of history. Daly could see that in spite of gathering all this information about the murder triangle, the priest had failed to understand what most needed to be understood: all the intellectual rigour in the world would never fathom the dark arts of terrorism and counter-terrorism.

Daly snapped the ledger shut. He felt overwhelmed by the darkness that loomed over Walsh's research. The only antidote to all this confusion was to confront his own darkness. Solving the case meant penetrating the central story of his life. He found a clean sheet of paper and a pen. He began to draw up a list of facts that pertained directly to his mother's death. He scribbled down the blunt forensic details. He leaned so hard on the pen that he almost made holes in the paper. As he sifted through the notes, he found it hard not to plunge into the stories of the other victims, into the web of connections including the descriptions of Hannon's intelligence gathering methods.

According to Walsh's research, Ivor McClintock and Kenneth Agnew had been among the police officers manning the checkpoint that stopped his mother's car. There was no further mention of Agnew; however, McClintock's name cropped up in legal documents obtained by solicitors working on behalf of some of the victims' families. He was arrested several times in the early 1980s and released without charge.

In December 1983, McClintock was again arrested because of intelligence received by the RUC. After twenty-four hours in custody, he finally admitted his role in the bombing of a bar in Armagh. Dressed in his police uniform, he had acted as a scout for the driver of the bomb. In his confession, he told police, 'At no point did I think or intend that anyone would be killed in the bombing.' He added: 'I know it's stupid to say that now.'

McClintock also confessed to a similar scouting role in the murder of the McKenna brothers in March 1981. On the day that he was formally charged, McClintock was made to resign from the RUC. The judge sentencing him praised the professionalism and courage of the police force in the face of extreme provocation. He said the accused was a man who had given service to his community, and it was obvious from the minor role that he had played in the operations that he was not a common terrorist, and had been misguided. The judge gave McClintock a one-year jail sentence.

Daly swallowed and stood up. He paced around the room. The sight of the murder map made him break out in a cold sweat. *I can't read any more*, he thought. *Already I have read too much.* Part of him wanted his old life back, the life he had before he first entered this room, but it was too late now to return to that more innocent time.

He gazed through the window at the abbey grounds below. The research shed more light on his mother's murder, but the picture still wasn't clear. He knew more about the men who had murdered his mother, but he still didn't know why they had singled her out. He turned to the other murders, looking for points of similarity that Walsh might have overlooked.

His concentration was broken by a sudden rapping that shook the door. He heard a muffled call but ignored it. However, the visitor was determined. The handle turned this way and that, but the door failed to open. Somehow, it had jammed within its frame. The handle rattled as the person frantically worked it. The hinges groaned and at last, the door flew open. To Daly's surprise, in stepped the journalist Jacqueline Pryce.

'Celcius.' She stopped in her tracks, glancing at the opened files. 'Why didn't you tell me you were coming?'

'Don't worry, I was about to leave. You'll have the place to yourself then.'

However, she was immune to his brusqueness.

'Is this your way of stealing a lead on me?' Her tone sounded light–playful, even.

'No, not at all.'

She took off her coat and draped it over a seat.

'Have you been able to make any sense of the murder triangle?'

'I hardly know where to begin.'

'No wonder,' she said, lifting a sheaf of sun-yellowed notes. 'It's total chaos. There are files here based on the testimonies of paramilitaries turned alcoholics and born-again Christians. All sorts of demented ramblings. He should have burnt them long ago. It will take days to go through them and sort out the rubbish.'

Daly stared at the files.

'I'd say weeks.'

A silence fell. He could sense that Pryce wanted him to explain what he had gleaned from his perusal of the files, but he felt more in the dark than ever before.

'Poor Father Walsh,' she said. 'He was so close to nailing the links that would prove his theory, but all he left us was this ugly patchwork of tit-for-tat murders and international conspiracies.'

'I doubt if anyone will ever work out the links and uncover the truth,' said Daly. 'The past is ebbing away. People die and evidence disappears.'

She shrugged.

'We might never know if he was right or just deluded. In my writer's imagination, I can see how it might all fit together. It would make such a powerful story.' She hesitated. 'With a little poetic licence, of course.'

He glanced in her direction.

'What do you mean?'

'I'm thinking about writing a different type of book than the one Father Walsh had in mind. Something along fictional lines.'

'You mean all this research might work in some sort of a novel, but not as a factual account?'

'Yes. A novel might be the most fitting way to tell the secrets of the murder triangle. To tie up all the loose ends and clear away inconsistencies.'

'Is that why you're here?' He kept his voice as neutral as possible. 'Researching a piece of fiction?'

He saw how Walsh's death might have upset her literary ambitions. A best-selling exposé on the Troubles put on hold indefinitely. Her motivations suddenly seemed mundane and cynical.

She seemed to sense his recoil.

'Not entirely. I want to help the investigation because Father Walsh's work is too important to be forgotten. It means a lot to me.'

She saw the look of doubt on his face.

'Of course, it's true there are too many unresolved issues to make the book a credible work of fact,' she continued. 'That book was Father Walsh's and it died with him.'

Her expression registered anger or disappointment, Daly wasn't sure which.

'But if I incorporated the story of your childhood it might make a different kind of book.'

Daly regarded her uneasily. He didn't like the idea of her prowling after him, sniffing out the details of his family tragedy.

'Have you been researching me? Is that how you knew I was an only son?'

She barely flinched.

'I did ask around for a few background details.'

'So that's why you went along with the first meeting when you knew I couldn't possibly be Father Walsh. That's why you're here today. You're collecting more material for your book.' He almost chuckled. 'You're following me because you're afraid of losing sight of your story.'

She smiled, a little unsure of herself.

'I should have admitted to you from the start that I wanted to turn Aloysius's research into another type of book, but I didn't have the nerve.'

'But why do you need to add my story? Haven't you enough material here?'

She shrugged.

'Every story needs a lead character. A sympathetic hero.'

He frowned and wondered if she was trying to pay him a compliment.

'But clearly I'm not a hero.' He struggled to describe what he was. 'I'm an outsider who arrived too late in the day to influence anything. When I think about it, there are no heroes in the story of the murder triangle. Except perhaps for Father Walsh, and he's dead.'

She smiled at him.

'Can't you see that you're perfect? A hero who doesn't want to be a hero.'

Daly sighed.

'There must be a better way for you to finish your book. One that isn't complicated by me.'

'I suppose I could work longer hours in the library, dig up more relatives and interview them. But that wouldn't be half as interesting as following you.'

Her eyes glinted. What sort of game was she playing? She reached out and ran her hand along the backs of his fingers. She held her hand there for a moment, as if inviting him to hold it, but Daly did not respond. It was the first time in ages a woman had touched him so tenderly, but he remained motionless.

'I could write about you sifting through Walsh's notes like you are now. Doggedly following a trail. Negotiating the obstacles placed in your way. Of course, I'll change the names; make sure no one can identify you.'

He felt a stab of annoyance, realizing she had already enrolled him in the plot of her book.

'Except that you'll never be able to follow the story to the end.'

'Why is that?'

'Because I have no intention of letting you find out what happens next. Anyway, why would readers be interested in my search for the truth?'

'Because you're a police detective, but also a victim.'

'Is that the impression I give?'

He could see the truth in her eyes. He was nothing more than a narrative device, a means to carry the interest of her readers. She was searching for a character made out of ink and punctuation toiling away at a knot of evil.

'I want to see you get closure on your mother's murder. Is that so bad? I worked with Father Walsh for months. Surely there's some way I can help you amid all this confusion and uncertainty.' She gestured at the murder map.

'For a start you can answer this question: Why was Walsh so interested in a British Army major called George Hannon?'

Her answer gave him a start.

'You can ask the major yourself.'

He hadn't considered the possibility that Hannon might still be alive.

'Where will I find him?'

'He's living somewhere in North Down. I'll see if I can arrange you an interview. He's retired now, but in the seventies he worked at British Army Intelligence's headquarters in Lisburn.'

Daly did a rapid calculation. If Hannon was still alive, he must be well over a hundred. It was highly unlikely he had worked for the army in the late 1970s as well as operating in Palestine during the 1940s. Unless he was some sort of ghost.

'Are you sure it's the same man Walsh was researching?'

'Judge for yourself when we meet him. I'll call you when I've arranged a visit. For the two of us.' She flashed him a winning smile.

'I've already told you, I've no intention of involving a journalist in this investigation.'

'At this point you need all the help you can get. Besides, this case is no longer a matter for the law. We can't leave it to Special Branch to deliver justice.'

Daly looked at her. He wondered whether she had even been born when the murder gang was doing its despicable work. He considered asking her what age she was but thought better of it.

'You can't use my mother's death as a source of inspiration for your book.'

He looked in her eyes and saw something that sickened him: grinding, writerly ambition. She had spent the entire conversation chipping away at his defences. He shuddered at the idea of her discovering his boyhood secrets, the lists of car number plates, his possible role in the intimidation his parents suffered. He gathered up his notes and stood to leave.

'I'm going, Ms Pryce. Your story ends here.'

'What if it's just the beginning?'

He let her question hang in the air and left. He walked back down the corridor, and passed an open door. He stopped. From inside, he could hear a group of women reciting the rosary. An echo from the past had startled him, the uncanny impression that his mother's voice was drifting through their murmured prayers. He crept in and took a seat at the back. The voice faded away. Perhaps the contents of Walsh's cluttered room had strained his mind. The pungent smell of incense filled the air. He listened carefully, and the voice returned. He sank deeper in his seat and tried to pinpoint its location. A man's voice began to pray at the front of the room, and the congregation fell silent. When the murmuring returned he detected her voice again, those soft syllables so familiar from his childhood. He stared at the backs of the women in disbelief. Her voice seemed to move within their ranks. He followed it like a ripple in water from one corner of the room to another.

To have this solemn echo of her, so close to him, must mean something, he thought. He began whispering the prayers, all the time listening to that reassuring voice floating through the others, as though it might give him some hint about her mysterious death. However, the voice was an auditory hallucination created by his imagination and the voices of living women who spoke in his mother's old-fashioned Tyrone accent. It had no connection to reality. It was precarious, a single thread guiding him through a maze of strangers' voices. He got up, a Hail Mary half-finished on his lips, and crept away.

17

All over the park the curling embryonic signs of spring glittered as Major George Hannon took his afternoon walk in determined good spirits. He skirted around an onrush of excited schoolchildren and pressed on along a path through the trees. He'd left the café with a coffee in hand and felt buoyed up by his surroundings and the countless signs that winter was over; the sense of creaturely occupancy amid the bushes and undergrowth; life shining and crawling onward in its endless war against death. *Mother Nature keeps her eyes wide open*, he thought with satisfaction. She knew instinctively how to outmanoeuvre the darkness that threatened to extinguish everything, even the sun and the stars.

He walked under trees that were already sprouting tender little leaves, almost hiding the skeletal branches. Feeling the warm sunshine on his face, he reflected that it was the perfect moment for a prayer of thanksgiving, but it had been years since he had mouthed anything holy, and he was reluctant to start now in case he might undermine his sense of enjoyment.

This feeling of light winning the battle over shade brought his mind back to the personal war he had waged during the Troubles.

He thought of the informers he'd handled back in the days when he worked for the Ministry of Defence, when intelligence gathering was pure power, when a single phone call could decide whether a man lived or died, when he was effectively carving out the history of Northern Ireland, before that history was handed back to the squabbling politicians who mired it in sectarian point scoring and flag waving. He missed that sense of control and precision, manipulating hidden strings within the paramilitary gangs. However, the faces and voices of that era were far removed from this spring afternoon and his bright path through the trees.

He was sipping his coffee, listening to the birdsong piping overhead when the figure of a man seated on a park bench distracted him. He blinked but the figure remained silhouetted against the sunlight. For several moments the major stood motionless, studying the figure's outline against the trees, stark as a freshly revealed target, an old ghost sitting in the sunlight. The major felt irritated rather than alarmed; his cheerful vigour drained away.

He approached the bench, and the elderly man glanced up at him and then looked away. His gaze was empty, without intent or focus. On his lap, he clutched a thin black briefcase.

Hannon stared vengefully at the man and sat down beside him. What was he doing here, disturbing the happy peace of his daily walk, like some half-dead corpse from the past seeking reanimation?

'I had to see you,' explained the man, sensing the major's hostility. 'This is urgent. There was no one else I could turn to.'

'That's not the case, Hegarty.' Hannon frowned. He stared straight ahead of him. 'I'm retired. It's extremely dangerous to contact me like this.'

'I've killed a man.'

The major sighed heavily.

'Who?'

'A shadow from the past. It was either him or me.'

'How did he trace you?'

Hegarty croaked his explanation. Hannon felt his spirits flag, infected by the old spy's doomed air.

'I need your help.'

'I can't help you any more.'

'Then let me preface my request.' He shifted his briefcase in Hannon's direction. 'The gun in my case is pointed at you. Like I said, I need your help.'

Hannon stared at the briefcase. He considered the possibility that the spy was bluffing and discounted it.

'You'd shoot me here in broad daylight?'

'Believe me, it would be less messy than the last shooting.'

'How much do you need?'

'How much what?'

'Money. How much to get you out of the country and off my fucking back?'

'I don't need to go anywhere right now. What I want are answers. A week ago, I arranged to meet a priest and now he is dead. Then a woman claiming to be a journalist almost lured me to my death. Who's pulling the strings? Is the journalist on the MOD's payroll?'

'I'm out of touch. I don't have those kinds of answers.'

The hand holding the object inside the briefcase shifted it closer to Hannon.

'Then you must go looking for them.'

'All you're giving me is an assumption. What makes you think that the MOD would use a journalist and her accomplice to assassinate you? They don't strike me as professional killers.'

'Perhaps the MOD persuaded them to intervene.'

'The MOD has its pick of agents. They don't have to go with anyone they can *persuade* to do the job. If they wanted you killed they would have arranged for it to resemble an accident.'

'Like Father Walsh?'

Hannon left the question unanswered and sighed. Hegarty was another searcher and puzzler trying to discover the hidden truths of the past. Like the priest and his journalist friend. He stared at the light fading through the trees with dismay. Everything precious about the afternoon was lost; cold shadows contending with the sunlight in every corner, the gracious burst of early spring warmth dissolving away. Hannon remained motionless, leaning away from Hegarty as much as he could. He grew aware of the vastness of the silence in the darkening trees.

'What else is inside that briefcase of yours, Hegarty?'

The spy sniggered nervously but didn't reply.

'Why did you arrange to meet the priest? What makes you so worried the MOD is out to kill you? What secrets are you carrying that might make you their target?'

'A copy of your old files. The ones you handed over to me.' Hegarty smiled and a drunken glow lit his eyes. Hannon saw the excitement of a man addicted to secrets and betrayal.

He tried his best to smile back. Inside, however, he felt hollow. He wondered if Hegarty had noticed the inner slippage, the psychological tremor induced by the mention of the files.

'You're devious,' he said. 'I'll have to grant you that, but foolhardy, too. Now I understand why your life is in so much danger. You should have stayed on the run, or got into some nice little racket, fuel smuggling or extortion. Small-time stuff. Nothing as big as holding on to those secret files.'

'Don't worry, I'm not so dumb as to carry them with me. I think more than one step ahead.'

'Where are they, then?'

'Why do you think I'd tell you? Let's just say they're in a very safe place, and if anything happens to me I've left strict instructions that they should be posted to all the newspapers in the country. I think of them as my insurance policy.'

Hannon stared at the spy's feverish-looking eyes. He saw betrayal upon betrayal, the reckless, heedless descent of an old spy into loneliness and death. Hegarty was like a lame dog that had been kicked out into the wilds to fend for itself. He might have a few old bones buried in places, enough to gnaw on for a few nights, but bigger, stronger animals were already circling him. If the MOD knew about the secret files, it was unlikely that he'd survive another week, unless they had some secret purpose for him, one final suicidal mission. The thought gave him some satisfaction.

'I'll dig up whatever information the MOD has on the journalist,' said Hannon. 'If she was working with Walsh, there's bound to be a file on her somewhere. Come back here in a week's time and I'll have it for you.'

Hegarty removed his bony hand from the briefcase.

'Consider it a deal.'

'Does that mean you're not going to shoot me?'

'Just answer me one more question. I want the truth now and no more bullshit.' Seeing the major squirm with apprehension made him more confident.

'I can only promise not to lie,' said the major with a thin smile.

'Who was in charge of the rogue police unit Walsh was researching? Who allowed them to wreak such havoc?'

Hannon leaned back and tried to look the part of a respectable retiree enjoying the faint sunshine. He wondered whether Hegarty expected a truthful answer or not. He was bound to an unbroken code – surely the spy knew that – a brotherhood of denial and silence.

'There were so many intelligence units back then. Operations hidden within other operations. The whole system was run on a need-to-know basis, otherwise the networks would have collapsed.'

'I want the name, you bastard.'

'You should do what I do, Hegarty,' the major said coldly. 'Keep your fucking head down and watch your back. This is still a treacherous, violent little country.' He shifted uncomfortably and tried to regain an upright bearing. 'Is this why you've risked meeting me today?' he continued. 'To rake over the past?'

A grimace tugged at Hegarty's lips.

'You're being evasive. Why won't you give me the name?'

'I'm protecting my privacy, not a gang of murderers. If there was such a unit operating it wasn't on my watch.'

'So that is all you're concerned with? Protecting your privacy.'

'Why should I let the past intrude on my life? It is of no concern to anyone.'

Hegarty leaned his face towards him, at once angry and vulnerable, like an offended beggar.

'Who wiped your slate clean of all your meddling in this shitty country?' he hissed. 'Who purged you of everything rotten? Who made you pure and worthy of this bright afternoon?'

Hannon leaned back into his corner of the bench. He tried to maintain his composure. He did not take kindly to the inquisition but in the circumstances, with Hegarty's gun still in his briefcase, he could not rise and walk away.

With increasing venom, Hegarty threw accusations at him, blaming him for the deaths of different agents, unsolved murders and other dark deeds from the Troubles. Hannon waited for him to finish his tirade. Hegarty's scrawny little face was lined and pale. A more dangerous light glittered in his eyes as he made impossible demands for the truth. Worse than impossible – crazy. He should not even be thinking about such topics. The spy was unravelling, realized Hannon, a threat to all who encountered him.

'Are you sick?' asked the major when he stopped for a breath.

'No.'

'Then why are you so eager to dig up the past and search for these ghosts?' Hannon grimaced. 'Why the interest in past causes and retribution? You'll never find answers in the fog of war. You'll only flounder helplessly in the quagmire, like poor old Walsh did, becoming more weary and entangled by the day. Take my advice: crawl out while you still have the chance.'

'Bad things were covered up.' Hegarty's face looked up at the sun, revealing his hawk-like profile. 'When that happens, there will always be someone searching for the truth.'

Hannon was unmoved by the veiled threat. He wanted nothing more than to continue his path through the fading sunlight and trees, and for the spy to be gone with his battered-looking briefcase.

'There's a detective working on Walsh's accident,' said Hegarty. 'He's interested in his research.'

'We've had police investigations before.' Hannon smiled. 'They never get very far.'

'This one seems more keen than usual. I've spoken to him on the phone. He must have got my number from Walsh's records.'

'Why don't you help him? Maybe he'll find the answers you are seeking.'

Hegarty grimaced.

'If he finds out who I am, he'll arrest me for murdering the man in the hotel. And then I'll spend the rest of my days in jail. If the paramilitaries don't get to me first.'

'Then you really are in a fix.'

'You concentrate on digging up what you can on the journalist,' said Hegarty. 'I'll look after the detective. We'll report back to each other next week.'

'Very well.'

Hegarty got up and limped off. 'You'd better not let me down,' was his final warning.

The sun had disappeared, replaced by something else – the sharp empty feel of winter. Hannon remained on the bench long after Hegarty had left. The advance of darkness was unflagging – the gathering shadows, the dark birds roosting in their nests high in the trees – like the weight of the past bearing down upon the present. Hannon absorbed it all with a precious sense of lingering life and hope.

Men like Hegarty were a species in peril, he thought; eventually their butchered bodies ended up face down in the dark little ditches of border country. He felt genuinely sad at the thought of what lay ahead for the spy. And more than sad, angry. Hegarty had been one of his most useful recruits, and his betrayals had played an important role in convincing the IRA to abandon its terror campaign. He wished the spy had retired to a quiet corner of the country, become a man of modest means and sober habits, like himself, rather than scuffling about in the dirt of his own grave.

Yet there was a sneaking euphoria to be experienced in darkness and death, especially when one man's demise meant another would live and breathe more easily. He stared at the unmoving trees, smiling at the notion that he was a spectre himself in the fading sunlight. Today and yesterday, the present and the past: really, there was no chance of ever separating the two. This feeling of vengeance more than compensated for the loss of his pleasant afternoon walk and the warmth of the spring sunlight on his face.

He sat stiffly in the corner of his bench like an actor waiting for his moment to return to the stage. In the fading light, the rest of the park turned into a desert of empty paths and shadows.

18

A flash-in-the-pan rainstorm kept Daly confined to his car outside an abandoned cottage, the roof hammering with raindrops, the windscreen wriggling with the distorted shapes of trees. He switched off the engine. The silence within the car felt equal to the silence emanating from the cottage. He rolled down his window, and listened as the ditches deepened their gurgling. He drove off again, bumping cautiously along potholed roads and then even more cautiously over rush-grown lanes.

The detective was driving through border country, following Walsh's dated map. It was the best guide he had to tracing the homes of the murder triangle victims, to untangling the network of minor roads the killers had once used. It struck him that this journey through the back roads was like travelling into that strangest of places – the past. The idea of summarizing what had happened along these roads daunted him; there were so many personal tragedies on both sides of the community, the murders of so many innocent Protestants and Catholics left unsolved, so much rumour and suspicion, that only bewilderment and fear remained.

The task ahead strengthened his feeling of not knowing which way to turn, this sense of not having a single clear thought in his head. He knew that his mother had been murdered and that her killers had escaped justice, swallowed up in the murkiness of the past. In his mind, he tried to juggle her murder with the other twenty-odd cases marked on Walsh's murder map.

As he drove, derelict cottages emerged from lanes like ghosts of his own cottage. He stared at each one; they were his obsession now. Something to take the place of his introvert's collection of vehicle registration numbers. Every thorn hedge seemed to hide another potential murder site; every ditch brimmed with murky mysteries, the hummocky little fields like rucked-up carpet hiding swept-away secrets. He got out, strolled around the wild margins of their plots, gawking at the extent of ruin. The similarities with his father's farm held him spellbound. They belonged to the same kingdom of slippage and neglect.

He drove down roads he had forgotten existed, trying to discriminate in his head between the different murders, sifting through the array of facts accumulated by the priest. He wanted to limit the cases to a significant few, the ones that had most in common with his mother's.

He played with the possibility that a serial killer had been at work, operating on a psychopathic level, killing innocent people because the justice system and the media were so overwhelmed with the deaths of so many Catholics and Protestants that they ignored his handiwork, his bloody trail of evidence.

He delved further into Walsh's map, going deeper into border country. There was no going back now, he told himself. The evening grew darker, the roads and thorn thickets and low hills became indistinguishable. He remained transfixed, hunched over his steering wheel, the car headlights groping the blackness.

He pulled up a muddy lane, and located another ruinous old house dimly visible through the trees, another fractured mirror revealing fragments of his past. He switched off the engine and got out. He could hear something moving through the trees. It was not the wind moving, but something darker, the unsettling nearness of the past. He stood for several moments, fused with the twilight, conscious only of the pale gable wall of the cottage, its outline slowly disappearing as night drew in. *I'm in danger of disappearing into this darkness*, he told himself.

He took out his flashlight and flicked the beam over the house. Straggling gorse thickets overran what had probably been a well-tended garden in the 1970s. To the side, he traced the same mounded heaps of earth overgrown with rank grass and briars that lay so mysteriously in a corner of his father's farm, the same sense of a half-buried pattern that eluded any interpretation.

He inspected the dark of the ruined interior and shivered. He saw what looked like an old boot with no sole lying in a damp corner. A shudder from the past doubled the cottage's dereliction. On 25 January 1979, 24-year-old Gregory O'Brien had been shot dead by a Loyalist paramilitary gang in the cottage's hallway. Daly suspected that no amount of renovation work could have remedied the disfiguring slippage induced by that evil act.

He fumbled in his pockets for his car key. He had seen enough. It was time he went home to the familiar folds of his father's fields. Perhaps the journalist or Hegarty would contact him, and they could unravel the mystery together. He turned back to his car and a light flicked through the trees. Warm, inviting light. He decided to walk towards it. He saw a silhouette framed in the window of a house. It was a young woman, staring in his direction. She looked peaceful, disturbingly peaceful through the restless trees, as though she belonged to a dream or some other dimension.

He drew closer to the light and came across a tarmac lane. He saw that a neat lawn had been bulldozed from the humped terrain, and a new bungalow built on the levelled site. He knocked on the door, and the young woman answered.

He introduced himself and said he was looking for the relatives of Gregory O'Brien.

The woman's face was motionless. She stared at him as if waiting for more.

'Why have you come now?' she said.

'A man died recently in mysterious circumstances. He was searching for new evidence relating to Gregory's murder.'

'No one told us you were coming.'

'I know. I won't trouble you for long.'

She held out her hand.

'My name is Ciara O'Brien. Gregory was my uncle.'

She reacted calmly to his appearance on her doorstep. She did not seem hostile, dismayed or badly interrupted to have her uncle's murder brought up by a strange detective calling unannounced at her door.

'He's a police detective,' she explained to the man who had appeared from an inner room. 'An Inspector Daly.'

The man had a slight beard, and was carrying a young child in his arms. He looked closely at Daly and then at the woman, as if trying to decide if the intrusion was going to be painful or bothersome.

'Your name doesn't ring a bell,' he said, a trace of scepticism in his voice. 'You weren't involved in any of the previous investigations.'

'That's correct. This is a new line of inquiry. Evidence has emerged that Gregory may have been murdered by serving police officers.'

His explanation did not appear to perturb them. If anything, it seemed to satisfy them.

'You must be talking about Father Walsh's murder map,' said Ciara.

'You knew him?'

'He visited us about a fortnight ago and gave us a copy of the map. He told us he was close to solving a mystery about the murders. He had questions to ask us.'

'What sort of questions?'

She took the baby from the man and placed it in a cot. The man returned to a back room. She sat at the edge of the seat, legs intertwined, pale knees jutting. She was wearing a loose woollen sweater that had been tugged awry, probably by her baby, giving her an air of frayed nerves and distress, yet when she spoke her voice was calm.

'Father Walsh asked lots of questions. About my uncle's life, his occupation, his friends. He wanted to know all about the harassment Gregory had suffered at police checkpoints in the weeks leading up to the shooting. He kept asking about neighbourly disputes, resentments, that sort of thing. He said that greed and envy were useful traits to exploit. He believed that the intelligence services had exploited local grievances, what he called mean little jealousies between Catholics and Protestants.'

'What was he suggesting? That neighbours scheming against each other could lead to murder?'

'You know what neighbours are like in these parishes. Always ready to help out in a crisis but secretly plotting each other's downfall.'

Daly looked doubtful. He stared through the window, wondering where was the root of it all, why innocent families had to suffer so much. If there was a web of connections between the murders, why did it entangle so many blameless individuals?

The window framed a stark vista. A thicket of thorns and Gregory's ruined cottage. The wind picked up, agitating the trees, multiplying the shadows and patterns that fell across the cracked walls of the old house. He felt as though he was getting closer to something difficult to understand. *Mean little jealousies.* What had Walsh been referring to?

'Tell me, Inspector, why are the police so anxious to find out what Father Walsh asked?' Her voice was firm. 'It shouldn't be any of your business. You shouldn't give a damn about his murder map, but you clearly do.'

Her eyes rapidly surveyed him as he held his silence.

'Why weren't we informed in advance of this investigation?' she demanded. 'Why have you turned up out of the blue at this time of the evening?' Her indignation mounted. 'Is this visit part of an official investigation into my uncle's murder?'

Her blunt questions silenced him. He passed his hand over his forehead, rubbed his stubble and looked out through the window. He caught sight of his reflection and saw something beggarly and vulnerable in the way he sat on the sofa with his shoulders hunched. He realized he had given himself away. He looked more like a lonely obsessive than a professional detective working on an important investigation.

'There is no new official investigation into your uncle's murder,' he said.

'Then why should I answer your questions?' There was a ring of triumph in her voice, but she was incensed now. 'What interest do you have in Gregory's death? Are you here to cover up the past, to keep a lid on things? Are you working on your own or for someone else?'

'I haven't come here to be interrogated like this,' said Daly. A part of him was drawn to the intensity of her fury, the energy of her questions. She adjusted her position, twisting her legs tighter. Her body grew taut, ready for attack. 'I'm here as a detective,' he explained. 'Searching for the truth. Nothing else.'

'But you're not telling me the truth. Your motives for coming here are more personal than what you're letting on.'

Daly levered forward, uncertain as to whether he should simply leave or reveal his secret. He had spent the afternoon scuttling from the shell of one empty house to another, like some introverted, raw-skinned creature seeking protection from the elements. She had sensed this need in him. In her eyes, his motives must have appeared suspicious – sinister, even.

'I'm trying to connect your uncle's murder to that of a woman called Angela Daly.' His heart beat faster at the mention of her name. 'She was killed on the second of April 1979.' He swallowed. 'She was my mother.'

Immediately, her anger flickered off, like a blown light bulb. Her face grew weary, strained by her show of emotion, Daly's reluctant admission and the fact that a bond now existed between them.

'And what connections have you discovered?'

'Nothing groundbreaking.'

She looked relieved.

'I know that they were killed by the same weapon and on the first Monday of the month. I also know…'

She raised her hand. 'I don't want to hear.'

'Aren't you interested in hearing the connections?'

'What I am is exhausted, Inspector. I want to get on with my life, look after my baby, go to bed and get some sleep. The same things you look as though you need.'

The glint of young motherhood shone in her eyes. Daly found it slightly intimidating.

'You sound more angry than exhausted,' he said.

She didn't reply.

Outside, the trees shifted, one behind another, realigning their branches. A line of sight opened, letting him see the darkness of the ruined cottage, and then the view disappeared. He felt a sudden longing for symmetry.

'Inspector?'

He started at the closeness of her voice. His thoughts had been miles away.

'Have you ever considered what good digging up the past will do?' she asked. 'All this searching for connections and conspiracies. How will it really help either of our families? Or anyone, for that matter? This baby of mine, do you think it will make any difference to his life, knowing exactly why his grand-uncle was murdered?'

Daly's face was a blank. His reference to Walsh's research had felt clumsy and rushed, and, in a way, he was grateful that she had stopped him in his tracks. He raised his eyes to the view of the cottage. He could not stop his thoughts from hovering with the trees, joining their dark consciousness as they churned in the wind. Their restless movement made the woman and her baby seem eerily calm and stable. Was he the only one of the victims' relatives in thrall to the past's restless shadows and silences? he wondered.

'Father Walsh died in a road accident a few days ago,' said Daly. 'Ordinarily that means his research would have died with him. However, he had a journalist working with him. She wants to publish a book on his findings. She's convinced the story should be told.'

'A journalist?' She laughed harshly. 'That's presumptuous of her. Why does she want to tell the story?'

'For the same reason that Walsh wanted to. Because she is obsessed with the idea of a murder triangle. Because it's a mystery that has never been properly explained. Isn't that the sort of story that needs to be told?'

The note of scorn persisted in her voice.

'Anyone can tell a story like that. The bookshops in this country are groaning with the weight of those sort of books. But not everyone can keep silent. The art of staying quiet is an underestimated talent.' She watched him closely. 'Tell me, what did your father tell you about your mother's death?'

'Nothing. Apart from a few vague lies that I took to be the truth.'

'Isn't that a better sort of a story to tell? One that protects you from the painful truth?'

Perhaps she was right, thought Daly; the only stories worth telling were the ones that hid secrets right to the final words. Weren't the best fairy tales labyrinths for the unpalatable truth?He remembered his father's bedside presence when he was a boy, helping him settle into sleep. He felt a pang of loss for his fatherly attention, his watchful eyes, his sustaining silence.

'Perhaps your father was right to hide the truth from you. He didn't want it to ruin your life.'

'But the truth doesn't ruin lives.' He could have said more, but he stopped himself.

'But it doesn't make us any happier. If I found out tomorrow that I had an incurable disease, how would that make my life any better?' She stared at him and shrugged. 'Perhaps I should know better than to argue with you about your father's motives.'

'It's OK.'

'About what you said, earlier, it is true. I am exhausted. With all this talking about my uncle's death. We should keep our mouths shut more often. We used to be good at doing that in this country.'

He took out a copy of Walsh's murder map.

'Before I go, I want you to have a copy of this. I want you to study it carefully.'

She gave it straight back to him.

'I can't look at it.'

'Why not?'

'I have a baby to feed.'

She looked at him with a hint of sympathy. What kind of image did he present? A courageous investigator following clues into the past, or a grieving son, hopelessly lost with only an outdated map for guidance? Her face clouded, gathering itself to tell him something important.

'Maps don't always lead you to your destination. Sometimes they just take you further away.'

Daly drove home slowly, chewing over what Ciara had told him. His father had mentioned in his letter something about the depths of evil their neighbours had sunk to in the weeks leading up to his mother's murder. The comment chimed with Walsh's line about mean little jealousies. He was tempted to go back to Walsh's room in the monastery and read the notes on each murder. However, it was getting late in the day, and he needed time to think.

He had the nagging feeling he had overlooked something important. Until now, he had assumed that Walsh's talk of conspiracies involved the intelligence services and perhaps the judiciary. But what if these weren't the principal characters? What if the conspiracies involved a different circle of people entirely? One more connected with the local landscape? This was where he should begin again, he thought. He would have to go through all the connections of the murder map from a different perspective.

The simplest way to give symmetry to chaos was to hold a mirror to it. The details of Ciara's family tragedy had aligned with fragments of his own: the ruined cottage, the harassment at checkpoints, the time of the week and the hint at neighbourly disputes. When he recalled the stories of the other murders he saw that the same details were mirrored, doubled, trebled. It was no wonder that Walsh had worked on the cases for years.

On an emotional level, he felt an odd sense of peace, satisfaction even, to know that invisible seams joined their family tragedies to his. On an intellectual level, he realized that Walsh was correct to have searched for patterns. He should be focusing on the most innocent-seeming details that the murders had in common; the more they were repeated, the more they took on meaning and importance.

For the first time in ages, he felt a sense of achievement. Back in his cottage, he stood for a long time at the scullery window watching the lights of houses winking in the blackness, and in the distance, on the other side of the lough, the string of towns lit up against the dark motion of the waves. He went straight to bed, hoping to hold on to his small glow of contentment.

In the middle of the night, a frenzied cry warning of murder stirred him in his dreams. He turned and twisted his blankets. The shriek sounded again. Semi-conscious, he sensed the terror of something that could not speak expressed in that blood-curdling cry.

For a moment, his brain could not make any sense of what was going on, but then he heard the cry again. An anguished squawk from the darkness outside. He woke up fully, realizing the sound wasn't human. He remembered with awful clarity that he had forgotten to lock up the black hen, and that it was a moonless night. Killing time for predators like foxes.

He jumped up, grabbed a torch and pulled on an old coat. It had been a while since he'd been tempted out for a nocturnal walk, and he was clumsy stumbling his way through the door and out into the overgrown garden. He knocked his shin against a low wall and cursed. He searched for the hen at her usual roost on the windowsill and then in the coop, but there was no sign of her. He made a circuit of the cottage. Scanning with his torch, he found a trail of black feathers leading into one of the thorn thickets.

The thought that a fox had made off with the hen made him feel sad and angry, but a part of him also felt relieved of a troublesome burden. He followed the feathers. After a few minutes, he heard a faint jumble of cluck-cluck noises emerging from the thicket. The hen was more resourceful than he had believed. The beam of his torch caught her bolting deeper into the thicket, but then she froze. She crouched close to the ground, still gripped by fear. Apart from the missing feathers, she appeared unhurt. He eased himself through the thorns on his haunches, groping with his hands until he encircled her tattered wings and then her trembling body. He dragged her out and hoisted her back to the cottage, talking softly to her all the time.

Fearing that she might not survive the cold night, he settled her into a box packed with hay and placed it next to the dying fire in the scullery. He waited until her agitation ceased and her attention turned inwards. Soon she settled into sleep.

He was unable to get back to sleep himself, and got up once more to sit by the embers of the fire. He sighed. He wondered whether he was wasting his life, living day by day with the silence of the cottage, his only company this black hen dodging from shadow to shadow in his tracks. They were both castaways, he realized, marooned in the past. He saw a little of his futile detective's life in the hen and her mannerisms, in the way she spent her waking life stooped over the ground, pecking at odd bits here and there, a life of scratching and vigilance, while the unseen predators circled perpetually in the darkness.

Pryce wanted a hero for her book, but he wasn't what she was looking for. He wasn't even a hero of waiting and procrastination. He had exhausted all his resources already. He closed his eyes and willed a voice to speak, a voice of reassurance and wisdom, advising him of the right course of action to take, his mother or father's voice, or his own voice from his childhood, any voice at all, but none were forthcoming.

19

Early-morning mist rolled in from the lough and gathered around the cottage, low-lying, serpentine, clinging in weird whorls to the tops of the thorn thickets. Daly stood at the scullery window watching it blanket his fields. The blackthorns seemed to collect the mist, giving it shape and menace. Dense and white, it advanced towards his lookout until all he could see was his reflection staring back at him with a look of haunted bafflement.

The phone rang in the hall. It took a while for him to register the fact. He did not want to talk to anyone. Still, he hurried out and answered it.

'Yes?'

'Hello, Celcius.' The woman's voice was warm, intimate. 'You left without a proper goodbye.' It was the journalist, Pryce.

He said nothing.

'Listen, I have to see you. We must meet up and talk things through.'

'Talk what through?'

'Aloysius's murder map. Your mother. The connections.'

He looked out at the thickening mist. The deepest of silences filled the air.

'I'm busy this morning.'

She gave a little laugh.

'Ever since we met I've been turning this story over and over in my head, but every time I sit down to write it I get bogged down and give up. Not a single word written. You've cursed me with writer's block.'

Blaming him for her procrastination seemed absurd and petty, even for a journalist, thought Daly.

'Perhaps it's no longer your story to tell.'

'Which is why I need to see you. I could come out to your cottage, or you could choose somewhere else to meet.'

'I told you I'm busy.'

Her voice grew softer, more winning.

'I really need to talk to you.'

Daly sighed again.

'I've spoken to Major Hannon,' she said. 'He's willing to meet us this morning.'

'What's the address?'

Daly wrote down the details. He understood why she needed him so badly. Who else would be desperate enough to follow her signposts?

'We should travel up together,' she suggested.

He had to hand it to her. She was stubborn and resourceful – the most dangerous type of journalist, brazen as long as she still had the scent of a story in her nostrils.

'This is a police investigation. I don't want you in the way.'

'Why?'

'I don't need to explain my decisions to you. For a start, you don't know the type of people we're dealing with.'

'I don't know?'

'Correct. You don't even begin to know. And let me remind you that in normal societies, police investigate crimes and journalists report them.'

'But I have a duty to this story and to Father Walsh, not to mention my career. I can't give it up now. I'd never be able to live with myself otherwise.'

'You might not have much of a career left – or a life, for that matter – if you keep interfering,' warned Daly and hung up.

An hour later, the sun was splitting through the mist and drenching Daly's car in light as he pulled up the gravelled drive leading to Major Hannon's home. He got out and stared at the impressive three-storey Victorian building with that slightly mesmerized feeling one gets when arriving in a warmer, more colourful country. He felt as though he had ascended through a fog of worry, sleeplessness and moral uncertainty to alight on this golden gravel. He climbed the steps to a pair of oak doors, with the uncomfortable sensation that he was dragging his tangled story behind, like a monstrous tail from the past.

Hannon was large, square-headed, dressed in a cashmere cardigan, polo neck and cream slacks. He looked as though he had just dropped off his golf clubs at the putting green. He was fat for a former military man, and it was more than retirement weight, Daly noticed.

On greeting the detective, Hannon swung his bulk to the back of his heels and forward again, his teeing-up position. The expectant look on his face turned a little desolate when he realized Daly was on his own.

'Ms Pryce said you wanted to talk to me,' he said, shaking hands. His voice was abrupt with a hint of tension in it. 'Where is she?'

He looked Daly up and down carefully. The detective guessed that not too far below Hannon's overweight golfer's persona there still lurked a razor-sharp intelligence agent.

'Ms Pryce is a journalist. I want to keep our conversation between us and no one else.'

'Very well,' replied the major. 'You'd better come in.'

He led Daly into a conservatory with potted orange trees and a tiled floor scrubbed to the bright polish of a military barracks. From a drawer, Hannon removed an old-fashioned voice recorder, and placed it on the table between them. He smiled.

'How may I help your investigation?'

'What investigation?' asked Daly, wondering how well the major had prepared himself for the visit.

'I mean this – a police detective coming all the way from the sticks in Tyrone to interview me and rake over my past.' He stared at Daly as though he had dragged himself from a wild thorny corner of another country.

'This is not an official investigation. More a casual inquiry. I was interested in meeting you after I came across your name in some old files. I want to ask you a few questions about a number of murders that took place in the 1970s.' Daly cleared his throat. 'One of the victims was my mother. A completely innocent woman who was killed at a police checkpoint.'

It occurred to Daly that Walsh's research had made his mother's death public property. He felt an odd sense of vulnerability bringing up its details like this.

'If you want to ask questions then clearly you are conducting an investigation,' replied the major. 'What sort of questions?'

Daly sensed a note of contempt enter Hannon's regard for him. It prickled his anger.

'According to the records, you were a senior intelligence agent operating out of Armagh military barracks at the time of the murders.'

'Which records are you talking about?' Hannon's face and voice grew cold.

'I'm afraid that's confidential.'

'Then I'm assuming they were dug up by your journalist friend.'

'With the help of another source. A very reliable one.'

Hannon snorted.

'What sources are reliable these days? What do you know about your informant's real priorities and prejudices? Everyone is playing some sort of political game in this country.'

'I'm a detective. My job is to collar criminals, not play politics. Besides, I can assure you that this source was completely disinterested in anything but the truth.'

The major's face sharpened.

'Was? Sounds like your source is deceased.' He sighed and leaned his bulk back into the seat. 'Dear God, I can see why you're convinced; the only completely disinterested source is a dead one.' He regarded Daly for several moments. 'Very well, I will answer your questions. I'm retired now, and I've received no instruction from MI5 as to what I can or cannot say about that particular time of the Troubles. But first, you have to tell me precisely what you want to know.'

'Who murdered my mother? And who orchestrated the cover-up?'

'What makes you believe I can answer those questions?'

Daly told him what he knew of his mother's death, and the connections he had gleaned from Walsh's murder map.

Hannon shrugged pompously.

'I find it strange your mother was murdered by that particular gang of Loyalists and rogue police officers if she was, as you claim, completely innocent. Did she have any political connections or involvement with the IRA?'

'None whatsoever.'

'But you were a child at the time. It's not inconceivable that your mother's political leanings were unknown to you.'

'Neither of my parents was political in any way.'

'What about her relatives? Any black sheep in the family? A brother on the run, perhaps?'

'No.'

'A completely innocent Catholic, then?' The major looked thoughtful.

Daly pushed the memory of his car registration collection to the back of his mind.

'But that wasn't the Loyalists' style, you see,' said the major. 'Unless they had some sort of personal score to settle with your family. Why else would they target her completely at random?'

Daly felt a bitter black taste rise in his mouth.

'What do you mean? A personal score?'

'A neighbourly dispute. A business deal gone wrong. Remember, Inspector, these men were weak, mentally unhinged. They obsessed over things in the past, grudges, enmities, a perceived slight.'

The indifference with which he shrugged off the motivation for the murder increased the bitter taste in Daly's mouth.

'This was 1979,' continued the major. 'The entire country was slipping into chaos. If I tried to explain it, you wouldn't understand.'

'Try me.'

'Very well, then.' He sighed and leaned forward with the air of a man eager to talk, anxious not to conceal anything about the past. 'Before the Troubles started, sectarianism and bigotry were barely noticeable to people of my class and background. It was simply how the country got by.' He sighed. 'But then the Civil Rights marches and the IRA bombing campaign came along, and that pathology became something much nastier, a convulsion, which along with the IRA's barbaric terror tactics shook the country to its core. Many ordinary people were caught up in it – including a bunch of very misguided police officers and soldiers, over whom their commanders had no final control or authority. Remember, the IRA were rampant and the entire situation seemed out of control. Bloodlust and revenge can travel at lightning speed through the ranks of the very best of officers, men and women who had to bury their colleagues in the morning and return to duty in the afternoon.'

'And when these officers or security agents committed murder a blind eye was turned?'

'Of course not. However, in the atmosphere then, when it felt as though everything was falling apart, those of us in command and our contacts in the judiciary and media had a duty not to undermine public confidence in the security forces. In those days, secrecy wasn't a dirty word, it meant discretion. It was thought that some things were better kept away from public scrutiny.'

'So the conspiracy theories are true. There was a committee in regular contact at the highest levels of society.'

'No. But we knew who our friends were. Those in positions of authority who understood our predicament.'

'And with their help you kept the truth about the murder triangle secret.'

'Yes. A secret that was a bulwark to the policing of a society hovering on the brink of violence. Remember, we were only trying to do what was best for this country in the long run.' He leaned back again. 'Being loyal to one's country and to law and order is not a criminal offence. Despite what people think nowadays.' He smiled at Daly. 'But of course, you've heard all this before. This is nothing new.'

It was and it wasn't. Not to this critical extent. Not to the nihilistic point where the very people paid to uphold law and order were being protected as they propelled the country towards civil war.

'There is another theory,' said Daly. 'That there was an orchestrated campaign within intelligence circles to murder innocent Catholics.'

'Why would anyone devise such a plan?'

'Because it was the only way to detach the IRA from its bedrock of support. A cohort within the intelligence services wanted to prove that the IRA could not protect the wider Catholic community. The objective required a robust sectarian murder campaign. In a warped way, the more innocent the Catholic victim the better. Hence my mother's murder.' Daly stared intensely at the major, but Hannon gave nothing away. 'There must have been an order given at the highest levels of government or within the military. The pattern of murders, the cover-ups within the police force, the judiciary and the media. Something sinister is begging to be discovered.'

'Then discover it.' The major's voice had turned cold again.

'I don't have to. One man already has. A priest. He spent years struggling to find the connections. He wrote thousands of words about the similarities between these murders. He was on a mission to expose the entire rotten system until he died in mysterious circumstances close to the Irish border. His name was Father Aloysius Walsh.'

Hannon did not react to the mention of the name. He seemed to be expecting it. He rose, unlocked a drawer in his desk, and pulled out a slender file.

'I don't have any information on your Father Walsh,' he said. 'But I do have this on his assistant, Jacqueline Pryce. I'd assumed she was accompanying you here today, so I took the liberty of preparing myself with a little background reading. This is a copy of an MI5 file that was dispatched to me by courier this morning. It concerns your little reporter friend and her involvement with Walsh. She must be flattered to have warranted the attention.'

He sat down and opened the file.

'How well do you know her?' he asked Daly.

'I've only just met her.'

'Did she mention that she's married to a former IRA man, Eddie McKenna, a Republican dissident who doesn't subscribe to the peace process? Gives her persona a little more edge, doesn't it?' He stared at Daly. 'I have some background here about her employment record, and the people she has been talking to in the past few months.'

'Background?' relied Daly. 'What about this for background? Walsh was researching an incident that took place in Palestine in 1947.

The murder of a Jewish youth by a Major George Hannon. Why don't you tell me what you know about this man who shares your name?'

Hannon stared at Daly, seemingly fascinated by the detective's digression.

'I've examined the military records,' said Daly. 'He was your father.'

'You're correct. But that was seventy years ago, when he worked for the Palestine police service. You know that he returned from his stint there a hero. He was awarded several medals for bravery. For his service in Oman, too. If you like, I can let you see them.'

Daly did not respond.

'But I fail to see what relevance his military record has to your investigation. My father had no involvement with the modern-day Troubles. What you should be concentrating on is the foreground.'

'But he passed something else on to you as well as his medals. A strategy, a controversial military theory on countering insurgency in a native population. Walsh tracked its use in Palestine, Oman and Uganda. It was his legacy to you.'

'I see where you're going now, Inspector.' Hannon sat upright. 'If you're suggesting that I or my father had anything to do with Walsh's murder triangle then you will have my lawyers to answer to.'

'I'll pass your concerns on to Special Branch. They'll have to look into this, like everything else in the case.'

At the mention of Special Branch, Hannon visibly relaxed.

'Make sure to keep them properly informed. They might save you from a serious lapse of judgement.'

Daly got up to leave. 'One more thing before I go. Walsh was due to meet a man called Hegarty at the hotel the night he died. Do you know anything about him?

Hannon grimaced.

'He's a murderer, by anyone's definition.'

He went on to explain that Hegarty was a highly placed mole within the IRA working for British Intelligence.

'I recruited him many years ago when he was a young man. Unfortunately, since the peace process he has gone to great lengths trying to smear his former employers. He has stirred up a storm of rumour and conjecture that will tarnish the security forces for years. From what

I understand, Walsh swallowed his lies and came back for more. Be warned, Inspector, Hegarty is ruthless enough to kill anyone in his path. For the last forty years he has operated in a vacuum without any political or judicial controls.'

'He was also a British Intelligence agent,' said Daly. 'On this occasion, you're not showing much loyalty to an old comrade.'

'I'm only telling you this because I believe he's one of the most dangerous men I've ever met. To make matters worse, his life is under threat in a way it never was before. Republicans know there was a mole in their midst. They won't stop till they hunt him out.'

Hannon walked Daly to the door.

'Do you know his whereabouts?' he asked Daly.

'I have no idea.'

'Now is the time for him to leave Northern Ireland. I've argued with him over the years, begged him to emigrate to the US or Australia. But he's hell-bent on stirring up trouble. You must warn him.'

'As I said, I don't know where he is.'

'But you have some means of contacting him?'

'No,' lied Daly.

'Well, if by some chance Hegarty gets in touch with you, I want you to contact your colleagues in Special Branch, immediately. Your life may be in great danger.'

Daly said goodbye to him at the door. Hannon handed him a copy of the MI5 file on Pryce.

'I wish you luck in your search for your mother's killers,' said Hannon. 'However, I fear that you will discover only traces of the truth, brutal bits of information here and there, a few obscure connections, but the whole story will remained invisible, fragmented. Especially if you have people like Pryce and Hegarty as your guides.'

'My eyes are wide open, believe me, and my suspicions on the highest alert,' said Daly and left.

Driving back to Tyrone, Daly imagined that a dark-coloured car was keeping pace behind him on the motorway. Was he being followed? It was difficult to tell on such a busy road. He cut off on to the minor roads around Lough Neagh. It was easier to single out a tail on this empty maze of lanes that he knew like the back of his hands. He glanced in his rear mirror and saw the car swing into view. For several miles, the car kept its distance as Daly traversed crossroads and junctions, until he came across a police checkpoint in the middle of nowhere. He slowed right down when the checkpoint was a hundred yards away. He could see the group of police officers standing in the middle of the road with their guns, waiting for his car to approach. They seemed to be doing nothing but guarding the emptiness of the road behind. Two of them were wearing blue overalls. Why the overalls? Was it to keep the forensics clean? A sweat broke out on Daly's forehead thinking of what the officers might be planning. The snub noses of their guns were pointed at the ground but their eyes stared hard at his car, noting the registration. He reversed the vehicle at speed and turned off on to a narrow road. He hit the pedal hard, and drove straight to police headquarters. If a speed camera had caught him on those twisting by-roads, plunging by derelict-looking farms on one side and flooded fields on the other, he would without question have lost his licence.

Fealty appeared to be waiting for him as soon as he entered headquarters.

'We've had complaints, Daly, about your little visits.' The Special Branch inspector radiated barely controlled anger.

'What do you mean?'

'You can't go knocking on doors and barging right in like the old days. Especially at the home of a high-ranking former intelligence agent.'

'How do you propose I should conduct my investigation?'

'By sharing information and strategies with your colleagues. We work in an open-plan environment these days. You can't keep skulking and hiding in back offices or your car, and operating like a maverick.'

'I have questions that need answered. I need to find out what happened all those years ago, and uncover the links between Walsh's death and the murder of McClintock in the hotel room.'

There was a shift in Fealty's voice, a deepening of his anger.

'Remember you're a detective in the new police service of Northern Ireland. You shouldn't let what happened in the past cloud your better judgement.'

'Happened in the past,' replied Daly. 'You make it sound as

though what happened to my mother is over and done with, but it's not. It's not the past, at all. It's my front line. It's where my detective career was headed on the day I began. I've no choice in the matter. I can no more ignore what happened all those years ago than climb out of my own skin.'

'How can you be sure there are any links between what happened to your mother and Walsh's death?'

'What is there to be uncertain of?'

'Why would anyone want to kill Walsh and make it look like an accident?'

'That's the crux of the puzzle. Who would want to kill an elderly priest? And who would want to shoot another man in his hotel bedroom? I can only assume that Walsh uncovered something that became too dangerous.'

'And you suspect the major of involvement. What leads do you have?'

'Right now, I've none, except that his name was mentioned in Walsh's research.'

'Who else have you spoken to?'

'A woman called Ciara O'Brien. She's a niece of one of the murder triangle victims.'

Fealty sighed.

'It's been more than thirty years since those murders took place. What could be so dangerous about that time that threatens a man's life now? Haven't you noticed, for Christ's sake? We have a peace process; the paramilitaries have ended their bloody campaigns. No one wants to rock the boat. What ghosts can emerge into the light now?'

'What do you know of a former spy called Daniel Hegarty?'

Fealty's face darkened.

'He was an informer within the IRA. Unfortunately, he wants to keep the war going. We believe he was trying to manipulate Walsh into believing there was a grand conspiracy. He has gone to great lengths to smear Special Branch and his former employers.' Fealty paused briefly before continuing. 'You should know that we're launching a full-scale manhunt for Mr Hegarty. We believe he killed McClintock.' He looked sharply at Daly. 'Do you have any leads on Hegarty? What about Walsh's mobile phone? Any sign yet?'

'No,' lied Daly. 'I'll let you know when I have something worth pursuing.'

Daly noticed that his evasions were disturbing Fealty, who stepped up close to his face. The Special Branch inspector wanted to push his point across as firmly as he could.

'Listen to me, Daly. Father Walsh spun a web of rumour and suspicion for himself. He went looking for evidence to confirm his fears and prejudices, and he found it among disgruntled informers, alcoholic ex-police officers, journalists with an eye on the big scoop.' Fealty's thin lips carried an ugly sense of threat. 'They fed him with what he wanted to hear – in the end, his conspiracy theories entangled him like a snug little web. He wove it for his ageing mind, wrapping himself in thicker and thicker strands of darkness. That night he crashed his car, something at the checkpoint spooked him. It was not the fault of the police officers, who were just trying to do their job, as officers have always done in this country. Walsh misconstrued something he saw, or saw something that was not there. It was a bad habit he had developed. In the end it killed him.'

'I'll keep that in mind the next time a police checkpoint tries to stop me.'

Fealty did not react to Daly's comment. He nodded and made his way back up the stairs. Daly only stayed long enough in the building to check if any police patrols had radioed in the details of his car and his evasion of a checkpoint. The fact that there were no such reports heightened his suspicion that something sinister had been arranged on that lonely lough-shore road.

He made his way back to the entrance. He suddenly felt oppressed by the building and its sprawling size. He'd had enough of open-plan offices and long corridors. Part of him wanted to return to his old detective's life and his former shell, the fortified police station at Derrylee. He scuttled out of the doors. He missed the old smoke-filled incident rooms, the sectarian banter and the chat about drinking expeditions, trifling things compared to all this high-powered talk of a new police force for a new Northern Ireland. He wanted to hear the voices of those old RUC officers, sit down at the same table with them, look into their eyes and laugh at their grim jokes, even if he did not share their religion or political beliefs, and would always be regarded as an outsider. However, that was akin to talking and laughing with a circle of ghosts, among whom his mother's murderers might lurk. He could never partake of that world now. He could see those old RUC officers in his mind's eye, getting up and quietly vanishing.

He turned his back on the building, and drove off in his car, but there it was again, floating in his rear-view mirror, jutting into his consciousness, urging him to hit the pedal hard. His wheels bit gravel at the verge of the road, and the car skidded. The building swung back into his windscreen again, and he cursed. He started up his car and shifted straight from first to third, the engine whining with the strain.

Someone had chosen that his mother should die, and the fault lay at least partially with former RUC officers. But who else had known about it? Who else had helped orchestrate and cover up the incident? The questions demanded answers. We live in a world compacted from our past and unsolved crimes cannot be hidden forever. He began to suspect that Special Branch were fabricating one lie after another, burdening his mother's murder with secrets and darkness in the hope that it might plunge from view forever. That was the monstrous logic of military intelligence, the gargoyle-like behaviour of men like Fealty and Hannon.

Daly retired to the scullery fire that evening. He pulled up an old armchair with a sigh. For the first time that day, he felt his mind and body relax. Within the burning turf and the shadows cast by its flames, he had finally established a terrain under his personal control, where he could patrol his thoughts and keep an eye on his innermost anxieties. He opened a bottle of whiskey and sipped his way through several glasses, all the time watching the flames rise steadily. When he had done with the whiskey, he got out a pen and paper and wrote a letter, offering his resignation from the police force. He read it through a little while later. Perhaps it was the whiskey's fault, but the letter contained feelings so dark and embittered that he immediately tore it up and cast the scraps into the fire.

Though his mind still felt dark, in the midst of his dejection he experienced a moment of odd euphoria, a flicker of anger and professional pride that persuaded him not to resign. Nothing he could do would erase the actions of the police officers in the past, but he might still summon enough courage to fix things for the future.

20

Saturday morning, and Daly awoke with a fresh mind. He took a quick shower to rinse away the previous night's mood of morbid self-inspection. It was hard to keep holding on to loss and anger, especially when you needed to get out of bed in the morning. Keen to enjoy what was usually the most pleasant part of his day, he dressed and stepped outside without having breakfast. The sight of the farm foundering in the interplay of mist and dawn light was enough to keep him from regretting the discoveries he had made over the past week.

Shunning the enigmas of the landscape, the humped banks of soil and overgrown weeds, he strayed on to his father's old vegetable patch. He kicked aside the nettles and managed to locate the almost effaced drills where the vegetables he had planted last year now lay rotten with frost. He grabbed his father's lean spade and began digging as if he might tell the earth the depth of his troubles. The black hen came scuttling out and hurried after each fresh spadeful, picking out the worms and grubs.

The scrape of the spade hitting stones resounded comfortingly in the morning air. He worked himself into a sweat. At first, the clumps of root-entangled earth felt too heavy to lift, but then he struck a softer patch. He dug on, not looking up for an hour, fashioning a set of drills in the way he had seen his father do every spring of his childhood, head bent low, as if he were talking all the time to the spade. The ground had never been levelled or ploughed by a tractor and was full of quirky humps and dips, minutely adjusted by his father's annual digging bouts.

With the hen for company, he lost himself in the work. The mist hung level in the air above and behind him, robing the terrain in pale threads. He felt a quiet satisfaction that he was in some small way contributing to the levelling of the farm's patchwork of fields, which had been compacted and heaped by his forebears into this lopsided landscape. In short, he almost felt his old self again. It might be far from the normal demeanour of a well-adjusted, middle-aged man, but he was determined to hold on to the feeling at all costs.

He took a break, leaning on the spade, and surveyed the rest of the farm. If only he could take the sharp edge of the spade to the past, he thought, but that landscape had been twisted out of symmetry by far greater forces.

Back in his cottage, he was about to breakfast on a bowl of porridge when he heard a car pull up rapidly outside. He opened the front door to see the journalist Pryce waving from her car.

'Good morning,' she called, rolling down the window.

He returned the greeting without moving from his threshold.

'I was passing near and thought I'd drop by. I need to ask you a few questions.'

'Not if they're for your book.' He tried to smile politely but failed.

She switched off the engine.

'I thought it was country hospitality to always offer visitors a cup of tea.'

'The place is a mess at the moment. We can talk out here.'

She tried to examine his face closely but couldn't.

'I'm sorry. This is one writing assignment I can't shirk from. You must know how compelling a preoccupation it can be.'

'What do you mean?'

'As a detective yourself. You search for clues and suspects. I search for words and characters. But our compulsions are the same.'

He flinched at the comparison.

'The truth is, I've become obsessed by your story, Celcius. My instinct tells me you'd make a compelling character for readers. It would be professional malpractice for me to ignore that.'

She looked at him with a smile that showed both pleasure and apprehension at her revelation. Daly felt himself blush slightly. Her use of his first name made him uneasy. Her smile darkened, grew more purposeful. She was aware of his discomfort.

'I'm too stubborn and introverted to be compelling.'

'A stubborn character often makes the reader stubborn, too. Gives them the determination to keep turning the pages of the story.'

'Whose story are we talking about?'

'Our story. You and me pulling away the layers of fear and denial from your past.'

He nodded slightly. She understood the overarching narrative of his life.

'What do you want to ask me?'

'The questions come later. First, I have to jog your memory with a few clues.'

'What sort of clues?' He felt his suspicions return.

'Addresses. The first is number sixteen Derrycush Road. Jump in and I'll take you there.'

He was about to open the passenger door and climb in when she stopped him. Her face looked suddenly vulnerable.

'Do you have your service weapon with you?'

Her question surprised him.

'Why do you ask?'

'I don't know. I just have a feeling I'm being followed by someone. I don't know who they are.'

Daly thought of the car shadowing him the previous day and the checkpoint on the empty road. He went back to the house and retrieved the gun. He climbed into her car, knowing he had allowed her a small victory, that they were one step closer to becoming accomplices.

'I've a question I need to ask you,' he said when she had settled into driving.

'Fire ahead.'

'How's your husband Eddie McKenna doing?'

She barely flinched. He found it difficult to read the look on her face.

'Who told you that name?'

'Major Hannon. He has a copy of a British Intelligence report on you.'

A little of her prim, professional air drained away.

'What else did he tell you?'

'What else should I know?'

'Nothing. I've a Republican husband. That's all there is to it. Eddie did some time in prison for IRA membership. When he came out he set up a campaign group for ex-prisoners' rights. I interviewed him for a couple of stories and eventually he invited me out for a drink.'

'I take it that saying no would also have been tantamount to professional malpractice.'

This time she did flinch.

'You know you remind me of him.'

'How?'

'Another man stuck in the past.'

She pushed the car into a higher gear and drove fearlessly along roads that were little more than boreens, tapping the brakes only slightly as she swerved around blind corners. Potholes jolted the front wheels. A thorn branch slapped Daly's side of the windscreen.

'At least slow down,' he complained.

A crossroads loomed ahead and she braked hard. Daly lurched forward, held back by his seatbelt, and cursed. Pryce, however, was unperturbed, driving on in the same careless manner.

The low hills, the roads that were all corners and crossroads, the hedges bearing in on them, the water swilling over the rims of blocked ditches and flooding dips in the road, made it impossible for Daly to lean back and stare through the windscreen in silence. He found himself longing for straighter roads, for the smooth tar of the dual carriageway. The car toiled through the gears. Their eyes kept meeting as, several times, she had to extricate the vehicle from a muddy lane that was in the final phase before obliteration.

He took out Walsh's murder map and examined it in a bid to distract himself from her driving. He tried to penetrate the cramped townlands, the interlocking parishes of grief and death. From memory, he pinpointed the locations of at least half a dozen IRA murders. For some reason, they were more easily recalled than the Loyalist attacks – Catholic guilt, perhaps, for the sins committed in his name.

'Let me reassure you about one thing,' she said. 'I don't have a political axe to grind, in spite of my husband's background and what Major Hannon might think. I need to finish this book for financial reasons. Every journalist I know in this bloody country is broke. We're all mortgaged to the hilt and our bank accounts are empty.'

'I hope for your sake that your book never gets published,' he said, putting away the map. 'Otherwise some victims' relatives might come to regard you as worse than the murderers.'

'Why?'

'Because of the way you consume people's stories. Their tragedies. Like a cannibal of lost souls.'

She changed gears roughly and drove on in silence. At one point, the gleam of open blue water caught his eye, and, glancing over her shoulder, he saw the white gable of his cottage, half-submerged in the bumpy fields, but then he realized that was geographically impossible, even in such a labyrinth of wriggling roads. His gable walls faced east and west, and this one faced south. He turned back to the windscreen, his empty stomach heaving with the sense of dislocation and Pryce's reckless driving.

'I doubt you'll ever finish the book anyway,' he told her. 'There are too many blanks in the story.'

'You needn't worry. We're going to fill in several this afternoon.'

They drove along a long, lonely road that ran between a river and bogland. Daly glanced behind and saw a sleek black Audi following them. It wasn't the type of car you'd normally see on empty by-roads. Its presence made Daly feel uneasy. It stayed close behind them in a manner that seemed deliberate and ominous, just like his tail the previous day. He glanced behind again and memorized the number plate. *Old habits die hard*, he thought. He rehearsed the numbers in his mind. As a child, the practice had helped prevent his mind from wandering into unsettling territories. He glanced behind again and saw that the car had disappeared.

At intervals, the bogland gave way to plantations of pine trees and small, untidy-looking farms that had never shaken off the look of the bog, more cottages that had been abandoned and allowed to fall into ruin.

'It must be hard work, living in that cottage of yours,' said Pryce at one point.

'What do you mean?'

'I mean living cheek by jowl with the past. All those childhood memories mixed up with the present. Why not move to a new house in a nearby town?'

He'd often asked the question himself in the gloom of a winter night, rolling in an old blanket, listening to the cold wind rising from the lough. He thought of the twisted little garden and the hummocky fields that looked as though they were slouching closer to his bedroom window with the inexorable creep of the past, and his mind darkened.

'You must feel a duty to your forebears,' said Pryce, testing his silence. 'Why else are you still living there? Moping about that old cottage while the rest of the world moves on.'

He sighed.

'After my marriage broke up and my father died I grew tired of playing musical chairs with my life. I just wanted to stay put. The cottage is not that bad a place for a single man, despite the cold and the damp. It has its…' He struggled to think of the correct word. Not comforts. 'Refinements.'

'Like what?'

'I have a weakness for turf fires and the bottle of whiskey in the old press. Then there are the views of the lough. Some mornings when the water's at its highest I look out and imagine I'm in a little boat.'

She smiled. Was it because she thought she was gaining ground with him?

'But it must be lonely. Staring out at the same view, those same walls closing you in every evening.'

'I have my lodgers for company.'

She looked at him sharply.

'Every night I can hear the blackbirds crawling into the roof-space. And I have a homely hen living in the porch.'

She concentrated on driving. After a few miles, she pulled up at a lane leading to a rundown house.

'Recognize this place?' she asked.

Daly nodded his head in silence; 16 Derrycush Road: a ruined house that had once belonged to a young couple called the Corrigans. The ruin had been a familiar landmark in his childhood. He remembered asking his father why no one lived there, and had been told a tragic story of a newly married couple who had died in a fire, and whose ghosts still haunted the burnt-out remains.

'Why are we stopping here?'

'Because it's crucial to your story.'

'Why is it crucial?'

'Father Walsh's murder triangle is saturated with secret stories like that of the Corrigans and your mother. That was his predicament. He kept finding stories that could not be told until other stories were told first.'

They both got out and approached the house. Daly opened a gate that was creaking in the wind.

'I want to help you tell your story, if I can, but you have to be open with me. Do you understand? We can't let the facts of what happened to families like yours and the Corrigans fall back into the darkness.'

'What has my story got to do with what happened here?'

He was surprised by what she told him. According to Walsh's research, the Corrigans had married in the early summer of 1979. They had been painting their new house on the day after their honeymoon, when a Loyalist bomb, hidden in the hot press, had detonated, killing them both instantly.

'You've got it wrong,' he replied. 'I heard another story. One that has nothing to do with the Troubles.' He recounted what his father had told him, and in the telling of it, he realized how simplistic it sounded, stripped of any sense of evil or blame. A poignant isolated tragedy, constructed for a child's ears. The truth caught up with him, and he found himself resenting Pryce. Again, she had him in her power. She had the capacity for rousing in him conflicting emotions: this aversion for the truth combined with a stronger desire to hear how evil had ploughed its course through his childhood.

They approached the house and circled it. A blackbird bolted through a window. They stepped through what had once been the front door. At first, they could barely see where they were going in the gloom. He almost tripped over several pieces of furniture: an armchair crumbling with fungus, an upended cradle. At head level, electrical flexes and cracked light bulbs dangled in tortured silence. The rest of the house had been stripped bare, or perhaps had never been furnished or fitted out in the first place. A small ash tree had sprouted in a damp corner, a prisoner rooted in rubble, and a colony of slugs gathered where rainwater oozed from a hole in the ceiling. Now that he examined the roof closely, he could make out the path of the bomb where it had ripped through the ceiling and roof, shattering wood and tiles, buckling a steel girder.

'Now can you see?' said Pryce.

Her exaggerated patience felt like a form of mockery. In the half-light, he saw that she was smirking slightly. She had calculated his punishment correctly.

He cleared his throat.

'When you're a child you believe what your parents tell you.'

After a few moments of silence, they walked back to the car.

'You grew up with blinkers on, Celcius,' she said disapprovingly. 'You didn't see what was really happening. You didn't understand a thing.'

Daly got into the car and stared straight ahead, perplexed.

'Of course, your family weren't the only ones to ignore what was going on. It's human nature not to acknowledge evil in case it spreads and comes closer to home.'

'I don't need to defend my family to you. You didn't live through those times.'

'Correct. But you *did*. It's your responsibility to find out the truth. If you buckle and hide from it, you will never be able to live with yourself. You have a duty to your past, to your own self-respect.'

She was right, he conceded. He couldn't ignore the past any longer. He had his own journey to undertake. It was useless to keep closing his eyes, or turning his back. If their road trip proved anything, it was that the past was all around, in every direction, stretching all the way to the horizon. It was time to go back to his cottage on that morning in 1979. It was time to dig up the cottage's secrets, the precious family bones.

'You had a nice life, Celcius,' she said. 'A detective in the police service of Northern Ireland. With the Troubles over, life was safe, peaceful, prosperous. Then one day a priest is killed in a car crash, and bang! The past hits you. Suddenly you find out your mother was murdered. Life is not so nice and peaceful any more.'

Again, Daly detected more than a hint of mockery in her voice. Had his life ever felt safe and peaceful? he wondered. Certainly, there had been an absence of trouble, but that did not equate with feeling safe. His father's story about an accidental bullet had been a lie, but it had filled what would have otherwise been an all-devouring hole in his childhood. Pryce was correct. The idea of a random bullet had been so much easier to live with than puzzling over an evil motive. How much easier it was to forget a stray incident in the mix, beyond the concepts of good and evil, blame and retribution.

'Take me home,' he said.

'Wait. I've one more address to show you.'

The land changed from bogland to pasture and places where things grew. It improved so much that soon they were driving through leafless orchards. The farmhouses were clearly inhabited, comfortably off in appearance; the hedges well maintained, the whitethorn blossoming in neat, rectangular shapes. There was a sense of order at every level, from the rows of apple trees to the mown grass and mud-free farmyards.

The sun found a gap in the overcast sky and reached across the low-lying apple trees, their arched branches resembling sinews bracing for a calamity that had already happened. Daly and Pryce got stuck behind a tractor, bumping along the narrow roads. He had time to take in sharply defined details in the sunlight, an Orange Order Hall bristling with antennae and flags, and the first tentative apple blossoms of the year, so bright they seemed to sway over the trees.

'I haven't been down these roads in years,' he remarked.

'Tell me something more about your mother, Celcius.'

It was a test of his powers of recall to remember anything but the image of her that existed in photographs. All he could conjure up was the blurred oval of her face at the kitchen window, her back as he followed her about the house, and her blue nurse's uniforms neatly ironed. She drove a red Hillman. He remembered long hours in the evening, standing by the front window, waiting for her car to turn the corner and arrive home. But was that before or after her death? Had he kept vigil expecting her to come back, once, briefly, to say goodbye?

'There's not much to tell you,' he said. 'She led an ordinary life.'

'Was she the typical Irish mother? I want to picture her in my mind.'

'Why do you want to picture her?'

'No reason, really.'

'I don't want my mother to be a character in your book. Not now or ever. The subject is closed. Please don't mention her again.'

Pryce slowed her driving, hesitated at crossroads, and drove back down the same roads. She was lost. She pulled over and asked directions from a farmer, mentioning the name Agnew. Daly felt cold perspiration form on his forehead. Instinctively, he reached for his gun and felt its reassuring heft. A minute later, they pulled up at the front door of a two-storey farmhouse. An elderly woman watched them from an upstairs window, and then disappeared. She reappeared at a downstairs window and continued watching them, a fearful look on her face.

They stepped out of the car. The sunlight intensified, casting long groping shadows through the nearby apple trees, which swayed in the breeze. Daly felt tension enter his body, a tension so intense his shoulders shivered. He remembered the name Agnew. It was the name of the last surviving police officer at the checkpoint that had stopped his mother.

'Is this whose house I think it is?' he asked

She nodded and watched him carefully. Again, his hand reached into his jacket pocket and felt the gun nestling there. He wondered if they should turn back and arrange the visit for another day, when he was better prepared, but they had come too far already.

He heard footsteps approach the door, a halting tread, the sound of infirmity or age, followed by the clicks of keys turning, locks unlatched. His tension grew. The thought of confronting one of his mother's killers made him want to shut his eyes. Another part of him felt aroused by the thought of the gun in his pocket and the opportunity for revenge that now presented itself. *If I were some other person*, he thought.

He saw the handle turn. The door creaked open and an old man appeared. His gaze was hard and unwelcoming.

Pryce spoke first, her voice sounding uncharacteristically uncertain.

'We're looking for Kenneth Agnew. We'd like to talk to him.'

The old man's eyes looked them both up and down. He frowned, faltered for a moment.

'You're too late,' he said.

Pryce showed no change in her demeanour. She leaned closer to the doorframe. Daly noticed that she had planted one foot across the threshold. She exuded determination to find out more, yet at the same time there was sympathy in her voice.

'What happened?'

The old man spoke bluntly.

'Kenneth was my brother. He hanged himself at the bottom of the orchard a week ago. We buried him on Sunday.'

The tension evaporated from Daly's body, replaced in that instant by a larger feeling, of calmness – satisfaction, even. From her purse, Pryce took one of her calling cards and handed it to him.

'Have you come far?' asked the old man.

'No,' replied Daly.

The man's eyes flitted suspiciously over Daly, as though he were the odd man out.

'Where do you live? Do I know you?'

The farmyard stood still. The question hung in the air.

'It doesn't matter where I live. We came to talk to your brother.'

The old man examined Pryce's card.

'You're that journalist.' He stared at her with new interest. 'Kenneth said he talked to you a while back.'

'That's correct. I was hoping he might have helped me with a book I'm writing. About the Troubles.'

He handed her the card back but she refused to take it.

'They're my contact details,' she said. 'They're for you to keep. When you feel more like talking.'

He waved the card in the air.

'I don't know why you want to talk to me. I don't even know why you came here. There are things that belong to the past and should never see the light of day.'

'Thank you for your time, Mr Agnew,' said Pryce.

They went back to the car and drove off.

'Agnew was the last surviving policeman from the Loyalist gang,' said Pryce. 'I interviewed him a while back. He was an alcoholic, and completely unrepentant about his past.'

If the comment was meant to jar Daly, it failed. Instead, he felt a sense of peace. The men responsible for his mother's murder had suffered and were dead. Agnew had hanged himself in an empty orchard. *Does that mean I've won? That I can give up this search for the truth? That I am no longer bound by any obligation to pursue her killers?* At the very least, he had been released from the limbo between procrastination and revenge. The sense of relief made him look all around the landscape. The late-afternoon sun gave the rolling hills of apple orchards an air of peace. There was a shine upon everything that felt strange after the brooding greyness of the morning.

However, Pryce did not appear to share his mood. She ignored the signs at crossroads, unwilling to stop. She was riveted by something, her expression rigid, her eyes impervious to the shifts of light in the sky, the restfulness of the landscape.

'Now we might never discover why they targeted your mother, or who set her up in the first place.'

Daly realized that Agnew's suicide might have raised more questions than it had answered.

'We might never know if these murders were willed at a higher level.'

Her eyes flicked across his face, hardened, and focused straight ahead on the road with a tunnelled gaze. Daly began to feel travel-sick. Perhaps it was more than physical nausea; it was the strain of locating himself repeatedly in the spider's web of roads on Walsh's map, jarred by the perspective of slanting fields and thorn hedges, and Pryce's vicious regress into the past. Another empty cottage materialized before them: a gate hanging open in disrepair, the roof dipping in places and spiky weeds sprouting from the drainpipes. Someone had been digging in the overgrown garden, fashioning neat drills out of the black earth. He jolted with surprise when he realized she had taken him home.

That night, Daly found it hard to settle in the cottage. He paced back and forth over the floorboards. A biting wind blew in from the lough, and made the windows rattle. The frames had loosened over the winter and needed fixing. He walked outside to the turf shed and filled a basket with turf. He usually enjoyed puttering about the back yard but he felt cold and tired. He cleaned out the fireplace in the living room, the ashes enveloping him in their soft stink. He picked out pieces of crumbling mortar that had fallen down the chimney. The stack needed repairing and the roof needed new insulation. Everything about the cottage required something done, he grumbled. It was in mortal danger of becoming one of the ruined, forgotten cottages of Walsh's murder map.

The thought of the mounting odd jobs vexed him. Why had he not sold up and moved into a brand-new house? Everywhere he looked in the cottage, he saw accusing fingers pointing at him, demanding his care and attention: the dilapidated furniture, the peeling walls. Would it not have been easier to run away, to seek the comforts of a modern apartment? But there were other fingers oppressing him. What else did he lack? What else had he left undone? Where was his thirst for revenge, the determination to have the people who orchestrated his mother's death brought to justice? He gritted his teeth. He felt annoyed with his fate, the story of his mother's murder and now this dire sequel, his search for the truth, and the unravelling of his career as a detective.

Perhaps Pryce was right. The story was his story, and he could not escape the tale, no matter how dark the telling grew.

21

That Sunday morning, Daly needed time and space to think. He did something he had not done in a long while. He drove to early-morning Mass at his parish chapel. All his life he had aspired to being a good and careful human being, and when he went to Mass he was usually reminded of how much he had failed, and that his life was little more than a tortuous journey through regret and shame. However, within that huddled Maghery congregation, it was a comfort to feel he was not the only one.

He made sure he was early for the service. He liked the silence of the altar before the priest appeared, a silence that the mind could truly baulk at. He walked up to the chapel doors, feeling like a creature that had hidden for too long in the darkest reaches of a hole, hoping that the shadows of history would pass it by. He blessed himself at the double doors, and closed them gently behind.

Almost an hour later, he re-emerged, blinking in the early-morning sunlight. He sat in his car and waited for the other churchgoers to leave. His mobile phone beeped into life. He checked the number that was calling him and sighed. It wasn't God who had him firmly in his grip, he realized, it was a darker force entirely.

'Hello,' he said.

'I apologize for being curt on the phone the last time we spoke.' It was Hegarty. 'I ignored the fact we have so much in common.'

'Like what?'

'We are both victims of the Troubles.'

'You were a paid informer in the IRA. How does that make you a victim?'

'Everyone's story is special. Their struggle, their pain. When the complete history of the Troubles is told, everyone will have their say, including you and me, rest assured of that.'

'You might see yourself as a victim, but I don't.'

'Your mother was murdered by a gang of rogue police officers being manipulated by the intelligence services. Doesn't that change how you view things?'

'I still don't know that for sure.' Daly disliked the way Hegarty was trying to pin down his mother's fate in history. 'Until I find the hard evidence I'll always believe those officers were operating alone, and shot my mother in a case of mistaken identity.'

'Then you'll be pleased to know that I have in my possession the hard evidence that disproves that.'

'What do you mean?'

'A few months ago, I obtained a set of intelligence files from the 1970s. You might have heard of them. Special Branch refer to them as the secret books.'

'What's in them?'

'What do you want to know?'

'Do they mention anything about organized death squads?'

Hegarty laughed grimly.

'They talk of nothing else. During the Cold War, that was how the army dealt with internecine conflict. Palestine, Oman, Kenya, one bloodbath after another. They even had a killing quota.'

Daly kept his voice flat.

'How much?'

'About one victim per ten thousand of the native population. But with a certain flexibility, usually upward in the aftermath of a rebel strike. The military aim was to tear apart the fabric of community life, to make the victims appear complicit in their fate. Nineteen seventy-nine was a hurricane year. An upsurge in organized violence to sow mayhem and fear. The details are in the secret books. You can read them for yourself.'

'I'd rather not.' He wondered if Hegarty could sense his fear, the inner recoil.

'You want to work it out for yourself?'

'I'd rather not know the details at all. Are we clear about that?'

'But it's important for both of us to uncover the truth.'

'You're suggesting that our interests in my mother's death are identical? Forgive me for sounding cynical.'

'You're a police detective, trying to solve the riddle of your mother's murder. The files will abolish all the inconsistencies of the past. They are what you want most of all.'

'What else is in them?'

'Evidence of a cover-up. Officers were made to resign from the police force on the day they were charged with terrorism offences. The prosecution ensured they were described as factory operatives, farm labourers, part-time barmen. There's enough evidence in the books to tilt the balance of any further investigation and send senior Special Branch officers to jail.'

'Now I understand where our interests coincide. You want to have your former bosses put away.'

Hegarty gave a short, bitter laugh.

'That's how the deal works.'

The spy was obsessed, like Pryce, thought Daly with rising indignation. *These people are living in the shadowy world of the past and I'm their last chance at salvation. They're putting their hope in my grief, my need for vengeance.* With Walsh dead, they no longer had a focal point to lead themselves out of the labyrinth. They needed a propaganda tool, a victim, but the idea of shouldering that responsibility left him cold and tired. The anger he felt over his mother's murder diminished.

'What I want most' – Daly spoke more sharply than he intended – 'is for everyone to stop bringing up my mother's death. I'm not burning with anger and I'm not desperately seeking revenge. I've spent most of my life coping with her loss. Let me deal with these new revelations in my own time.'

'Are you saying you are going to wait and do nothing?'

'Yes.'

The phone was silent.

'You're scared,' said the spy. 'You don't want to revise the details of her death. You'd rather pretend her murder was an accident.'

'What do you expect me to do? Other than bringing those officers back to life and interrogating them there's not much I *can* do. I suggest you bring these files to a solicitor or a priest, and let them pass them on to the authorities.'

'I don't believe you, Daly. You won't be able to ignore the files. Otherwise, what will the future hold for you? Nothing but uncertainty, your life trickling away in guilt and regret.'

Daly felt resentful. The temptation to be led by Hegarty's whispering words, their solid assurance, troubled him. But he resisted the urge. He needed time to think things through. He would not go running to Hegarty like a child lunging at the truth, eager to hear all the answers.

'Where are the files?'

'Someone is looking after them for me. I'm due to meet him very soon.'

'You worked for Special Branch. You were an informer. Why should I believe you?'

'It's true. I am compromised. More so than most in this country. The same people who orchestrated these murders paid me. But in all this murk doesn't the man with one eye have a duty to lead the blind?'

Daly said nothing. They hung on in silence.

'Do you know the healing glen close to where Walsh had his accident?' asked Hegarty.

'Yes.'

'I can meet you there tonight.'

Daly hesitated and then ended the call without replying yes or no. It was a reflex gesture, but one he hoped would buy him more time to think.

22

The road seemed empty. Mist sizzled on the tarmac and cloaked the hedges. Hegarty eased his car through the still landscape and pulled into a lay-by. He sat at the wheel and watched the bus shelter at the other side of the road. He was alert, his eyes cold and hard. In his inside pocket, he could feel the muzzle of his gun, sniffing to get out. After a while, a ginger-haired boy appeared in a school uniform carrying his schoolbag and a small holdall. The spy checked for any suspicious cars, scrutinizing the twisting roads as though they were the wires of a live detonator.

He thought it prudent to wait several more minutes before he got out and walked over. He allowed himself a flicker of a smile. It had been a stroke of luck that he'd spotted his niece's son at the wedding in the Clary Lodge Hotel. Their chance meeting had transformed that stressful morning waiting for Walsh, fearing the worst. It had rescued him from the trap the journalist had set. Now that the boy had turned up as requested, he knew his judgement had been correct. His grandnephew had been the one person he could trust that morning to look after the secret files.

'How's your mother?' he asked as the lad sat down beside him.

'She said she doesn't want to see you. She's told you that before.'

Hegarty sighed. Surely he had a right to see his nearest relatives from time to time.

'She said you shouldn't call again. It's too dangerous.'

He seized the holdall next to the boy, and ruffled his hair. The child lowered his head but not before Hegarty saw in the glimmering whites of his eyes a nervous glance along the road. He sensed that something was wrong. The boy fidgeted with the strap of his bag. Hegarty checked the road in both directions. He had been given a secret sign but he didn't know what to do with it.

'Tell your mother I'll send her some money soon,' he said, trying to look deeper into the boy's reluctant face.

'She said she doesn't need your money. She has a new job.'

'Not working in the Sinn Fein centre any more?'

'She had to leave when they found out about you. She said people are looking for you. They're calling you a traitor.'

He swallowed at that. Some more schoolchildren arrived at the shelter. A bus trundled by. He stared at the destination sign on its front as though the answer to this new dilemma might lie somewhere along its route. The children stared at him as though they had never seen an old man waiting like this, a look of unease growing on his face, uncertain of what to do next.

The boy climbed on to the bus, and Hegarty contemplated following him. The children jostled around him and then the bus left. He waited another while. A car pulled in at the bottom of the road. A sleek, dark-coloured vehicle. He got up and climbed into his car, tossing the holdall into the passenger seat. He contemplated the changed nature of the morning. Someone was watching him, he was sure of that. He stared at the dark car, trying to think of a new plan. The driver did nothing. The tension increased in Hegarty's body as he started the engine. Thinking that it was too late to slip away unnoticed, he drove towards the watching vehicle at speed.

The driver's face was a blur through the tinted windows. After Hegarty passed him, the driver wheeled the car sharply and turned in the opposite direction. Hegarty heard the tyres lose rubber against the tarmac. The driver's getaway technique, his haste, the determined expression on his face were odd enough to increase Hegarty's alarm. He pivoted in his seat. The road was empty again. He drummed his fingers on the steering wheel. He turned on to a minor road and checked the rear-view mirror. No one was following him. The car rocked over a series of potholes that seemed to spell out a warning message. He knew what he had to do. He rolled down his window, lifted the briefcase and flung it as hard as he could. The case arced through the air and sailed over a field wall. For a second he watched it in his wing mirror, suspended over a group of cows, which, surprised, lifted their heads to follow the strange flying object before it flared in an explosion of red and yellow flames and descended in a slow-motion spiral of what felt to the spy's tired eyes like red-hot blood. His foot pressed the accelerator pedal flat.

He drove deep into the dark hills and secrecy of border country, wondering when it might be safe to abandon his car. Along the road, the houses petered out until there were no more. He pulled into a narrow culvert half-hidden by overhanging trees. Below him, the shadows of the valley hid the healing glen. He waited for a long while. When he was satisfied that no one had followed him, he got out and put on his backpack. He stood and listened carefully. The only sounds were the stirring of branches and the rushing of water somewhere. *What will I do now that the secret books are gone? What options do I have without my only bargaining tool?* He walked down to the holy well and stared at the tree's sinuous branches. Somehow, it seemed to entangle all his fears in its silence. He watched the river. He hunkered down beside it. His breathing and his thoughts began to settle. Strange that so much moving water could induce this sense of stillness, he thought, as though the river itself was more of settled thing than any human being. He felt helpless. He said some prayers but forgot to bless himself. Peace eluded him. *Some Catholic I am, crouching next to this dark river with just the violent past for company.*

When it was almost dark, he rose and climbed the side of the glen. He followed a hidden path until he came out on the exposed mountainside. He feared that someone might be watching him from the trees below. He waited and stared back into the glen, and at the river coiling through the thorn thickets. All was still. He kept walking until he came to an old cottage surrounded by a flock of half-wild mountain sheep.

Ever since he was a boy, the cottage had appealed to his fugitive's mind. Its remoteness – the nearest road more than a mile away – made it feel like a highwayman's refuge. His grandfather had once lived here and tended to his flock of mountain sheep. Since his death, it had lain abandoned. Hegarty pushed through the sheep and stepped inside. To his surprise, the sheep followed him into the damp rooms. He prowled through them, smelling their fetid odour. He shouted at the sheep, waved his hands, but now that night had fallen, they were reluctant to leave the shelter of the cottage. They stalked him through the rooms. He took out his sleeping bag, made his bed as far away from them as he possibly could, and waited, thinking through his options.

Perhaps Special Branch did not want him dead after all, he began to hope. They could have killed him back then, but instead they had delivered a warning in the form of a firebomb. Was it because they still planned to use him? But for what purpose? They had orchestrated Father Walsh's death, of that he was sure. Perhaps that had been a warning, too. He looked through the doorway at the dark shape of the mountain.

He picked up his phone and dialled Daly's number, but there was no answer. He thought of the detective, his stubborn defiance and his pitiful naivety about the past. He'd detected a loneliness in Daly's voice, the sense that he was marooned in a detective's limbo, frustrated and paranoid. Perhaps to Daly, he was just another lost shadow from the Troubles, babbling about the past, about a story that was of little importance to anyone any more, a story of murder and the fog of war that was both dangerous and pointless.

But untold stories had a way of hanging in time, unfinished, haunting.

He took out his phone again and rang Major Hannon.

'Where are you?' snapped the major.

'I'm in a difficult spot.'

'Again?' The major sounded exasperated.

Hegarty briefly recounted the events that had befallen him.

The major almost chuckled. 'I knew your luck would run out, Hegarty. Let me tell you a little secret. Things are going from bad to worse for you. Tomorrow you will encounter a new predicament that will make this pit you're in now seem like a picnic in the park.'

'What are you talking about?'

'Someone has leaked your identity and back story to the media. In the morning, your photograph will be plastered all over the newspapers and the internet. The story of a mole at the heart of the IRA, feeding back its secrets to British Intelligence for over thirty years. It will travel like the wind. Everyone will be on the lookout for you. You've come to a dead end, Hegarty. There's nowhere else for you to run.'

Hegarty said nothing. The thought of Special Branch blowing his cover made him feel cold and sick. However, he was too deeply committed to this fugitive life to give it up that easily. *I must be tough-willed and not relent. I have only one plot, while they have many, but my plan to be free will in the end prevail over their countless conspiracies.*

'The last time we met, you talked about getting me out of the country. I want to avail myself of that opportunity now.'

The major grunted.

'Yes.'

'Yes I want to, or yes you'll help me?'

'Yes, it's never too late to come to your senses,' said the major after a hesitation. 'I can arrange flights and a new passport, but we'll have to work quickly.' He paused. 'Rest assured, in a few days, you'll be out of this country and your only regret will be that it took you so long to give up the game.'

Hegarty felt a wave of comfort at the major's promise.

'You know I'm not cut out for this type of subterfuge any more,' grumbled the major. 'I should be tending to my garden and enjoying my retirement rather than getting pulled into your messy one-man war with Special Branch.'

'I understand,' said Hegarty. 'Where do you intend to send me? Will Special Branch know?'

'Do you have to ask so many questions and make things complicated? Just give us your location and I'll have you picked up within hours.'

Hegarty hesitated. The brevity of the major's replies made him feel uneasy, and who were the 'us' he referred to?

'Refusing this offer is tantamount to signing your own death warrant,' said the major.

Did he have no say in where he was going to be relocated? It was the way the intelligence services always worked, invisible people playing games with the lives of others. However, his discomfort overwhelmed his doubt. Other than Inspector Daly, there was no one else he could rely on. In spite of his distrust, he gave the major the details of where he was hiding.

'We'll pick you up in the morning. Sit tight until then, and don't let anyone else know of our plans. Have you got that?'

'Yes.'

'Good luck, Hegarty.'

23

That night, the spy lay down on his sleeping bag and tried to nod off. However, it was impossible. He felt suspended between relief and dark suspicion. He listened to the occasional bleats and footfalls of the sheep, and almost drifted away, but then their sudden silence brought him back to alertness.

He switched on the light of his phone and saw that the entire flock had gathered around him, stifling the air with their rank breath. Their muddy faces and dugs tottered closer. They had stopped chewing the cud and their mouths were slack, their green saliva sickening his stomach. Their eyes gaped at him.

'What is it?' he asked the mute assembly. 'What's happened?'

What were they doing, crowding around him like a confused search party? Something must be worrying them, he concluded.

'Is it me?' he asked.

He stared at their silent black faces, and without thinking began to play a mental game, finding similarities between them and the faces of people he knew, former comrades in the IRA, and his handlers in Special Branch. He remembered men in cramped dark rooms, entrenched in conspiracy, eyes flashing in the dim light. He thought of the countless rooms he'd sat in, rooms with listening devices recording everything, rooms where he'd plotted murder and betrayal.

He stared at the sheep until his eyes began to throb. Here and there, he glimpsed the faces of dead comrades, murdered neighbours. They seemed to disappear as soon as he caught sight of them. He was filled with a desire to hear their voices, to look into their eyes and have a conversation with them. He prowled through the flock, moving from one animal to another, his mind filling with the paranoid thought that the ghosts of the past had gathered to warn him, telling him he could not go on living like this, that he had reached a dead end. The more he shouted at them, the more resistant the sheep were to moving. They seemed to know he was just a harmless old man, crazed with loneliness and fear. He clenched his jaw. What a pity he had lived to this stage of his life, searching for familiar company in the faces of beasts.

Suddenly something in the dark disturbed the sheep, and they began bleating. He forgot himself and began scolding them.

'Look at your filthy faces. Look at the mess you've made,' he muttered. 'This is entirely your fault. The trouble I'm in. Stop crying. It's too late for crying. Be silent and give me peace.' He vented a torrent of resentment upon the sheep that swelled in ire the more they surrounded him meekly and refused to speak back. 'I don't want to see any of you again,' he shouted, on his feet now.

He swung his arms and ran at them, but they darted out of his path and re-formed, bowing their heads and refusing to move, stubborn and oddly calm in the circumstances. He beat his fists in the air, frustrated and breathless.

He only stopped his tirade when a further chorus of warning bleats broke out from them. He watched as a few of the sheep turned to stare at the opened doorway and the moonless sky beyond as though it held an invisible threat. He listened carefully. At first, he could hear nothing but the wheeze and snort of the sheep's breathing. Then a faint rumble, more like a tremor in the sky. Was it thunder? He was fully alert now. He could see through the doorway the silhouettes of the thorn trees against the starlit sky. They stirred in the wind, like a river of tossing shadows. The thunder returned, louder now. Up in the sky he spotted a light that was not a star. He pushed his way through the flock and saw the lights of a helicopter and its search-beam combing the glen below.

In frantic, awkward haste, he packed his bag and tried to slip away into the night, but the sheep blocked his escape. They grew panicked, bleating loudly, following his progress through the doorway. He stopped and stared at their startled eyeballs.

'Come on, get a move on,' he whispered. But they made no effort at flight. 'You filthy beasts, move away or you'll finish me right here.'

He waved his arms in the air and hissed, but if anything, the flock thickened around him, butting his legs.

The helicopter turned away from the glen and came thundering up the mountain. The searchlight swept towards the shepherd's cottage, the air brimming with the roar of the blades. The sheep panicked in different ways, some fell sideways, or backwards, and then they picked themselves up and ran off.

He stumbled after them, keeping his body low. He looked behind. The field was dazzled with light, the blades of the helicopter drawing closer, smacking the air, beating out a threshed circle of grass. The searchlight picked out one or two of the outlying sheep. The helicopter was almost above him now. He plunged into the herd of sheep and ran with them, almost on all fours. They had grown used to his presence in the cottage and were not alarmed to have a human trotting within their ranks. The helicopter passed overhead and continued along the mountain.

For a blessed interval, Hegarty was a wolf among sheep, feeling sharp and alert, heading towards a dark forest. Their trampling hooves would erase any footprints or sign of occupation, his scent, the trail of evidence, anything that might link him to the cottage. The helicopter swept over them again, and the flock closed in around Hegarty, so near he could feel their agitated breathing on his face. It was hard to believe that he had been reduced to this half-wild state, seeking refuge among animals and thorns. His hands and knees grew cold, sinking into the boggy ground.

The helicopter hovered overhead and passed. He took off for the cover of the forest. Again, the sheep circled in behind his crouched figure. Swiftly, he forged into the flock's lead position. He felt vigour in his legs that he had not felt in years, as if he were part of a mass escape in the good old days. They came across a river and toiled along its rocky course.

He savoured the sensation of the cold water. The sheep's hooves plunged along the riverbed. His neck and back strained to keep as low as the rest of the flock. The closest beasts eyeballed him with side glances, anticipating his next move, his next turn of direction. All he had to do was nod his head and they understood, bursting into a chorus of energetic bleats. He found himself looking at them with companionable curiosity, their black tongues, the paleness of their eyes, their pointed hooves churning the muddy sides of the river. He was surprised at the sense of satisfaction he felt to have fallen into the company of these dumb creatures, the sense that he might count as something in their tribe. What mistakes had he made all his life, running on his own, he thought, a solitary fugitive, when he could have been hiding with a pack and enjoying this freedom, this sense of indifference to his individual fate? All his life he had been thwarted, he realized, cheated out of this sense of belonging.

The river grew deeper, the water rougher. The flock churned alongside him with grim resolve. He groped in the dark. Several times, he slipped and collided with the body of one of the animals. Each time he picked himself up and kept running, but then in a lapse of concentration his foot struck a submerged rock. He wavered, staggered and fell, knocking his head against an outcrop. He stood up again and felt dizzy. He stumbled for a few steps and then sprawled face first into the river. This time he lost consciousness. The sheep crowded around him, ramming their heads against his prone body, turning him over, and then they fell silent, unmoving, their hooves sinking into the watery quagmire. Somewhere, not too far away in the sky, the helicopter persisted with its tiny tumult.

24

Daly drove to the healing glen and cautiously searched around the holy well with his flashlight but could find no trace of Hegarty. He thought he saw something caught and struggling in the branches of the tree overhanging the well but when he shone his torch all he saw were ribbons of material and religious medals dangling from the branches. That evening, in the darkness of his cottage, he had decided that whatever fate had in store for him it was entangled with Hegarty's destiny. They had in common a unity of suspicions, fears and hopes that was strong enough to suspend any sane or professional judgement. The intensity of Daly's loneliness also propelled him towards this dangerous rendezvous, and fuelled the fantasy that the spy might help dissolve all the murk surrounding the past.

Daly drove back out on to the roads that surrounded the glen. He had no idea where he was going. There were no other vehicles about. He saw the searchlight of a helicopter in the distance and drove in its direction. He wasn't even sure if he was on the right side of the border. It was a landscape of straggling forest, winding rivers and empty farms.

Abruptly he braked to a standstill. His headlights had picked out the shape of an old man, a wraith-like figure, at the side of the road. Daly stepped out into the night air. He thought he heard a moan but the throb of the helicopter and the roar of a nearby river drowned it out. The figure of a man stepped into the pool of light cast by the headlights, a figure that buckled as Daly hurried to support it. The man's clothes were soaked through and moulded to his back. His eyes glowered like someone deranged and his face was streaked with mud.

'Hegarty?'

'Yes.' The spy shivered with the cold.

Daly introduced himself.

'What the hell happened to you?' he asked the spy.

'I had a little accident.' Hegarty looked at Daly as though meeting like this was the most natural thing in the world.

'A genuine accident, or did someone arrange for it to happen?' Daly glanced uneasily at the blinking light of the helicopter in the sky, and thought of Walsh's crashed car.

'No,' growled Hegarty. 'Normally they don't let their victims limp away.' He leaned heavily on Daly, who felt the chill of a mountain river on the old man's body.

'We should bring you to a doctor.'

'I'm fine. I can take care of myself.'

'Where are the secret books?'

Hegarty groaned.

'Special Branch got to them first. They booby-trapped them with a firebomb.'

'Then we'd better get you out of here,' said Daly, pushing him towards the car. 'We'll go back to my cottage and figure out what to do from there.'

Hegarty shook his head.

'What about the others?' he asked. He grabbed Daly's sleeve and pointed back towards the trees.

'What others?'

Daly heard a set of voices, all sounding alike, a few plaintive phrases, repeated over and over again, difficult to comprehend. The sounds grew louder, broke into a commotion, and then he observed a stream of shadowy lumps hurtling out of the trees, piling on to the road. He made out the woolly heads of sheep, and their trembling bodies. They stood and blocked the road, bleating noisily.

Daly helped Hegarty into the passenger seat and jumped in himself. The sheep churned around the car, as if they were trying to keep up with the spy, who lay back in his seat, eyes half-closed, his face set in a grimace. The sour smell of sheep filled the car.

'What are they talking about, Daly?' he asked. 'What do they want of me?'

The detective did not respond. He assumed the spy had concussion and was confused, but right now he was more worried about the helicopter in the sky, and the possibility of checkpoints along the road. He eased the car through the flock. They jostled and pushed against the vehicle. Hegarty raised his hand to the side window in an attempted gesture of farewell. He strained against his seatbelt and tried to get to his feet.

'Sit where you are,' ordered Daly.

The spy obeyed immediately. The sharpness of Daly's voice brought him to his senses. He looked at the detective.

'I thought you weren't going to come. What took you so long?'

'I came as soon as I could.'

'Did anyone follow you?'

'No. I took the back roads.'

'Are you sure?'

Daly hesitated.

'We'd better get a move on,' said Hegarty. 'They'll be here soon. Switch off your headlights; otherwise you'll draw in the helicopter.'

This time Daly followed Hegarty's instructions. It was pitch-dark and he drove at a snail's pace. However, he soon found that if he unfocused his eyes he could see more in the dim starlight: the avenue of fir trees, the emptiness of the road, the tunnel of deeper darkness ahead. In his rear-view mirror, he saw flashes of light, the helicopter's searchbeam, a mile or so behind, sweeping through the forest.

'What's going on?' he asked.

'Hannon double-crossed me. He was meant to get me out of the country but instead he sent in the hunting hounds. He was my handler and I trusted him.'

Daly glanced at Hegarty and, for a moment, he thought he understood the terror and loneliness of intelligence work. The safest thing to do would have been to put as much distance between himself and this elderly spy.

'We'll have to get you to a safe place.'

'There are no more safe places for me now,' replied Hegarty and sniggered.

The spy's behaviour was unsettling, but Daly did not feel too unnerved. Instead, he felt strangely at ease in Hegarty's company. Under the circumstances, this car journey was probably one of the most dangerous things he had undertaken, but it also felt straightforward and uncomplicated. They had no history together, and neither of them felt it necessary to put up their guard.

Indifferent to his fate was how Daly felt. And he thought he recognized the same air about Hegarty. A dangerous nonchalance hung about both of them, as around two gamblers who realize they have nothing left to lose.

When they returned to the main road, Daly flicked his headlights back on. For the rest of the journey, neither of them said anything. Daly's eyes flitted between the road ahead and the rear-view mirror. He kept thinking that cars behind were following them. What were Special Branch up to? *Perhaps they want us to know they're in pursuit and are biding their time to pounce.* He was now as much of an outlaw as Hegarty. *How have I ended up as an IRA informer's last refuge?* he wondered bitterly. On the final stretch to his cottage, he looked behind and breathed a sigh of relief. The roads were completely empty.

25

It had been raining and the moon peeked out as Daly pulled up at his cottage. The detective walked around the old house several times looking for any sign of disturbance. Then he stepped into the unlit porch and listened to the sound of the drainpipes channelling the rainwater. He heard crows scrabbling along the rooftop and then the flap of their wings. The lack of any moving lights and the stillness in the terrain leading down to the lough reassured Daly. He felt as though he was the only one staring at this landscape of irregular fields and bogland.

He helped Hegarty into the house, got him some dry clothes and stationed him by the fire. In the kitchen, he sorted through a sink of unwashed glasses. He wiped two of the least grubby ones and took them with a bottle of whiskey over to the fire. The smell of livestock coming from Hegarty was stronger now, accentuated by sweat and the heat of the burning turf.

'Tell me, why are Special Branch so desperate to find you?' asked Daly.

'Have you seen them?' said Hegarty, his eyes protruding. 'Are they out there waiting for us to make a move?'

God, the man was a wreck, thought Daly. He could almost taste his panic in the air. He tried to imagine Hegarty as a master-spy, tricking the leaders of the IRA for decades, and his mind boggled. The spy looked more like a feeble-minded farmer who had wandered into a war zone, and hadn't the wit to get out.

'No. I think we are safe. At least for now.'

Hegarty kept fidgeting, but with the help of the whiskey and a warm blanket, he eventually settled into his armchair and began telling Daly snippets of the events that had brought him to this wretched state. The spy repeated himself as he grappled with the plots in his head. Sometimes he lost the thread of the story. Memories from his childhood drifted through his account, and his face would crack into a smile, before dark suspicion puckered his mouth again.

Daly listened carefully and piece by piece began to put together the story. It was by no means the whole story, and there were several significant gaps, but it was enough to guide Daly out of the darkness. Hegarty spoke of cold half-drownings in border rivers, his recruitment by Hannon, the fear and uncertainty of sterile interrogation rooms in secret military barracks, and then of IRA operations, sleeping in ditches or outbuildings, always fully clothed, always with a gun nestling beside him, the insects and the cold gnawing at him as he waited further instructions from his commanders.

Daly asked whether any of his IRA colleagues had ever suspected he was a traitor.

'Those that did had a habit of dying off quickly,' replied Hegarty.

Daly learned that some years previously the British government had set up a special investigation team of mostly English police officers. Their job was to investigate the allegations of collusion between the security forces and Loyalist terrorists. The team contacted Major Hannon and interviewed him several times. Inevitably, men like Hannon began to feel the heat. The political winds were changing with a ceasefire in place. Newly elected Republican politicians were bandying about collusion claims. Mud was beginning to stick and Hannon began to fear for his reputation.

'The major photocopied some of the unit's most sensitive intelligence files,' explained Hegarty. 'What he called the secret books. He gave me the copy to deliver to a Dublin-based lawyer.' He stared at

Daly. 'It was his insurance policy in case the legal hammer should ever fall on him. He had no desire to be a sacrificial lamb. He planned to open a Pandora's box if he was ever dragged to court.

'The English investigation team had some of the most honest cops on the force. The problem was they were so bloody slow. By the time they got round to investigating the gang of officers involved in the murder triangle, they were almost impossible to trace. Only a few had managed to stay afloat and avoid alcoholism or mental illness. And those who had, maintained a pact of silence.'

Daly heard a tiredness in Hegarty's voice. A tiredness made up of forty years of denial and silence.

'In the meantime, the top brass made sure the secret books were destroyed. Every effort was made to hamper the investigation team, including the firebombing of their offices within a secure facility. The investigation eventually turned into a charade. When the file was finally sent to the government department that had commissioned the inquiry, it was decided the best thing to do was to bin it. It turned out no one was interested in the truth. Military Intelligence weathered the storm and soon got back to business as usual.'

Daly went on drinking whiskey, saying nothing. He listened to Hegarty, and stared at the embers of the turf fire, the sparks rifling up the chimney, chased by flakes of soot. In spite of his proximity to the fire and the heat of the whiskey, he felt a shivery gloom descend. He threw on more turf. The flames turned bluer, licking the dark chunks of peat. He thought of the wind-filled orchard where Agnew had hanged himself. And the other dead members of the gang. They all had their stories to tell, too, but their time had passed. Perhaps they had decided it was best to keep silent forever, that it was better not to add their voices to the history of the Troubles, that taking their secrets to the grave was a favour for future generations. Should he not respect those wishes? He understood another reason why his father hadn't told him everything about his mother's murder. He had tried to obliterate the evil in the act, as though years of denial could erase the truth.

Out of the corner of his eye, Daly saw Hegarty search the pockets of his overcoat. What was he looking for? A piece of paper or the butt of a revolver? Whatever it was, Daly did not feel afraid. Where else could a man feel as safe as sitting by his own fire, with a bottle of whiskey at hand?

In the wavering light of the flames, the spy's figure grew still and deadly, as though he were the weapon that was about to be fired. Daly watched him expectantly, waiting for him to resume speaking. The spy coughed and lit a cigarette from the grubby-looking pack he had unearthed from his coat.

'When the investigating team went back to England, I held on to a copy of the secret books and contacted Father Walsh. I thought he was the only one trustworthy enough to bring them to the public's attention.' Hegarty exhaled some smoke. 'But in the end I signed his death warrant. Special Branch were following Walsh the night he crashed. They had him frightened almost out of his wits. They were only interested in him because they believed he would lead them to me. They were after the secret books, you see.'

It made sense to Daly now. Walsh worried that he was being followed. The checkpoint looming unexpectedly out of the darkness of border country. The officers in blue overalls; the startling similarity to the modus operandi of the 1970s murder squad. The loneliness of the road ahead. All must have conspired to make the patrol seem more menacing in Walsh's imagination, all those years of research into the Troubles breeding a swarm of paranoid fears. Thus, he had sped off along the line of misplaced traffic cones, entering the murder triangle's labyrinth for good.

'Special Branch won't rest until I'm dead, too,' said Hegarty in a hoarse whisper. 'They have me firmly in their sights.'

'Surely the state has a duty to protect you? Have you spoken to a solicitor? Taken legal advice?'

'I haven't sought legal advice and I don't intend to.' He glared at Daly in the half-light. 'I've been an IRA informer for forty years. My situation cannot be improved by any solicitor. I am beyond legal protection.'

'What about taking your story to a politician or the media? You could explain your predicament. Highlight the terrible dangers you were subjected to.'

'My predicament? That can be summed up in one word.'

Daly waited for the reply.

'Guilty.'

'Of what?'

'Murder. Betrayal. Of everything that the security forces and the IRA want to pin on me.'

'But there must be some way out of this nightmare.'

'What do you mean? Some way of continuing my career as an informer? Some way of keeping my cover?'

'What about the lives you saved? Surely that must count?'

Hegarty snickered in the flickering light. He finished smoking his cigarette and threw the butt into the fire. He lit another one and stared at Daly.

The detective began telling Hegarty all that he'd learned about his mother's death, the cover-up by the police, his father's silence, the letter in the bible and the documents from the family solicitor.

Hegarty pointed his cigarette at Daly.

'The only thing that counts now is the truth,' he said. 'It's time the public heard your story. Not the story your father gave you. The one you figured out yourself.'

'But why should I publicize the truth after all these years? How will it make my life more tolerable – or anyone else's, for that matter?'

'Because the truth hurts,' said Hegarty. 'It will hurt people like Hannon.'

Daly topped up his glass with whiskey and as an afterthought did the same for Hegarty. He was unused to playing the host.

'My father kept me in the dark all these years,' said Daly. 'Not telling the truth can hurt, too.'

'Sometimes the biggest silences exist between fathers and sons,' replied Hegarty. 'Perhaps your old man never broke that silence because he wanted to shield you from the truth, and then as the years passed he didn't know how to bring up the subject and correct your misunderstanding. Perhaps you never asked him the right questions. You of all people, a detective, did not know how to get the truth from your father. But in the final reckoning, everyone wants to tell their story and reveal the truth. Even the dead.'

Daly felt Hegarty's stare. Now that he had invited him into his cottage, the spy's nagging presence was going to be at his side forever, he feared, like a gloating ghost's, shaping his story, goading him on.

'What do you mean, even the dead?'

Hegarty leaned into his armchair and muttered something.

'Come out of the dark,' whispered the spy. 'The inspector wants to see you.'

Daly turned sharply. His neck had grown stiff with stillness and the tension of the evening. He had been submerged within the glow of the fire while the rest of the room was plunged in darkness.

Shadows streaked the spy's face. He appeared to be staring at something in the blackest corner of the room. He said nothing, just nodded his head from time to time, his features sharp and alert.

'I see you. I see you,' he said. He turned to Daly. 'Do you see how many there are?'

'All I see is the dark,' said Daly.

Hegarty rubbed his eyes and sighed. 'I'm talking to my ghosts. They come and go without saying anything. It is enough that I see and recognize them.'

'If you wish, I can turn on the light,' said Daly, unwilling to be drawn any further into the spy's psychological vortex.

'No. I don't mind them. They're comfortable presences. They've been with me since the Troubles ended.'

'The end of a war can be a strange and haunting time.'

'Yes.' Hegarty snickered again. 'It's been a difficult period of adjustment.' His eyes darted from right to left as though the room was full of drifting shapes. 'You see, all through the Troubles I kept turning my back on them.'

'Who are they?'

'The men and women whose stories were silenced by torture and murder.' Hegarty settled back into his seat. 'The forgotten ones.' He sighed and lit a cigarette. 'I read a book a few years ago. A crime thriller by a local writer. About an IRA man who is haunted by the ghosts of the people he murdered.' He chuckled morbidly. 'Unable to bear their constant presence, this IRA fucker comes up with the radical solution of starting a killing spree in revenge for their deaths.' He spat out smoke. 'It irritated me, leafing through all that murder. As if more violence might alleviate a guilty conscience. I don't think he knew it, but the writer came so close to getting it right. The dead do haunt you. But their ghosts don't have scores to settle. The dead just want their story told. They want the truth to live. The submerged truth. That's the reason they never go away.'

It grew cold in the room, or perhaps Hegarty's words made Daly feel cold. He got up to put on an extra jumper. Instead of returning to the fire, he stood in the dark kitchen. He stared at the dim outline of the table and chairs, the Welsh dresser and the cupboards. It was a relief to look at these familiar domestic objects. Perhaps Hegarty was correct. The story of his mother's murder was never going to disappear without a trace. The more it was ignored the more it expressed itself in fear and unverifiable suspicion, the more it resurfaced and reformulated itself, like the fields his father had worked into his old age, full of uncovered lumps and obstacles. The landscape of resignation and silence.

Daly caught sight of a beam of light illuminating the kitchen window. From a sideways position, he looked out and saw that a car had pulled up at the front gate. He remained motionless. The lights went out and a figure stepped out of the car. There was just enough moonlight for Daly to make out a tall, stiff figure and the blur of a face. The figure stood by the car, staring at Daly's cottage, as if waiting for some sort of signal. It took Daly a few seconds to recognize his forlorn gaze, the upright bearing of his shoulders, the hesitation of his stance.

Christ, what's Donaldson doing here? he thought in dismay. *It can't be a coincidence.* Who else could he want but Hegarty? He hurried back to the fire and warned the spy, who immediately stiffened at the news.

'Who does he want? You or me?' asked Hegarty.

The spy stood up and moved to the window, wanting to see Donaldson for himself. Daly was unnerved. He pulled the curtains and ushered Hegarty into the back bedroom. The old man crouched by the door and looked up, staring right through Daly, his eyes glinting with an unstable light. Daly closed the door and left him in darkness, hoping that in the panic, Hegarty's ghosts had fully abandoned him.

26

Daly walked outside to where his former commander stood in the moonlight, silhouetted against the thorn trees, and in the distance another wild border, the shore of Lough Neagh, its waves jostling together in the moonlight. It seemed to be the detective's fate these days to have unwelcome visitors flocking to his cottage.

There was a silence between the two men. Donaldson looked at Daly as though waiting for a welcome or a question, neither of which were forthcoming. Daly could see that Donaldson had come alone, but he sensed that this was not a simple friendly visit.

The former commander had not shaved for a few days and the stubble gave his face a drawn, shifty look. He walked over to Daly's old Renault.

'Look at that,' he said. 'The roads round here must be a real mud bath.' He pointed to the rear bumper and licence plate, which were almost obscured by dirt. 'If you're not careful you'll get bogged down in the quagmire.' His voice was almost ironic. He smiled at Daly. It was a contracted smile. Even his voice sounded thin. There was another silence.

'What brings you here?' said Daly eventually.

'The lough. At this time of my career, I'm considering my plan B.'

Neither of them said anything as a few bats twirled overhead.

'Nothing to do with police work. I've spent the evening looking round for a retirement cottage. One that has a berth for my boat. With Dorothy a permanent resident in the nursing home, I need some sort of a distraction.' Donaldson's wife had taken sick a few months previously and had been unable to care for herself since.

His tone was apologetically cheerful, but the look in his eyes and his movements were wary.

'Why would you want to retire here?'

'To get in touch with the elements.' He breathed deeply. 'The wind and the water.'

Daly grimaced. The lough shore was already in danger of becoming a refuge for transient souls, outlaws and people with a past to hide. Somehow, the strangeness of that vast body of inland water made visitors feel they could suddenly become anonymous, and end their days puttering about in boats.

'So why did you call by?'

Donaldson seemed more interested in the humped fields surrounding the cottage. Daly had never seen anyone looking at the farm in that way, as though the former commander had known the lie of the land a long time ago and was making an effort to recognize it. He seemed to be experiencing a tentative revelation. His eyes swivelled about, unwilling to absorb some dreadful fact he saw written in the uneven landscape. Daly followed his gaze, trying to decipher the secret. The dappled moonlit fields looked false, lit up with nocturnal contours, the mysterious places multiplying now that daylight had receded.

'I was passing and I remembered how heated our last conversation had been. I wanted to get some things off my chest.' His usual irritability and condescension were absent. 'Can I come in?'

Daly hesitated.

'If you're busy, I can come back some other time. Perhaps you have a guest?'

'No, not at all. Come in. I've been clearing the attic, so excuse the mess.'

Daly tried to control his apprehension. His nerves were all over the place. Steady, he told himself as he led Donaldson through into the kitchen. If Donaldson knew nothing of Hegarty's presence, he didn't want his discomfort to alert any suspicions. He thought of his ex-RUC chief in one room and Hegarty the informer skulking in another. It pained him deeply to have his privacy, so carefully constructed during months of loneliness, gatecrashed in this manner.

At the sink, he fussed over some cups and the kettle. He wondered if Donaldson could detect the whiff of whiskey on his breath. The place seemed darker and more cluttered now that he had two unwelcome guests. Donaldson paced up and down the flagstones, bumping into bits of furniture.

'Sit down,' ordered Daly and handed him a cup of tea.

'Where's your travelling companion?'

Daly flinched.

'Who?'

'Your journalist friend. I hear you and she have been travelling in circles. You should find a better guide, Celcius. One who really knows the way.'

'I thought you said there was something you wanted to get off your chest.'

'My chest?' His voice stiffened and he avoided Daly's eye. 'I'm not sure if that is the case or not. They aren't my secrets to confess, after all.' He glanced at Daly. 'Excuse me for talking in this roundabout way. I've come to tell you another side of the story.'

'I've heard enough stories to last me a lifetime.'

'Well, I would like to tell you this one, if you have the time to listen.'

How much time would it take to hear everyone's story? wondered Daly. Days of non-stop confessing, weeks, months, perhaps even years.

'You know,' began Donaldson, 'one of the laziest assumptions people make these days is that guilt and shame are morbid things to be avoided. Really, the opposite is true. Guilt should be embraced like a trusted friend. It is usually a warning that bad things are at hand. To avoid feelings of guilt is the worst form of cowardice imaginable. Even if the bad things were done by others.' He looked at Daly again. 'I'm speaking about the actions of men under my command, the men responsible for your mother's murder.'

'Why should you feel guilty if you had no involvement in it?'

Donaldson nodded.

'I feel guilty because I was preoccupied with maintaining the good reputation of the police force, when I should have shown courage and an instinct for justice. In those days, loyalty to one's profession was not regarded as a virtue or a defect. It was a basic premise.' He was now staring meaningfully at Daly. 'I wanted to tell you this. I lied earlier when I said I happened to be passing by. I came here specifically to see you.'

Daly felt tired of his unwanted visitors, their shadows, their complications. He wished their stories were tidier, easier to comprehend and file away. He longed for open space, the clean sound of the wind swelling from the lough, rather than the stillness of this cramped cottage with too many traps and bodies to bump into.

'I want to tell you that you have my backing for an official investigation into what happened during these murders,' said Donaldson. 'In my early career I did not speak out as much as I should have done. Loyalty held me back. And the shame that my officers could be capable of harbouring such hatred. If we can't speak of those times now, when shall we ever?' He stood up as if to go. 'You will be hearing from Special Branch soon.'

'I want a press conference to announce the inquiry,' said Daly. 'The maximum publicity possible. I don't want the investigation hidden away and quietly forgotten about. And I want the promise of cooperation from serving and retired police officers.'

'Very well.'

'Before you go, I want to show you something.'

Daly unfolded the notes he had been gathering of his mother's murder and the links to the other murders in Walsh's triangle. He laid them out before Donaldson, whose eyes flicked over the connections and cross-references.

'So many links,' he said. 'Most of them sketchy, to say the least.'

'The dates intrigue me. They must be connected by some sort of calculation.'

Donaldson's jaw clenched.

'You understand I'm not obliged to discuss the matter until the inquiry is fully under way.'

'The gang picked their victims for whatever reason and watched them. They waited. And then on the first Monday of every month they struck. There's a strange logic at work there.'

Up to now, Donaldson's words had a rehearsed air. Suddenly, he seemed unprepared and didn't know what to say.

'I fear there are many things about the gang's modus operandi we will probably never know,' he said.

His evasion stimulated the interrogator in Daly.

'Why was it always the first Monday and not the third or fourth? Or a Tuesday, for that matter?'

'Maybe it was the only time they were off duty together. I can't recall their rosters. Maybe the dates are irrelevant. They murdered when they could get away with it. That's all there was to it.'

'There's something else I find odd. The geographical spread of the murders. They all took place within the Armagh Council boundaries except for three. My mother's murder, the Corrigans' and the Hacketts', who all lived in the Dungannon Council area. However, I've done some research. The council boundaries were changed in 1984. Before that date, this part of the lough shore fell into the Armagh Council jurisdiction. What do you think that means?'

'Perhaps Walsh should have spread his map further. After all, there were just as many people murdered in neighbouring districts.'

'But not by this particular gang.'

Donaldson looked properly rattled now.

'You're trying to make these random connections deliver evidence that doesn't exist.' He stared at Daly with a desperate look in his eyes. 'I came here to get things off my chest and you make an interrogation out of it.' He sounded aggrieved.

'There is something else we're missing about these murders,' pressed Daly. 'What does it mean that so many of the victims were living in dank cottages, and that after their murders their families remained trapped in ruined old houses?'

'You're serious?' Donaldson glared at Daly. 'If there's a meaning to that, surely it's too deep for a police investigation to plumb.'

'But what do you think it means? What secret lies in their refusal to move into new houses?'

'If people want to live in decrepit homes, then so be it.' He glanced about the small kitchen. 'If you want an answer take a look at this cottage of yours, Daly, rotting into the ground. The only reason you prolonged your stay is because secretly you want to follow its example. You want to disappear back into the past. Melt away into darkness. You and your…' He hesitated to say the word.

'Co-religionists?' suggested Daly.

'Whatever. I have to go now, Daly.'

Donaldson strode out of the kitchen and into the night. He looked right and left, anywhere but straight ahead at the fields slouching in the moonlight. He knew more than he was saying; Daly was convinced of that. It wasn't a case that he didn't know or found Daly's questions unreasonable. He turned back to Daly before climbing into his car.

'Remember, Daly, the truth comes at a cost. It will not make your life simpler or easier. It will complicate your way of seeing the world and it won't bring your mother back to life. It won't even bring you back to life, out of this sad old shell of a cottage.'

Daly stood for a while at the door and watched Donaldson's car disappear. The idea of an official inquiry daunted him. The unravelling of the snarl of clues around his mother's death might have been invigorating in the initial stages, but with an official inquiry he would be at the centre of an investigation he no longer controlled. He would be its prisoner. The more he probed, the more the labyrinth would unroll its twisting paths into the past, a vista he had ignored his entire adult life.

Hegarty emerged from the bedroom and followed the detective back into the fire. The spy seemed reanimated, freed from the tenacious hold of his ghosts.

'An official police inquiry with the backing of an ex-RUC chief?' Hegarty's eyes glinted as he watched the detective. 'Why, you're all set now. The truth will finally out.' He had obviously overheard every word of the conversation with Donaldson.

Daly pulled closer to the fire, scraping his chair against the floor.

'I told you before. I don't know whether I have the appetite for the truth or not. Part of me would rather live with questions rather than answers.'

'Then you are just as guilty of the cover-up as any of your senior officers.'

Daly stared at the fire. He spoke in a low voice.

'I don't want my mother's name plastered all over the newspapers and the internet. I don't want her grave vandalized by Loyalists. I don't want her story to end up on YouTube. I want her to rest in peace. If that makes me complicit in a cover-up then so be it.'

'But there is something very flawed with this notion of peace you have for your mother.' Hegarty's voice intensified. 'If it is secured by lies and denial then in my view it is not real peace. That is just my way of looking at things. You obviously have a different way. In your mind, the end justifies the means. Isn't that what the politicians maintain as well? Isn't that the principle this harmonious new society of ours is built upon?'

The spy leaned closer to the fire, crouching forward, his knees almost bundled up to his chin, while Daly leaned back into the shadows. Hegarty turned his face to check for the detective's presence, not to seek his agreement or concession but to reassure himself that his words weren't disappearing into a void.

'No,' said Daly from the darkness. 'That is not my guiding principle at all. My principle is to adopt the passive path. Because any other path leads to pain. To anger and the danger of more bloodshed.'

'But what about the truth? Shouldn't that be the moral code of any peaceful society? Rather than allowing lies and half-truths to flourish? It is your duty, Daly, and the police's, to root out the truth.'

'Perhaps what we need in this country is not the truth,' replied Daly. 'What we really want is a fabrication. A made-up truth, one that we can all live with. Until we get that, everything else must be suspended, the rule of law, common sense, dealing with the past, even forgiveness.'

Hegarty stared at Daly. He lowered his voice to a whisper and craned over the fire.

'You and I are beyond that now, Inspector. We've crossed into unknown terrain.'

Daly didn't move in the flickering shadows. He felt a pang of jealousy. It would have been foolish to describe Hegarty as an authority on the past, but with his access to secrets darker than Daly could imagine, the spy had developed an insight that was probably only a finger's breadth from the real truth.

'The past surrounds us,' said Hegarty. 'Try as we may, we will never disperse its murk, only illuminate it.'

A set of sparks charged up the chimney and distracted them into a prolonged silence.

'The murder triangle is part of your past, too,' said Hegarty softly. 'You've done nothing all of your adult life but secretly seek it, and now that you have the truth within reach, and it's too late to walk away, you realize that it will destroy you, and everything around you: your career as a detective, your life in this cottage, your peace of mind.

'You should have foreseen this. You should have ignored the past, the tantalizing clues within Walsh's research. You shouldn't have rung my number. You should have thrown it away instead.'

Hegarty was right. Daly's personal life was in turmoil. He had lost faith in the police force, which had been the focal point of his life, the source of meaning to his existence, or at least the one source that had an illusion of meaning. What he had discovered was the worst thing possible for a policeman to discover: that the organization he had pledged his working life to had hidden his mother's murderers. He had begun to fear that his true vocation wasn't detective work. He wasn't a true detective. It was simply that detective work had been the only tool he'd had at hand to challenge the darkness.

Daly had only a vague recollection of the remainder of the evening. Hegarty's words made him feel uncomfortable, but he felt unable or unwilling to stop their flow. He grew steadily drunk, while Hegarty talked on, without pausing, wetting his dry lips, determined to tell his story, even though his voice began to croak. It was hard to have the last word with a man who had whispered brutal secrets for thousands of nights.

27

The next morning Daly awoke with a sense of dread. He showered, dressed and while he was making a pot of tea, his phone rang. Hegarty had yet to emerge from his room, but Daly could hear him moving about, so he took the call in the porch.

He tried to make his voice sound as though he wasn't the ghost of the competent detective he had once been. It was Irwin. He told Daly there was to be a press conference at headquarters and his attendance was required. Fealty was due to make an important announcement about the investigation into Walsh's death and the secret links that existed between Special Branch and the paramilitaries.

'I'll be there as soon as I can,' said Daly.

About half an hour later, Irwin met him as he entered the building.

'You're late,' said the younger detective.

'I wanted to shave for the cameras,' replied Daly.

Irwin said nothing, just ushered him through to one of the conference rooms.

'The meeting's about to begin. We'll have to slip in at the back.' He opened the doors. 'By the way, Daly,' he whispered. 'There's been a complication. A shift in the investigation.'

'What shift?'

'We now know that Walsh had entangled himself with some very sinister elements.'

The two walked into a room filled with noisy journalists.

'This media frenzy is all down to you, Daly,' hissed Irwin. 'I hope you're happy with the can of worms you've opened.'

They stood at the back of the room. At the front, next to a projector screen, sat Inspector Fealty. He appeared comfortable in the full glare of the media. His uniform looked impossibly neat and trim, as though it had been ironed a thousand times that morning. He was flanked by two officers from the press department, but there was no doubt as to who was in charge of the show. There was a professionalism and precision about Fealty's persona that had been absent in the old police force. Once upon a time police commanders had been dour, stolid figures, reliable but completely lacking in media skills. The peace process and its political climate had changed all that. The media had developed an appetite for castigating the old institutions, stripping them of any trace of their former prestige. They would have crucified police chiefs like Donaldson, who regarded it as an emblem of his professionalism that he had never issued statements to the press. Fealty belonged to the front ranks of a new breed of officer that had emerged from the anonymous grey corridors of the old police stations into the smart arena of public relations.

Daly heard a nearby reporter whisper, 'I hear Special Branch are going to lift the lid on collusion.'

He felt a sense of gratification – victory, even. He glanced over at Irwin and wondered why he was smirking.

Fealty leaned towards the gallery of journalists and photographers and began speaking.

'The extraordinary thing about what I am going to reveal to you today on this issue of the links between the police force and the paramilitaries is that the details exist nowhere in the official record.'

Daly sensed a shiver of excitement pass through the room. The journalists were electrified by the prospect of Fealty's revelations.

'In many respects they were lost amid the fog of war,' continued Fealty. 'However, that doesn't mean that the police force and the paramilitary organizations cannot be held accountable for what happened in the past.' He paused for emphasis. 'At a point in the mid-1970s the intelligence services came to the grim conclusion that the only way to beat the IRA's terror machine was to plant a mole at the heart of its operations. The simplest way to destroy the IRA's chain of command and crack its morale was to have a number of highly placed informers reporting on the running of the organization. Today I am going to reveal the identity of one of those men.'

Daly edged closer to the back of the room. What sort of trap had Fealty fixed for him? When was he going to start talking about collusion between Loyalists and the police? He looked up at the screen behind Fealty and his heart missed several beats when he saw Hegarty's face appear.

'His codename was Lethal Ally,' said Fealty, pointing to the screen. 'But his real name is Daniel Hegarty.'

Voice recorders were thrust towards Fealty and cameras flashed.

'Ideally it would have been preferable to keep the issue of Special Branch's links with the IRA out of the glare of the media. However, we are a new police force, operating in a new form of society, one where full disclosure is the norm. I regret to say that Mr Hegarty is no longer under our control. He is beyond the scope of law and order.'

It took a moment or two for what Fealty was talking about to take full effect on Daly. A quiver of dread ran through his stomach, but he decided not to let himself be intimidated by Fealty's subtle ploy. He stood as still as a statue, listening carefully to the journalists' questions and Fealty's concise replies.

'Help us with the chronology, Inspector,' said a journalist at the front. 'When precisely did Mr Hegarty's career as an intelligence agent begin? Who contacted whom?'

'Hegarty was recruited in the winter of 1974. He was first contacted by the Force Surveillance Unit.'

The cameras flashed again. Fealty's face shone. He seemed wonderfully sharp and alert, sure of himself, playing this game of cat and mouse with the truth, laying down a trail for the journalists that would divert them from Daly and his claims of collusion between the police and Loyalists, overshadowed now by these more shocking revelations about the police force's links to the IRA. The entire performance might have been scripted, analysed and researched within the highest levels of the intelligence services. In the eyes of the media, Daly's association with Hegarty would make him damaged goods, a police detective relying on the evidence of an informer and murderer.

Daly could see the look of surprise – astonishment, even – in the journalists' faces. Fealty was revealing a conspiracy so profound that they found it hard to believe. What sort of man could operate at the heart of the IRA for forty years and carry off such a lonely deception? The strategic impossibility of it. The emotional discipline. Already, Daly could hear the overtones of mobile phones ringing; editors ringing their journalists back to check the improbable facts; seasoned journalists purring with delight. This revelation of a top informer within the IRA would release a flood of speculation and headlines from the media, a swarm of claims and denials from politicians, with enough riddles and lingering questions to keep countless journalists occupied for months on end.

'Why now, Inspector? Why release this man's identity?'

'We are concerned for the safety of the public.'

'After forty years of supporting this agent's activities as a terrorist isn't it a little late to be concerned about the safety of the public?'

'We have specific concerns at the moment.'

'Has Hegarty made threats?'

'We are searching for him with the highest degree of urgency. A manhunt is already in progress.'

Fealty adjusted his position in his seat. He seemed to be looking towards the back of the room, straight at Daly. A coded glance, like an invitation to speak, his eyes cold and gloating. Irwin looked over at Daly and studied his reaction. A silence fell in the room, an uncomfortable silence in which Daly felt himself sharply etched and exposed. Had Fealty conjured up this media circus entirely to deter his investigation? He closed his eyes and thought of a question to pose, but all he could see was the searing outline of the murder triangle, replete with arrows, connections, dates and names.

Fealty resumed speaking from his prepared lines.

'Right now, my detectives are investigating Hegarty's role in the murder of Ivor McClintock at a hotel in South Armagh the week before last.'

The smartphones and voice recorders jabbed closer.

'Are you saying that McClintock's murder is connected with the intelligence services?'

'I can't comment on that.'

'Do you feel responsible for any murders this man may have committed during the Troubles?'

'No comment.'

Apart from the odd hesitation, Fealty handled the barrage in a brisk and efficient manner.

'Did you use Hegarty to manipulate the IRA in terms of their political direction, or did he simply disclose its secrets?'

'Hegarty gave us options, both in terms of military action and also broader political strategy. We were able to make things happen, and we knew when they would happen.'

Daly saw the politicians' and media's will for a collusion investigation deteriorate before his eyes. He was powerless to prevent its collapse. Fealty had hoodwinked him with this ploy to expose Hegarty, a spy whose secrets would tantalize the media and create waves of runaway speculation. The room seemed to grow more crowded, the mood urgent, a reflection of Daly's state of mind, which boiled with frustration and anger. Secrets and deception lay all around. In every direction, he stumbled upon his own ignorance, each fresh revelation leaving him fumbling in greater darkness.

Daly's breathing grew heavy and his shoulders slumped. He glanced up at Fealty, listening to the shouted questions of the journalists, waiting for the Special Branch inspector to deliver the final blow, to point the pack of journalists in his direction and utter the condemning words: *We have reason to believe that Inspector Celcius Daly knows Hegarty's whereabouts.*

But for some reason, the words never came. Perhaps Fealty had not exhausted him enough, he thought, perhaps he had yet to reach the fifteenth round, the point where he would no longer be fit to throw a single punch.

'Are you saying that the intelligence services were able to pull the strings of the IRA, thanks to this lone agent?'

'Correct,' replied Fealty.

'There must be more informers than this man. Who else do you have working for you?'

'No comment.'

'What murders did you know of in advance and were unwilling or unable to prevent?'

Fealty's tone changed.

'Spies like Hegarty operated in a grey zone, serving the public interest, but beyond the protection of the law. In many ways, the legal system has yet to catch up with their role during the conflict.'

Daly found it difficult to breathe. He wished the room wasn't so crowded. He had been careless of his own reputation and safety, he could see that now. He wished that Hegarty had not returned his call, that he had crawled away into the deepest hole of border country and taken his secrets with him. The media pack had the spy firmly in their sights. They would not rest until they had hounded him into the light. Tomorrow all the newspapers would have Fealty's revelations plastered over the front pages. They'd send out teams of journalists to pick over the traces of the spy's life and flush him out from hiding. He was too precious a commodity to the media. He was like the Abominable Snowman or the last of a primitive race, a creature left over from a darker, more violent time. They would drag him blinking like an ancient coelacanth into the blinding glare of notoriety. They would not let him skulk in the shadows any longer.

'Would it be fair to describe this manhunt as a setback to the peace process?'

'You'll have to ask the politicians and Mr Hegarty's former comrades in the IRA that.'

'What disciplinary procedures had Mr Hegarty been subject to in the past?'

'What do you mean?'

'I mean what punishments or sanctions were imposed whenever he broke the law?'

'I don't think I need to remind anyone here today of what it was like in this country during the Troubles. Spies like Mr Hegarty struck a fatal blow at the heart of terrorist organizations, and their actions helped steer this country towards peace.'

'Nevertheless, there must have been times when he exceeded his position as an intelligence agent in order not to attract suspicion.'

'Again, no comment.'

'Is Hegarty's life under threat?'

'From whom?'

'Under threat from members of the IRA. Now that he has been exposed.'

'I can't speak for his former associates.'

'Who can you speak for?' For a moment, the pack of journalists grew still, the scent of blood hanging in the air.

'If you study the press statement we have released, I think that you will find our position very clear. If you have any further questions...' Fealty paused and glanced at the back of the room. Once again, Daly thought he was going to point towards him, but the inspector gestured to the two officers flanking him. '... I suggest you put them to our press team.'

Fealty rose and quickly made his exit through a side door. The journalists headed, with the synchronicity of a herd, in the same direction. Bodies jostled against each other in a competition in journalistic greed. They were within touching distance of career-making scoops, the point where professional rivalry borders on gullible irrationality. Fealty glided through the doors and several police officers were forced to bar the reporters from following him.

Daly waited for the room to empty, wanting some peace to untangle his thoughts. Journalists drifted past him, pocketing their phones, shelving their questions, their skirmish with the murky past over for another day.

'What did you think of that?' one of them asked another.

'Betrayal. Deceit. The fog of war. That was the mother lode.'

Daly began to think clearly or at least with enough focus to understand what had happened. Intelligence services rarely sacrificed their own people to the media in this way. It wasn't good for business, for the recruitment of future informers. Cutting Hegarty loose like this was an unprecedented step.

However, the spy had clearly overstepped the line, reasoned Daly. He had threatened to open a window on to the shadowy intelligence environment, and what lurked there was unpleasant and potentially ruinous for many reputations. Everything Fealty had revealed was most probably true, but the elements of truth were also mechanisms for a much deeper deception, and a means to tarnish Daly's reputation and the trustworthiness of Hegarty's testimony forever. Fealty's officers were probably in the process of raiding his cottage and arresting Hegarty right now, if they had not already done so, with a carefully contrived leak to the press beforehand to give the story a little extra push.

With a sick feeling of dread, he made his way down the corridor towards the exit. He bumped into Irwin, whose face was almost ecstatic-looking.

'Watch out, Daly, you can't run with the wolves and hide with the sheep,' he shouted after him.

28

When Daly returned to his car, he saw Pryce standing there, a black scarf wrapped round her throat and chin, her stockinged legs planted close together for comfort against the cold. She looked as though she had been waiting for him.

'You look worried, Celcius. What's up now?'

He couldn't keep himself from scowling.

'None of your bloody business.'

He climbed into the car and rolled down the window.

'I've told you before. I don't want to be part of your book or answer any more of your stupid questions.'

She hurried over to his window.

'I did a quick interview with Fealty about your investigation.' She studied Daly for a reaction. 'He doesn't seem to like you.'

'There's a surprise. The investigation has entered a very dangerous phase. Too dangerous for meddling journalists.'

Her voice was casual, relaxed.

'You can't stop me searching for the truth, Celcius.'

'You're right. I can't stop you.'

'It's fun watching you try.'

Daly accelerated away. He caught sight of his face in the overhead mirror. It was the face of a doomed man. He took the back roads to his cottage, driving rashly, his only comfort the possibility that at any moment the car might swerve or career off the road in the way that Walsh's had done. He felt simultaneously lost and pinpointed, like a red dot in the middle of an unfinished map, denied and dislocated by the changing terrain of the past. Adrenalin coursed through his body, which gave his predicament a kind of levity, a detachment from reality. What was there to stop him driving south across the border, and keeping going for hours until he was as far away as possible from this dark corner of Northern Ireland?

However, he reminded himself that a wanted man was residing in his cottage. He needed every ounce of his strength to stay ahead of his enemies. He had to think clearly, stay sober and practical, rather than submit to this internal panic. His car got stuck behind a school bus. He drummed the steering wheel impatiently. He thought it incredible that the world was keeping to its unchanging course while a separate stream of events had turned him into a host for a murderer and a spy.

He slowed on approaching a police checkpoint less than half a mile from his cottage. Unexpectedly, they waved him through. He stared at the police officers in his rear-view mirror. They stood still in the middle of the road, watching his car.

He drove up the final stretch to his cottage and parked the vehicle. He stared at the old house. He was surprised to see no outward sign of disturbance. The place looked just as he had left it. *I am back home,* he said to himself, *to attend to a wanted man.* He grimaced. It was a topsy-turvy domestic arrangement for a police detective, but what choice did he have in the matter? He stared at the cottage, reluctant to move from the safety of the driver's seat. He wondered who else was watching the scene, waiting for Hegarty to reveal himself. Perhaps Special Branch were going to leave him alone with the spy for a while so that he would wallow in cold anticipation. Allow his imagination to go to work. Wasn't that their standard procedure in the run-up to arrest and interrogation?

My eyes have been sealed for years. Pryce was right, I have grown up with blinkers on, and now that the facts of the past are unravelling, I have no choice but to follow them through to the end. He got out of the car, and strode towards the cottage door. Inside, there was no sign of life. Secretly, he hoped that the spy had fled, but he was wrong. He found Hegarty in the shadows of the scullery staring at the cold fire grate. The detective was right back where he had started that morning.

Hegarty appeared unconcerned when Daly relayed the details of the press conference. He was content to wait. 'If they want to arrest me, let them arrest me here,' he told Daly.

However, the detective was determined to work out some plan of action that would resolve both their difficulties. Different plots emerged out of tense little conversations that they took from room to room, window to window. They could see the police checkpoint at the bottom of the road, the officers standing about, stopping the occasional car. The house filled with the unspoken fear that the police would swoop at any moment.

'We must find a way out of this impasse,' said Daly doggedly. 'You can't hide here forever.'

'I have no plans to run anywhere else.'

Daly sighed in frustration.

'I am sorry to be a source of trouble,' said Hegarty. 'But it is not my fault you are at war with Special Branch, too.'

It alarmed Daly to see that Hegarty was resigned to wait for the police to make the next move. It was as if Daly's complicity, his search for the truth, had provided him with a temporary refuge. The spy settled into an armchair in a corner of the scullery, and ignored Daly, mumbling to himself, his eyes darting from right to left. Daly slammed the door shut on him. Not for the first time that day, he found himself wishing for his own life back, the one he had before he discovered Walsh's murder triangle. He thought about crawling into a chair himself, closing his eyes and willing sleep to come. But he did not want to be lying defenceless when Special Branch arrived at his door. He prowled from room to room, glancing through the windows, alert to every sound and noise. He checked on Hegarty, who seemed half-asleep, a secretive smile playing on his lips. He wanted the spy out of his life, but was unable to evict him from the cottage. He hungered for privacy, to be left alone with the shadows of the past.

It was late afternoon. The stand-off could not continue indefinitely.

'Do you want something to eat?' asked Daly.

'I've no appetite.'

'You must eat something.' His voice was gruff rather than sympathetic.

Daly went into the kitchen. Unfortunately, he did not have a lot to work with. He took out some bread and told Hegarty to boil the kettle. He didn't think it right that he should fetch and carry for the spy. In the circumstances, domestic lines had to be drawn, and Hegarty needed to understand that.

They stood and waited for the water to boil. Daly found a knob of butter, a tin of beans and a can of pears in syrup. Hegarty set the table and Daly dished out the food. It was a fugitive's feast, enough to hold themselves together for the trials ahead.

A haze settled over Daly's mood as he drank his tea. Together, they made the effort to wash the dishes and put away the plates. Any prospect that Hegarty would help Daly discover why his mother was killed had evaporated. Anxiety that he was sheltering a fugitive had turned to despondency. The fantasy that gaining the confidence of a disgruntled spy would shine a penetrating light on the past was revealed as the desperate ploy of a powerless detective. All he had found was another blank wall in the heart of the labyrinth. Worse than that, he now had the problem of working out what to do with his unwelcome lodger.

Daly got out the bottle of whiskey and poured two small glasses. They sat at the kitchen table.

'I have to help you escape from this cottage,' he told the spy.

'You want rid of me.'

'No, but I can't wait on you any longer. We have to settle on a course of action and commit to it. You are your own man with your own enemies, while I need to go back to my old life and figure out what to do next with Walsh's murder triangle.'

'A good spy never acts out of fear. The police are waiting for us to make the first move. Why give them the satisfaction of seeing us run?' Hegarty flashed Daly a crooked smile.

Daly was silent. He sipped his whiskey. Through the window, he watched the sky darken with the premonition of rain. The light grew so dim it could have been evening. He always thought best when the light was like that. At one point, a helicopter hovered low over the cottage, its scythe-like blades disturbing the air with so much violence the windowpanes rattled in their frames.

Daly went through a methodical analysis of the options they had and came up with a plan. He made another pot of tea and convinced himself that helping Hegarty escape in this way was an act of mercy in accordance with an unwritten code of rights, the charter to a country he represented, the townlands of Walsh's murder triangle and its parishes of grief.

Determined now in his course of action, he got up and packed Hegarty a small holdall with a sleeping bag, tins of food and winter clothes, enough to help him survive a few nights in the open. When he had finished, he returned to the living room and picked up the phone. Pryce answered his call almost immediately.

'Celcius?' She sounded surprised.

'I need to meet you.'

'Why?'

'I want you to do me a special favour. I can't discuss it on the phone.'

'I thought you didn't want to see me again.'

'At the moment, you're the only person I can rely on.'

'Are you saying you've discovered something important?'

'I believe so. I need you to give me a lift into border country. Hegarty has told me where he hid a copy of Hannon's old security files. There's enough there to help fill in the gaps of Walsh's murder map.'

'Those files mean everything. Once we have them, the balance of power will swing towards us. I'll come to your house immediately.'

'Wait. There's a police checkpoint just down the road from the cottage. Meet me at Gillen's crossroads. It's less than a mile away through the fields. I'll be there at about five p.m. when the light begins to fade.'

'I'll see you there.'

The line went dead. Despite the caution he had shown on the phone, he hoped Special Branch had been listening to the exchange. The success of his plan depended on it.

'It's important you look after yourself as best you can,' he told

Hegarty as they waited. 'Don't try to contact me until you are safely over the border.'

The anticipation of escape had brought a flush to Hegarty's face but he said nothing. Daly felt his own heart begin to pound as the time came closer to leave.

29

The checkpoint was there, at the bottom of the road, waiting for them. A policeman carrying a gun loomed out of the twilight drizzle, a squad car blocking the road behind and more officers pacing about. Daly brought his car to a halt. The armed officer was so close Daly could see the firm line of his mouth and his marksman's blue eyes. Had he been instructed to shoot Hegarty on sight? Through the windscreen wipers, he peered to see if he recognized the officer, but there was nothing familiar about the man, who just stood there, cradling the gun in his arms, his expression a blank.

Daly caught sight of his own reflection in the car mirror and saw a stranger behind the wheel. He realized that the rules of this checkpoint were different from all the others he had encountered. He was no longer on the right side of the law. He was a fugitive's driver, about to go on the run from the police. There was no more time to wait patiently in the shadows. From now on, he had to draw his enemies towards him.

Above the sound of the wipers, he heard the rasp of Hegarty's heavy breathing. The spy's presence felt uncomfortably close. Daly's hand on the wheel shook slightly. He watched the wipers repeatedly clear the web of raindrops, revealing the policeman's figure, still and alert in the middle of the road. He thought of his mother and Father Walsh, and how they must have felt confronted by a similar checkpoint on a lonely road, watching the figure of a police officer, waiting tensely for what he was going to do next.

The policeman gave a little nod, almost a greeting. He seemed to be expecting Daly to bring the car forward.

Hegarty tugged his seatbelt loose.

'Wait,' ordered Daly.

The detective hunched his shoulders and watched the policeman. As the seconds ticked by and the rain kept falling, the officer grew more alert and uneasy-looking. Two of his colleagues got out of the car and joined him. They were all in their early twenties. Daly sighed. The empty expressions on their faces did look familiar. He might be back at the new police headquarters, sitting in front of a group of eager trainees, all of them born in the dying shadows of the Troubles, a new generation of public servants, marching under the banner of inclusive policing, whilst their senior officers withdrew into the shadows, reconciling themselves with silence and secrecy.

The wipers swept back and forth like a metronome, roughly in time with Hegarty's harsh breathing. The rain began to fall in earnest, welding them shut in a drum of noise.

Daly had made Hegarty wear a bright yellow raincoat, which made him look older than he had seemed in the cottage, a ghost bristling in the cold twilight. Suddenly Daly felt strangely protective of the spy. There was no simple way out for the old man. His life would always be hemmed in by checkpoints and suspicion, while those who had pulled his strings moved on in their careers, or retired on fat pensions.

The officers drew closer to the car. Daly stuck the gearstick in reverse and accelerated back towards the cottage, watching more police officers gather on the road from their hiding positions. The wheels bit into the verge, grinding against gravel and earth. He reversed the car hard into a hedge and told Hegarty to get out and run. On the road behind, there was a flurry of movement, police shouting instructions. Daly saw the lead officer advance towards them, running with the long strides of youth.

Daly glanced back at his cottage. From this perspective, his home place resembled a stubborn atoll of thorns and nettles, an untidy blot on the landscape. He pushed Hegarty by the shoulders into a gap in the hedge. They stumbled through a tunnel of hazel and blackthorn and emerged into a small meadow. He could hear the rumbling sound of cars moving off on the nearby road but apart from that, the only sound was the pattering of rain on the thick grass.

They ran together across the meadow, through a hedge and into another larger field. They followed the hedges of several more fields, wading through ditches that were filled with muddy water. They were careful not to entangle themselves in the briars and thorns as they hurried along the planned route. Their clothes were already soaked through, slowing their progress. Hegarty panted hard to keep up with the detective, spittle drooling from his mouth.

Soon they were crossing bogland along the ragged fringes of Lough Neagh. They dodged shadowy crevices that might have hidden bottomless bog holes. At one point, the bogland disappeared and they found themselves on an overgrown lane. It was clear it hadn't been used by anyone in a long time. They were surrounded by silence but soon a noise, growing louder, made them look up. They came upon the bank of a fast-flowing river. Checking that they could not be seen, Daly took off his raincoat and handed it to Hegarty.

A grey stupor had overcome the spy, and Daly had to help free the yellow raincoat from his shoulders. This was what it meant to be on the run, thought Daly, relying on guile and the lie of the land, scuttling away into the wild corners of the Lough Neagh hinterland.

They kept moving. The rain eased off, and in its aftermath, a mist crept in from the lough. They crossed the expanse of several fields and came upon another bend in the river. There was a flurry of movement from a thicket and several sheep emerged, their black faces staring at them in mute surprise. Hegarty shouted 'Baa' at them, and they trotted back into the mist.

The sound of traffic grew louder. They must be nearing a road, thought Daly, but they could see very little ahead. He stopped and stared at the broken outline of trees, trying to get his bearings. They forced their way through a tangle of blackthorns and came out into another field. Hegarty was still panting heavily and struggled to keep up. There was a wild look in his eyes and he kept glancing all around as though he could see invisible enemies.

The reverberations of the cars faded away, replaced by something else, the drone of a helicopter hovering far above. The mist floated thickly around them as they pushed ahead. Daly urged the spy to run faster as they kept to the cover of a small wood, but the fog had caught up with them. The detective watched as an army of ghostly figures emerged from the trees and hollows. In that soundless flight of water droplets, he saw a stream of shapes pour around them, hundreds of ghosts entangling themselves in their flight.

What if there were more fugitives on the run? he thought. Hundreds more than anyone imagined, their secret paths intermingling? Not just fugitives from paramilitary organizations, but fugitive policemen and fugitive soldiers, fugitive lawyers, politicians and journalists, all desperately trying to hide their secrets, overcrowding this dark landscape with their restless fears of punishment and revenge. What if the fugitives outnumbered the searchers? What if the country was nothing but a long line of fugitives in flight from one end to the other?

30

The mist cleared and Daly emerged from the hedge on to an empty road. Ahead, he saw a crossroads, and Pryce's car, the headlights on and the engine idling. He walked towards it, his eyes blinking in the full glare of the lights. He had almost reached the vehicle when a deafening roar erupted in the sky. A blur of deeper darkness hovered above him, the shape materializing into a low-flying helicopter. Daly hunkered down and hurried to the car. He barely had time to wipe the mud from his shoes and hands before climbing in. The helicopter flew off over the trees and disappeared.

'What's going on, Celcius?' asked Pryce, staring in surprise at his yellow raincoat.

'Just drive.'

She accelerated away.

'There was a police checkpoint outside the cottage. They thought I was hiding Hegarty.'

'And were you?'

'Yes.'

She glanced at him, her look of surprise intensifying.

'Are you insane? Running away in a luminous raincoat and

arranging to meet me like this. No wonder you've attracted their attention.'

That was the plan, he thought. To draw danger towards him and away from Hegarty, at least for the vital hour or so until the spy had made his escape. He and Hegarty had parted ways before he had emerged on to the road. He had directed the spy to follow the river's meandering route until he reached its mouth at Lough Neagh. Daly had given him the location of a small rowing boat hidden along the bank. The plan was that the spy would use it to ferry himself to Coney Island, where he could lie low for a few more days. In Daly's imagination, the island had always been a place of final refuge, where only the sound of the wind and the waves reigned. If it came to it, he could join Hegarty there.

'Don't be surprised if we end up with a police escort,' said Pryce.

'Just drive towards the border.'

'We should go back and get Hegarty,' she said. 'He can help us with the connections between the murders. It's the only way to make the murder triangle measurable or real. Without him, the map is just a mess of lines.'

'Hegarty's already gone. Keep driving and I'll tell you more.'

She pressed him several more times about the spy's whereabouts.

'I told you, I don't know,' he snapped. On a deeper level, it was the truth. He didn't know what was going to happen to the spy, nor was he sure what exactly Hegarty was going to do. He took comfort and strength from the uncertainty. It meant no one following them could understand them; they were impossible to plot against.

With his directions, Pryce took them further into border country, driving at her usual reckless speed. The hedges swerved closer. They seemed to twitch at the corner of his eye, alive, squirming with darkness and loose bits of the past. He kept checking in the rear window, but the roads were empty.

'It would be helpful to hear what you found out from Hegarty,' said Pryce. Her voice was mellow – seductive, even. 'Did he give you any clue about his plans?'

'He told me he was leaving the country, and he wanted everyone to forget about him.'

She laughed.

'No bloody chance of that happening now.'

They drove on.

'Did he say anything about me?'

Daly turned to her in surprise.

'Why would he?'

She flicked back her hair and flashed him a smile.

'Just wondering. What impression did he make on you?'

'He's a man addicted to betrayal. He gets a thrill from risking his life. Reckless – suicidal, almost.'

Crossroads after crossroads opened up before them. Pryce ground the car through the gears, paying more attention to Daly and his body language.

'You don't like him.'

'What makes you think that?'

'I can tell from the tone of your voice. He disturbed you.'

'Yes, of course. He's a killer.'

'Then why cover for him?'

'I'm not covering for him. I have no idea what he intends to do. With all the money Special Branch gave him, he might be planning a trip around the world.'

'You seem sure he's out of harm's way. You're not telling me everything you know.'

'Just concentrate on driving.'

They drove on. Some of the colour had left her face and apart from the movement of her hands on the wheel she sat completely immobile, concentrating on Daly's instructions and the implications of what he had said.

'What else did you find out?'

Daly glanced at his watch. By now, Hegarty should be well out on the waters of Lough Neagh.

'Enough to question your real motivations in wanting to find Hegarty. He told me you tried to trap him the day after Walsh's murder. In the Clary Lodge.'

Her hands gripped the steering wheel and her professional mask slipped for a moment.

'I guessed it,' she said with a voice that mingled triumph with contempt. 'You know a lot more than you're letting on.'

'What about you? You never mentioned a single detail of Ivor McClintock's murder. You met me at the hotel the next day, but never thought to bring it up.'

'I'm a journalist. Sometimes that means holding on to information, working out the best person to share it with.'

'But you knew I was trying to contact Hegarty. You never thought to warn me he was a killer.'

'Where are you going with this, Celcius? What are you trying to get out of me?'

He had no choice now but to confront her with his suspicions. He was convinced that she would not lie without his noticing.

'I'm trying to find out who you really are.'

She exchanged glances with him.

'I'm a journalist.'

'But who are you working for? More importantly, who are you working against?'

'I work for no one but myself.'

'That's a lie. I'm putting my job and my personal safety on the line by trusting you.'

'I give you my word. Your secrets are safe with me.'

'That's another lie.' He stared through the windscreen at the road ahead. Her lies were buying him time, ensuring that Hegarty made good his escape.

She looked at him sharply.

'If you had doubts you should have asked me these questions much earlier. Before you got into the car. Why now?'

'I'm a detective. I decide when to ask the questions.'

Daly felt the momentum of her speed, shadows streaming by the window as if border country were flinging all its trees out of the darkness at them.

She grew agitated.

'Where exactly are we?'

'I have no idea. If I had a destination in mind don't you think we'd have reached there by now?'

'Then why have you brought me down these godforsaken roads?'

'To throw Special Branch off the scent.'

She braked the car to a sudden halt. Her face was smeared with anger now, blotting out her usual self-possession.

'I knew you had some ulterior motive. What have you done with Hegarty?'

'Why are you so concerned with him? What other purpose does he serve for you?'

She didn't answer. She stared back at him with eyes that were unrelenting and steady.

'You've been helping Walsh research his murder triangle but in all that time you've been stalking your own demons,' continued Daly. 'Why do you want Hegarty? Is it to have him killed?'

She gave a bare monosyllable of a laugh.

'Don't be ridiculous, Celcius. I'm a writer, not some sort of monster, in spite of what you might think.' She hesitated. 'Hegarty is another one of my little writing assignments.'

'What do you mean?'

'I'm interested in him for creative reasons. Any man who kills another man right under my nose automatically earns the right to at least a chapter in my book.'

She was a dangerous woman, Daly realized. In the circumstances, he was glad he had steered her as far away as possible from the spy.

'My journalistic instincts drive me towards men like Hegarty and Hannon,' she continued. 'Men like you, Celcius, and Father Walsh. Men whose destiny has been determined by acts of violence. I seek you out and put you in touch with each other because I'm interested in seeing the collision of truth that emerges from your encounters.'

'So this is your mission. To entangle me with men like Hegarty and Hannon and write up the consequences?'

'Correct. Think about it. Each of you occupies such different terrain. There is so much distance between the paths you have chosen. You might think of people like Hegarty and Ivor McClintock as monsters but they weren't. They were like everybody else during the Troubles. They were just like you and me. Only they chose a certain path that took them beyond the realm of normal human behaviour.'

'So that was why you brought me to Kenneth Agnew's house that day.

You were curious to see how I would react. Dear God, you even made sure I was carrying my service weapon.'

Daly now saw that the former policeman's suicide had been a fortunate reprieve. Who knew how he might have reacted if Agnew had opened the door. And all of it would have been observed and recorded in detail by Pryce.

'I wanted to see how you behaved when you looked your mother's killer in the eye. A police detective who'd spent his life not wanting to see or know. For me you were the key, a symbol of this country's blurred view of the past, its willingness to ignore the crimes committed during the Troubles and the stories of its victims.'

Daly was aghast. She appeared stupidly proud of her meddling, her series of blind dates between sworn enemies. He saw that the past week or so in her company had been a process of persuasion to involve him more deeply in her unfinished book, to draw him down towards all those leaden figures from the murder triangle, Hegarty and Hannon, Agnew and McClintock, and below them the ghosts who could never recount their stories. But instead of a flow of words, her actions had triggered a flow of blood.

'Hegarty's meeting with McClintock in the hotel room. You orchestrated that as well?'

'Yes. Only I hadn't envisaged it would end so badly.'

Daly understood the full horror of that year in the 1970s. Walsh's interpretation had been incorrect. He realized that now. The image of a triangle was too naïve and plain, as if such darkness could be contained by simple geometry. There had been countless triangles of death operating in the year of his mother's murder, so many interconnecting spheres of evil, perpetrated by violent men on both sides. Hegarty was right. One could never dispel the murk, only illuminate it.

She turned her glittering eyes towards him.

'My only motivation was the creative impulse. You must understand that.' Her eyes flicked a little, scouting the margins of his doubting face. 'If it wasn't for my involvement, these ghosts would never have come out into the light. They would have had no chance of meeting each other, connecting their stories. Don't you understand? This country needs to coax its ghosts into full view, to see what they look like in the light.'

Daly stared back at her. She was so close he could feel the tingling warmth of her breath. What annoyed him the most was that she always seemed to be flirting with him, even now. However, in spite of the intimate setting of the car, he sensed a cold gap form between them. He felt a surge of physical energy much stronger than any creative impulse. Pure unadulterated anger.

'You forget that we're real people,' he said. 'Our lives are more than just words and punctuation.' He flung open his door and climbed out. 'Good luck with the rest of your book,' he added. 'I hope that you have your ending in sight, or that at least you have some idea how your book is going to finish.'

'I thought you were going to give me the ending tonight,' she said, leaning out of her seat. 'But I was wrong.' She looked genuinely sorrowful, as though her life depended on the completed book. 'Can I call round tomorrow?'

'No, you can't.'

'When, then?'

'When you've finished your book.'

'Finished it or killed it?' Suddenly she looked tired – bored, almost. 'The story needs you, Celcius. Why should I continue with it if you walk away now?'

'Because you owe it to Father Walsh. To the victims.'

The light went out of her eyes.

'OK then, you have given me the ending. It ends like this.' She reached across and slammed his door shut. The engine revved and she drove off into the darkness.

31

Daly stood in the middle of the road, watching Pryce's car disappear around a bend in the road. He stared at the darkness around him. It seemed innocent of surveillance. Where were Special Branch? he wondered. He began to walk back the way they had come.

A vehicle engine coughed in the darkness and a set of headlights lit up the trees in front of him. From a hidden lay-by, a car eased on to the road and pulled alongside Daly.

The dark driver's window slid down, revealing Inspector Fealty's face.

'Need a lift, Daly?'

Daly climbed in. He heard Fealty click on the central locking, and then engage the slick gears.

'For God's sake, what's going on, Celcius? What were you and Pryce doing, driving all the way down here?'

'She wanted to take me for a spin.'

'You'll have to give me more information than that.'

'I'd rather not say anything more.'

'What exactly is your relationship with Pryce? You know her husband is a dissident Republican.'

'She's a frustrated writer trying to finish her book on the murder triangle. She's been manipulating victims, pushing them physically around, cannibalizing their words and feelings. When she discovered I wasn't another puppet she ran off into the darkness.'

'Are you OK? You don't sound yourself.'

Was he himself? Daly was no longer sure. He tried to push away the feelings of guilt and lethargy that had been plaguing him.

'I've had a long day,' he said. 'I need a chance to reflect on things. Perhaps a leave of absence for a few days.'

Fealty nodded.

'You should take some sick leave. I don't think you realize how concerned we are for you. We've been keeping an eye on you – for your own good, of course. We knew you were in a tight spot. After the press conference this morning we didn't want to let you out of our sight.'

'Did you notice anything to heighten your concern?'

Fealty paused for a long time.

'No.'

'Well, then, that's good news, isn't it?'

'I don't know.'

Fealty's blank expression told Daly that Hegarty must have made his escape from the cottage as planned. Daly looked through his side window as the darkness of border country gave way to the lit-up motorway. He and Fealty had the two lanes to themselves. And the entire night ahead of them. They could travel anywhere they wanted.

'Why did you help Hegarty?' asked Fealty.

Daly thought about the question. An answer might have been because he needed Hegarty's help. A deeper one would have been because they were both outsiders and vulnerable. Neither he nor Fealty spoke, both waiting for the other to break the silence. Fealty shifted his narrow frame behind the wheel. He glanced at Daly with a bitter smile.

'You should have turned him in. He's not worth sacrificing your career. Or your integrity.'

'Is that what you think I've done? Sacrificed my integrity?'

'Yes. You might believe that you have operated professionally in this investigation, but your detective work has an emotional component. It is grief and anger disguised.'

Daly stared grimly ahead. Hegarty had gone, leaving him with more questions than answers. It hadn't been the most constructive of relationships. What he longed for, the truth, whatever it was, had not come. He was still waiting for the breakthrough, the final revelation. He had a hunch that the clues still lay enclosed within the walls of his cottage, or tucked under the fields that were his inheritance.

'Take me home,' he said.

Fealty drove on without saying anything. They passed the turn-off that would take them back to the lough shore.

'Where are you taking me?'

'There's been an unexpected development.' Fealty's voice was grave.

The Special Branch inspector drove him up a side road that eventually led to Donaldson's house.

'Why are we here?' asked Daly. 'Why are there so many police outside?'

'Donaldson, God rest his soul, is dead.'

'Murdered?'

'No. It looks like a tragic accident. Another one.'

32

Fealty explained how, early that morning, Donaldson had taken his wife from the nursing home in which she was a patient. He had left her at the pier in her wheelchair and taken his boat out on to the lough. Staff at the marina had raised the alarm that evening, when they found her wrapped in his overcoat, sitting close to the pier, with no sign of Donaldson or his boat.

'What did his wife say?' asked Daly.

'She can't speak or communicate in any way.'

Daly remembered that since her stroke she had been unable to take care of herself.

'Does she know what happened?'

'I doubt she ever will,' murmured Fealty. 'Maybe it's the best for her. The Lough Neagh rescue service found his body a couple of hours ago. The initial reports say there was no evidence of foul play.'

'The lough can be a very dangerous place at this time of year.' Daly looked at Fealty. 'You look worried.'

'I am.' Fealty's tone grew confiding. 'I'm afraid I'm suffering from your complaint.'

'What's that?'

'A heightened degree of suspicion.'

'As police detectives we work in an arena of suspicion.'

'I may be mistaken but I believe the poor bastard was driven to kill himself.'

'How?'

'He'd complained to me that Pryce was harassing him with details of his past. Pestering him into telling his story.'

Daly's face darkened at the mention of her name. He felt a rush of blood to his head.

'What are you suggesting? That she had something incriminating on him?'

'I hope not. God forgive me for my suspicions if they prove wrong. But Donaldson had been behaving like a man with a guilty conscience. He said that Pryce was trying to blackmail him.'

So Pryce had shepherded another man to his death. It was as easy as making sheep hop over a stile. She had asked for his story, demanded it, and he had given her his life instead. What sort of exchange was that? Had the woman no heart at all?

'In what way had she been blackmailing him?'

Fealty shrugged.

'He didn't tell me. But it appears that the RUC did not always have the leadership it deserved.'

'What leadership did it deserve?'

'No comment.'

'I spoke to Donaldson in person last night. He called round to my cottage. He seemed agitated.'

'Did he tell you anything about his fears?' Fealty's curiosity sharpened. 'Have you any idea what Pryce had on him? What drove him to such a desperate act?'

In a flash, Daly knew why Fealty had brought him here. It wasn't to help the investigation into Donaldson's death. It was to discover how much he knew of his former commander's secrets.

'I'm not sure what he was trying to tell me.'

'You're not sure? How?' Fealty stared at Daly, waiting for a response. His eyes looked alarmed. By contrast, calm had settled over Daly, which seemed to make Fealty more apprehensive.

'Donaldson promised me that he would help launch an inquiry into the murders. He said that he had devoted too much time to covering up the past.'

'A pity he'll never have the opportunity to fulfil his promise.'

Daly nodded. It seemed that Donaldson had changed his mind, buying his own silence in the most drastic way possible. But who or what had he been trying to protect? His own reputation or that of someone else? Someone with a more direct role in the killings? Someone to whom Donaldson still felt a loyalty in spite of the passing of so many years?

Daly followed Fealty into the house. He trod carefully through the rooms. It was clear from the police presence and the hum of activity that Special Branch were giving his sudden death more priority than that of Walsh, or Agnew or McClintock, for that matter. Even Irwin had rolled up his sleeves and was rooting through a set of drawers. The officers carried with them forensic bags but they were empty of anything that might prove useful to the investigation.

'You're not going to get very far here,' said Daly. 'You should be looking for what is missing. The secrets he took to the bottom of the lough.'

He slipped into the study, and inspected the ornaments and framed photographs in the glass cabinets. Donaldson's florid face stared back from one of the pictures. He was dressed in the full regalia of the Royal Ulster Constabulary. Most human beings were different things to different people, thought Daly, but with Donaldson what you saw was what you inevitably got – a tedious, slightly pompous police chief. There were other photos of him. Donaldson as a raw recruit, wiry and tall, and then later, rising up through the ranks, more dignified-looking with a large moustache, decorations on his uniform and a look in his eyes that suggested he had witnessed dark days. In the latest pictures, he looked at his most exalted and proud, grey-haired, moustache bristling, his eyes heavy and appraising.

Daly wandered through more rooms. He checked for ashes in the hearth, but the grate was empty. He watched the officers sort through drawers and cupboards. He searched down the backs of the sofas and seats. He had no idea what he was looking for, and he found nothing at all. He paused, sinking back into one of the seats. Something was missing from the house, his instinct told him. The air of gloominess was down to more than Donaldson's tragic death. Something else had been wiped from the house with a dreadful finality.

He caught sight of Fealty in the corridor, staring intently back. The Special Branch inspector was not much of a man for getting physically involved in a search. However, there was nothing passive or relaxed-looking about his eyes, which were full of restrained energy, looking at Daly as though he were the dark corner that most needed searching.

It occurred to Daly that, in spite of the intensity of the search, Fealty was just killing time, wondering what to do with him next. He was killing his own time, Daly realized, when he should be following his hunches.

He continued rummaging through shelves and drawers, searching for the information that Donaldson was trying to deny him. The more he saw its absence, the more determined he became. He worked with a sullen tenacity that attracted the smirking attention of Irwin. Several times, Daly returned to Donaldson's study. He sat down at his desk and checked if anything had been sellotaped to the back of the drawers. He stared blankly at the empty walls, sensing the actions of a very troubled but thorough mind.

No doubt Donaldson had been rigorous in his efforts to hide anything incriminating, but, in the end, Daly got lucky. Lifting a book out of a dusty box in the bottom of a cupboard, he found the lead he was looking for. It was an old volume on local planning laws. It had been well thumbed by someone in the past. He was about to put it back when something slipped out of its pages and fell at his feet. It was a black-and-white photograph of a young woman leaning against a car. He glanced around. No one had noticed his find. He examined the picture. The girl was posing in a summer dress, her hand raised to her brow, her eyes screwed up against the sunlight. It could almost have been his mother, but her hair was too light, and there was something tainted and tense about her smile that made it somehow less natural than his mother's. He couldn't make out her eyes, which were shaded completely by her hand. Behind her stood the shape of a large farmhouse, and beyond, just visible, a row of apple trees.

The car dated the picture. It was a dark-coloured Hillman Hunter.

He stared at the registration number. AIB 726. A shadow fell across his heart. A memory of the gloom and suspense he had felt collecting licence numbers as a boy. The car number looked familiar. He felt certain that it had been one of those listed in the documents he had found hidden in the family bible. He examined the woman again. He saw the stiffness in her slender frame, the hand raised in defence against the light, like a ghost begging not to be given away. He scanned the car looking for evidence of more ghosts. He felt certain that there were other presences just out of the camera's field of view.

At last, he had found a mental foothold. He thought about everything he knew of the murders and the possible role that the woman might have played. He wondered if he was mistaken in his assumptions. Perhaps he was misinterpreting Donaldson's state of mind. However, he couldn't think of any other possible reason to explain the former commander's behaviour. He was going to have to follow the lead. He slipped the photograph into a pocket.

In the corridor, he nodded at Fealty.

'Seen enough?' asked the Special Branch detective.

'Yes,' he replied.

Fealty hesitated for a moment. Then he nodded and said goodnight.

Daly walked out and asked one of the younger officers patrolling the grounds to drop him home. He needed to find the woman in the photograph, a woman who had left no trace of herself. Father Walsh had been exhaustive in his research, and so had Pryce, but neither of them, with their ability at ferreting out secrets, had found a single piece of information relating to the woman. Nothing that revealed her role in the killings, nothing that verified her existence, not even her name.

33

The front door of Daly's cottage lay slightly ajar and all the lights were on. He approached with caution, straining to listen, but he was unable to make out any sounds from within. He stepped inside with a sense of despondency. He stood in the hallway and glanced into the rooms. There was no sign of Hegarty anywhere, and the place was a mess. Clothes and books lay strewn across the floor, drawers hung open, their contents disordered. His house had been ransacked, its dark corners searched through, and the perpetrators had not even bothered to cover up their tracks.

It had been years since the army had conducted their last search of the cottage. He remembered their loaded guns grazing the narrow walls, their heavy boots echoing through the warren of rooms. He also recalled the entangled feelings of guilt and fear he had experienced as a boy, as though he had been found out. As though he had been the wrongdoer. Now it had happened again. More than three decades later. This time without any warning or fanfare. He wondered how the cottage had stood up to the poking and probing after all these years. Had the searchers found anything incriminating, rummaging through the rooms? Had they noticed how unclear the dividing line was between the past and the present? That the ghosts of the dead occupied more rooms than the living?

Considering that a wanted man had taken shelter here, it was fortunate they hadn't taken sledgehammers to the walls and ripped up the floorboards. He inspected the insides of his drawers and cupboards. It was impossible to tell what they had rifled through, and what they might have removed. He thought of phoning Irwin, and asking him outright, but perhaps that would break some professional code. It wasn't the type of question you asked your Special Branch colleague.

The fire had gone out in the scullery. He lit it and waited. He prowled through the rooms again and took a tour outside the cottage. The only trace of the spy's presence was a thin smell of sweat from the room he had slept in. Daly sat alone with the fire and the sound of the black hen pecking at the window.

When he was sure that Hegarty wasn't going to return he opened all the windows wide and the doors as well. It wasn't just the spy's smell, it was the dusty stench of the past that filled his nostrils, the bitter aroma of old furniture, the empty rooms and the corners full of cobwebs and dust. The wind blew in, driving out the stale air and memories. He stared through a window at the impenetrable hedges, the circle of moonlit fields, the swelling grass, the shadows of the past creeping forwards with a ghostly presence. He felt impatient and tense, breathing in the lough air through greedy nostrils.

Midges and moths drew in towards the light of the fire, their shadows creating a flickering show on the low ceiling. Spiders emerged from their nooks and crevices, their swags of dead insects wafting in the breeze. Last year's leaves gusted in through the front door and out through the back. The fire roared and crackled with the fresh ventilation.

Was it the joy of liberation he suddenly felt? The sense that the cottage itself was breathing and stirring with life? A bat twirled in through a window and out through another. He wished that his relationship with the cottage were just as transient. But human beings were different from animals and the creatures of the night, more like ghosts than living things, filled with memories and the darkness of the past. He couldn't leave the cottage now because to do so would mean dishonouring what haunted him, including the ghost of his nine-year-old self, the introverted little boy already acquainted with death and loss. If he avoided him, he might as well avoid life altogether. Perhaps Pryce was right in the end. Remembering ghosts, bringing them into the light, was a dangerous but necessary thing.

The wind blew through the cottage with greater force. The eaves in the roof creaked and shifted, as though the cottage were a boat finally on the move again, a rising storm shifting it from its moorings. Daly thought of the young woman in the picture and the car registration number. He went through all the stories and names in his head: his mother, Angela Daly, Father Aloysius Walsh, Ivor McClintock, Kenneth Agnew and now Ian Donaldson. Their fragmented stories overlapped like a restless sea of waves. He hunkered in the light of the fire, like the captain of a vessel decked out with billowing sails, plotting its course through the darkness.

34

The wind was still blowing fiercely the next morning. It hustled Daly out of sleep, blurring his dreams, rattling his opened bedroom window, flaring the curtains, filling the room with raw light. He got dressed in a hurry, feeling full of energy, even though a glance in the mirror revealed a face lined with fatigue and anxiety. He skipped breakfast and grabbed a mouthful of hot tea. He took the photograph of the young woman with him. Finding her represented the one clear path he had left.

Outside, the thorn trees swayed under the force of the wind, as if ready to leap into space, loose twigs and old leaves whipped into a panic. For the first time that year, he noticed a light green glimmering in the hedgerows. Overhead, birds were on the wing, prospecting for nesting sites. He sighed. Most of February had passed by without him noticing that the first signs of spring were afoot. He hoped that the woman and her story were still within reach, otherwise winter would have passed with the truth still no closer.

The woman he intended to visit was now elderly and infirm, but there would be no trace of compassion shown by him. No allowance made for old age, no politeness beyond that of an interrogator interviewing a suspect, sifting for secrets. He stuck the gearstick straight into third and the engine laboured as he pulled on to the road. His destination, a nursing home, was about ten miles further along the lough shore; however, it took about twenty minutes to drive there, traversing the bumpy roads, driving past slanting fields, braking hard at the corners and hidden crossroads.

In the clear light of morning, he thought again about Donaldson's death on the lough. Even though Pryce had been plaguing the former commander with her research into the past, it did not necessarily mean that his death was a direct consequence of her meddling. It might have been the conclusion of another set of events entirely, perhaps one that involved his domestic affairs. He thought about the empty feel to Donaldson's house, the sense that it was guarding a secret in his past.

The large three-storeyed nursing home overlooking the lough had once been a popular hotel in the time before cheap flights and overseas holidays, and a look of disuse had overtaken its façade. A flock of rooks was busy building nests in its high chimneys. Their rasping caws sounded half strangled and aggressive. This was the true accent of the lough-shore hinterland, thought Daly as he climbed out of his car, the kind of incomprehensible roar you once heard in the old fishermen's pubs. He nodded at an elderly man who had been pushed out in his wheelchair for a smoke, his head drooping like his cigarette. Inside, he found the nurse in charge and introduced himself. He explained that he wanted to talk to Dorothy Donaldson, the wife of his former commander.

'You're the first of her husband's colleagues to visit,' she remarked. She studied him for a moment. 'Were you a good friend of his?'

'No.'

'A pity. She hasn't anyone left to visit her since her brother passed away and now her husband too.'

'What happened to her brother?'

She thought for a moment before answering.

'A suicide. About a fortnight ago. He hanged himself in the family orchard.'

'What was his name?'

'Kenneth Agnew. He used to visit her all the time.'

He had thought he might have been seeing connections where none existed, but now he knew his hunch was correct. Donaldson had been protecting his wife and her link with the killers all along, and had tried to take the secret with him to the bottom of the lough. Daly felt the sense of apprehension he had been carrying around since Walsh's death intensify into deep dread. He followed the nurse down a silent corridor. He could imagine the advantages a nursing home might provide for someone hiding from the past.

'What's wrong with Mrs Donaldson?' asked Daly. 'I heard she had some sort of stroke.'

'Physically, there is nothing wrong with her at all. Her doctor says she has a form of hysteria. A silent hysteria. She hasn't spoken a word in six months. Shows no interest in anything and eats very little. She became a complete stranger to her husband overnight. He was at his wits' end before the doctor found a room here for her.'

'How does she keep up her silence?'

'I suppose she keeps her head in the clouds. Everyone gets a little like that with old age.'

Daly waited at her room door while the nurse entered. He heard her say loudly, 'There's an Inspector Celcius Daly here to see you.' There was a pause and then the nurse reappeared. 'Go on in, I'll be in the nurse's office if you need anything.'

The moment Daly crossed the threshold his sense of dread drained away. He smelled a strong odour of lavender almost overpowered by bleach and antiseptic. Propped with pillows in an armchair by the window, Dorothy Donaldson regarded him with a blank doll-like stare. She didn't have the haggard or ill appearance he'd been expecting. Her grey hair was finely brushed, her skin so pale it was almost transparent and curiously unwrinkled. A shadow-dweller, thought Daly, a ghost hiding from the light. She looked as though she had been pretty in her youth, but there was an emptiness now in her facial expression. Her sitting pose was elegant, but lifeless. Her hands clutched an old-looking teddy bear, as though it was the one toy she'd ever had. She didn't register his presence in any way; her only movement was the barely perceptible rise and fall of her chest.

Space was short in the room. Heavy furniture had been transported from her home, along with a complement of fringed lampshades, ornaments and framed photographs, which covered the dark surfaces of the furniture. Most of the pictures were of Dorothy, charting her journey through her wedded life. He saw that she was always wearing sunglasses, or her eyes were half-closed against the light, a hand raised to shade her face. The photographs were what had been missing from Donaldson's house, their absence making the place feel strangely empty for a married couple's home.

There was nowhere to sit, apart from her bed, so Daly stood in front of her. Through the window, he could see a small boat disappear into the dinge of a drizzly day on Lough Neagh.

He introduced himself slowly and carefully.

'I'm investigating a number of murders that took place in 1979 within the Armagh district,' he said. 'Including that of my mother. I have some questions I need to ask you.'

He detected a carefully veiled wariness in her eyes. He could tell she had understood what he had said. The corners of her mouth were dragged down by what at first he took to be sadness but now looked more like determination.

Why have you come here? her eyes seemed to ask.

'Angela Daly. Do you remember that name? From Maghery.'

A physical tremor appeared in her face. Was it the result of illness or a physical reaction to his question? Her mouth tightened into a puncture hole.

'She was shot dead by your brother Kenneth.'

Her chin lifted in defiance.

Daly mentioned the other victims of the murder triangle.

'I've been trying to find out what the common denominator was. What made these innocent people the targets of your brother's gang? Who supplied their details? And why?'

She turned away slightly and gazed through the window, at the watery murk of the lough. Then she rolled her eyes back at him.

'Their homes were important, weren't they? Their rundown cottages. Their dreams for a better future.'

For a moment, her hands clutched the teddy bear tighter. Daly noticed it and her hands went still.

'Someone in the background provided the gang with names and addresses.' He let the words settle for several seconds. 'Who do you suppose could have done something like that? If you don't tell me what you know, I'll find out for myself.'

Leave me alone, her eyes seemed to say. *Get on with your life.* Her frail fingers squeezed the teddy bear's arms.

'You can't dupe me with your act,' he said. He could hear the bitterness creep into his voice. Her silence felt like a provocation, an affront to justice. He saw that she had been preparing for this interrogation for years, building up her jaw muscles' strength to gag the tongue. The obstinate staring of her eyes. The silence that was like the din of a bell filling the room.

However, he was determined to break down her defences.

'I'm going to keep visiting you every day until you tell me what you know. I'm going to wait every day by your side until you tell me the truth.'

Her hands clawed at her teddy bear but her face gave nothing away.

'Your brother hangs himself. Then Ivor McClintock is shot dead. And now your husband drowns on the lough. Something is begging to be revealed.'

She cleared her throat with a little growl at the mention of her husband, but no words came out. She was locked into her muteness, he realized, as committed as a long-distance runner. A final marathon of unwavering silence. He could see that she probably had it in her to succeed. The toughness lying behind those pale eyes. The resolute line of her lips, the steadiness in her thin frame. She had said all she was going to say months ago. He could ask her questions all day and night, attempt to coax some utterance from her, uncover exactly what role she had played in the murders, but his efforts would be in vain. He had to hand it to her. As an experiment in hiding the truth it had worked so far. Retiring to this nursing home in silence. Waiting for entropy, for the truth to wither up and die. Wasn't that the irrevocable course of all things? From dust to dust, ashes to ashes; from that bright spring morning in 1979, his mother heading off to work, to this, an old woman dying in a corner of a nursing home.

'This story of yours is not going away, despite your silence,' he said.

He could almost read the unspoken words on her lips. *I'm dead already. What does it matter?*

He began moving around the room, examining the photographs, tantalized by the sense that he was missing something in them. Why had Donaldson been so careful to remove all trace of them from his house? Her eyes swivelled and focused on him with suspicion. He could sense her annoyance as he touched the pictures, turning them towards the light of the window. Perhaps he might be able to provoke an outburst. However, the closest she gave to an outcry was the lurch of her head as she followed his movements, and a rapid series of eye blinks.

One of the pictures appeared to be of her retirement day from the council. He studied it closely. Smiling officials presenting her with an award for long service. He saw the details of the department she worked in, her job title. A shadow fell over his heart, and with it a moment of insight. The haze that dimmed his vision of his father's humped fields and cottage lifted with an appalling clarity. He knew that he was looking at the truth, the same truth that had been hidden for years by the other ruinous cottages in the murder triangle.

He glanced back at the sight of Dorothy Donaldson staring at him and the photograph. Perhaps he wouldn't need to hear from her own lips the account of her role in the murders, after all. The secret lay much closer to home.

'Inspector Daly?' A voice disturbed him from his reverie. 'Are you OK?' It was the nurse.

'Yes, of course,' he said, turning, but that wasn't the truth either. 'I'm just leaving.'

He looked at the old woman one more time. The words came to him like a revelation. *She is trying to kill herself with silence. It's the perfect way out for her. Relentless silence. Losing contact with the world bit by bit.*

'Have you worked out why she won't speak?' asked the nurse.

'Yes.' They left the room together and walked down the corridor. 'Because she's afraid of the world discovering who she really was. She's simply holding out, waiting for death to complete her silence.'

35

Daly left the nursing home with more questions than answers. However, the most important one was the puzzle that had been haunting him since he first encountered Father Walsh's murder map. Why had someone directed that bloodthirsty gang to his mother? The question was like a box he'd been carrying around for years without knowing it. The box did not belong to any police investigation. It was his box, the burden of his family's past.

There was a small pier at the bottom of a footpath leading from the nursing home car park. He took a walk down to the lough shore. He was far away from cars and people now, the only sound that of the water lapping against the wooden jetty. The lough was full of light and waves but the land lay dark. He could see further along the shore where cattle had trodden the margins of the fields into quagmires. In places, clumps of earth lay crumbling in the water. In an attempt to slow the erosion, farmers had placed boulders and thick sleepers on the banks, but their efforts had merely channelled the water around the obstacles. More entropy, he thought. It was impossible to avoid or resist it. All around him, a shamed landscape slowly sinking into a restless lough.

The shore was almost a mirror to the society he had grown up in during the 1970s. Everything on the verge of capsizing into chaos. Two tribal communities on perpetual guard against anything that might threaten them, where stability, the status quo, was more important than anything else. A fragile society spinning around itself a protective web of denial, lies and cover-ups in a bid to keep from slipping over the edge.

In the distance, he spotted the outline of Coney Island. He thought of Hegarty and wondered if the old spy had found a sanctuary there. Last night, he had violated the most fundamental rule of police work in helping him escape the police checkpoint. In hindsight, he felt it was a mistake, one prompted by his shaken confidence in his police colleagues, but a professional error all the same.

What other mistakes had he made? he wondered. For a moment, he questioned his judgement about Dorothy Donaldson, but then he became convinced that he was right. She was the key link between the rogue police officers and their victims. He had to concentrate on finding the vital evidence that would prove this link before it disappeared forever. If he was correct, that evidence lay in two places: his father's back garden, and in a file somewhere in the council archives.

After a while, he walked up to the car and drove back through the labyrinth of lough-shore roads. As soon as he reached home, he ran from the car and into the back garden without bothering to change his clothes or shoes. He grabbed an old spade and ploughed into the nettle-infested banks at the bottom of the field. He cleared the weeds and began digging into the ground, as though his spade might hit upon the hard corners of the truth. Eventually his foot juddered as the spade struck something unyielding. He exposed the pale glint of concrete. He counted out about twenty paces, the average length of a bungalow, and began digging again. About a foot below the surface, his spade rang against another slab.

He found a sledgehammer in the shed and pounded the concrete, but it refused to break. It was at least a foot thick. He cleared more soil and watched the slab widen for several feet. He stopped, stood back, trembling with exhaustion. He attacked the northwest corner of the field and uncovered another concrete slab. Again, this one refused to break under the pounding of his sledgehammer.

He gave up and followed a path through the grass back to his car. Without thinking, he threw the spade into the back of the vehicle and set off. After several miles of driving, he parked his car outside the cottage of another of the murder triangle victims. He avoided the ruined house and hurried into the back garden.

The humps in the grass were his pointer. He tried to follow a straight line but the weeds were so thick and entangling that he lost his sense of direction. He thought of contacting a relative of the murdered man for guidance but then he realized the secrets of the rough ground had probably died with him. He picked a corner and began digging through the nettles and thistles. His knees almost buckled with the effort of clearing the invasive roots, gouging at them with the blade of his spade. He grabbed hold of them with his bare hands and loosened their hold. He went back to attacking the ground with his spade, only taking a breath when he hit a hard surface. He scraped away the soil and found concrete. He grunted with satisfaction. He counted out about twenty paces running south, just as he had done in his father's back field and began digging again.

It wasn't long before he encountered more concrete. He stood there motionless, staring at the patterns in the grass. He broke into a trot, criss-crossing the field in apparently aimless lines. In his mind's eye, he was able to draw a diagram connecting the spots where he had struck concrete. He had uncovered the concrete foundations of a bungalow that had never been built. Sweating but determined, he ran back to his car and sped off. A neighbour saw him leave and watched him with a puzzled stare.

He drove deeper into the townlands of Walsh's murder triangle. He stopped at the farms of several more victims. There was no one to stop or question him as he paced through the rough fields with his spade, trying to uncover the ungraspable outlines of the forgotten past. He groped around in the black earth of border country for the rest of the afternoon, striking concrete slabs at some of the farms, and finding nothing at the others but mud and a chaos of weeds.

Part of him wanted to drive to all the locations pinpointed on Walsh's map and dig up their humped fields, but he was too tired to complete that Herculean task. At about the tenth farm, he realized he had dug up and seen enough. He leaned his back against an old tree trunk. The afternoon grew cold, and his sweat made his clothes feel damp and chilly. He sank down on to the mossy grass, breathing heavily. He stared at the landscape of broken cottages, outhouses, craggy gables and gardens full of weed-covered banks where diggers had once piled the soil for the foundations of homes that had never been completed. For the first time he could clearly follow the fault line, the dislocation in a generation's dreams for the future, and the rotten inheritance they had left behind.

36

The schools had just opened their gates and Armagh town was full of running children and teenagers, faces babbling into mobile phones, figures with headsets sauntering in front of traffic. Daly drove cautiously through the busy streets, which were tinged with early spring sunshine. It was impossible to think that the terrible spectres of the past could touch this forward-looking town. Whereas the lough drew the haunted, the betrayed and the broken to its thorny shore, this part of the province had managed the trick of escaping the stranglehold of the past. An avenue of budding cherry trees led Daly towards a clean new building dappled with the light of a happier future. He had arrived at the headquarters of Armagh District Council.

When he asked to see the old planning files, the clerk at the desk frowned.

'Normally you have to apply in writing,' he explained.

Daly could barely conceal his impatience.

'This is related to an urgent police investigation.'

The clerk grumbled and led Daly down a set of stairs to a basement archive. Daly could sense his reluctance. Was he a stickler for protocol or just being lazy?

'What period are you looking for?'

'All the files related to 1979.'

'What is it you want to know about that year in particular?'

'I already know everything I need to know about that year.'

'You've come all the way here just to check something you already know?'

'Correct.'

The clerk shook his head and opened the door to the archive.

'You'll find all the planning decisions passed in the late seventies at the back.' He withdrew and went up the stairs. Daly walked between the aisles of boxes and folders. Darkness closed around him. He stood for a while without flicking on the lights. Then he found the switch and pulled up a chair.

Unlike many retiring police officers, Dorothy Donaldson had not cleared out her old files on the day she left her post as secretary to the chief planning officer. And unlike the remaining files in the police archive, none of hers had pages missing or redacted passages. After all, how could council staff have known they might contain such incriminating evidence?

An alertness came over Daly as he flicked through the pages of one dusty file after another. The amount of information he now had at his fingertips was a welcome relief compared to the evasion of Donaldson and the reticence of his wife. He spent an hour whittling his way through documents, reading the details of council meetings and the legal intricacies of planning committee decisions. As secretary, Dorothy had been responsible for recording the minutes of all the planning department meetings. Gradually the floor around him became covered in stacks of files.

There was a four-month period at the end of 1978 when her name disappeared from the list at the bottom of the minutes. Perhaps she had suffered some sort of mishap or illness. He began to wonder if he had been wrong in his assumption, but then her name reappeared at the start of 1979.

Several times, he stopped at the sound of approaching footsteps. He got up and looked down the empty aisles. The metal shelves rattled.

'Who's there?' he called out, but no one answered. A ghost, he thought, and returned to the files.

One by one, he examined the planning permission letters from that year. He lifted down a creased black folder with the word 'April' written across it. He sifted through the letters until he found what he was looking for. The file had his father's name on it and their address with a case number. He looked through the documents.

They included the architectural plans for a new bungalow and a site in the corner of the field behind the existing cottage. There were letters from Roads Service, the Water Board and the Building Control Department. More maps of the farm outlined where the water and electricity supply lines would go, the septic tank and a new access point on to the road. And then the planning procedure itself. Minor officials scratching along in their meticulous way, listing the number of objections to the planning proposal, fifteen in total from their neighbours, and some small alterations to the building to comply with fire safety regulations. A few paragraphs on the relevant planning law and then the decision stamped in bold red letters. *APPROVED.*

He looked up at the date of the decision, two weeks before his mother's death and then the line at the bottom: 'Decision to be ratified at the next monthly meeting of Armagh District Council, 2 April.' The date of his mother's death. The meeting had been scheduled for 7.30 p.m. After ratification, the council would send letters to the successful applicants informing them of the approvals.

So this was it. A single signature granting his mother and father planning permission for a new bungalow. Had that been enough to seal his mother's fate? He shook his head. He found more letters granting planning permission for other families of the murder triangle. All of them bearing the same red-inked word *APPROVED*, and the dates of the murders coinciding with that of the council meeting that ratified the decisions. How strange to see that word repeated again and again, and taste the high hopes it should have heralded. However, by the time the letters had landed on their appointed doorsteps, the dreams they promised were over and consigned forever to dark nettle-infested corners of fields.

The letters helped fill out the blanks in Walsh's murder map, moving it towards a state of greater coherence. A new pattern showed through the mesh of country lanes, not a complete one, for the map would never be finished. But it was as though it had been swilled in a bath of photographer's ink, allowing ghostly images to emerge, the bright new homes that had never materialized, the bereft families trapped in their cottages.

He could see how the murder gang had operated within the boundaries of the old Armagh District Council, following its triangular shape, driving up remote lanes with their loaded SMGs, to the farms and cottages of upwardly mobile families, young couples dreaming of a better future, planning new houses for their children, houses with proper foundations and insulated walls, tiled roofs and central heating, houses that would not sink back into the damp earth.

The fact that the murders had taken place on the first Monday of the month no longer seemed like a macabre joke by the killers. It was a conscious effort to communicate something to the victim's families, to keep an entire community alert and fearful. His mother would have been alive at the time the decision was passed, but dead by the time the letter arrived on their doorstep. Apart from the chief planning officer, Dorothy Donaldson would have been the only person with prior knowledge of the planning approvals. It must have been she who divulged the dreams of these families to the murder gang, passing on their addresses in that short band of time before the decisions were made public knowledge. In the warped logic of the gang, it must have seemed that families like the Dalys were advancing themselves dangerously, encroaching on their Protestant neighbours, stirring up the mean little jealousies Father Walsh had written about, raising the old spectre of the native Irish rising up from bog and mountain to cast aside the colonial invaders.

Daly sat gazing at the stack of files. For some reason he felt reluctant to leave. Eventually, he lumbered to his feet. He felt weary. It had been a busy day of revelations. His father had been exposed as a man of secrets, but also a man of flesh and feeling, the father of a son who still had to make his way in a dark world full of unpleasant surprises, a boy who innocently collected car registration numbers without realizing they might have made him the carrier of a plague, the shadowy violence that visited home after home in the murder triangle. He realized how thankful he should feel towards the old man, for holding his silence and allowing him to grow up untainted by anger and bitterness. He was grateful for that at least. He removed half a dozen of the letters from the file, folded them up and placed them in his jacket pocket. He reassured himself that he had found the most probable reason why the gang had targeted his mother, but somehow he still felt marked by guilt and uncertainty.

The receptionist at the front desk smiled at him sympathetically.

'Would you like a cup of tea, Inspector?' she asked.

'No, thanks.' His tongue had almost dried in his mouth. 'I should be on my way.'

He drove straight to the nearest post office and dropped the letters in an envelope. He sealed it and wrote an address on the back: 'Jacqueline Pryce, c/o The Belfast Mail'. He gave no details about the sender or any explanation about the contents. He posted the letter and drove home, back to the edge of the hidden world. There was still enough light in the day to do one last thing.

37

It was almost dark when he drove down the winding road that led to the mouth of the Blackwater River. He got out and walked along the banks. No one was about. The water had darkened to the colour of the blackthorn thickets. He wanted to make sure that Hegarty had made good his escape, and headed straight for the secret berth of the fisherman's boat.

He was surprised to see its dark hull just visible beneath a clump of willow and alder branches. It hadn't moved from its hiding place. He felt nervous, and looked all around him, his mind alert for signs of danger. The only sign that the spy had been to the boat was a letter Daly found underneath the seat boards. It was addressed to him.

Dear Celcius,

I have decided not to take you up on your kind offer of a few days' vacation on Coney Island. This tale of the murder triangle is yours, not mine, and I've interrupted it long enough, so I will slip away quietly rather than be a further hindrance to you.

You are an intelligent man, and I'm sure you will work out a way to save the truth from darkness, from your father's silence and the death of all those who took their secrets to the grave. Afterwards, you will decide the best thing to do with the story, whether it should be made public or passed on to a higher authority to investigate. I hope that I have been of some assistance to you in your search for the truth.

I know it is not easy to dredge the past, but you must not give up. Remember, too many stories are never told or are lost along the way. Who knows how many stories are hidden in people's hearts? One thing I am certain of is that their time will not pass, in spite of all the silence and cover-ups, since there is always someone who knows something, and the truth, no matter how twisted or incomplete, has the strength to filter through the tightest of defences.

For my part, I can no longer keep secret my forty-year career of lies and betrayals. I have decided to write my own story. When I am finished, I will send it to you and you can decide if it is part of the tale you want to tell.

Rest assured, by the time our stories are told, the Northern Ireland we grew up in will be finished. Whatever this country was during our childhoods, it is already disappearing. The paramilitaries terrorizing families with their Semtex and Armalites, and the garrison towns with their fortified police stations and army bases. It is all ending. Those violent men who murdered and bombed, and the shadowy figures who orchestrated the cover-ups, their day is almost over.

Carefully, Daly folded the letter and placed it in an inside pocket. Deep in thought, he walked along the bank and then back again. He should have foreseen Hegarty would disappear like this. The old spy was a maverick, a man of contradictions, and unlikely to follow a path that had been charted by anyone else, let alone a police detective. Daly stood there for a while, unable to force himself into thinking or acting like a detective. He was still the bewildered son of a murder victim, rather than an investigator solving a three-decade-long mystery on a contentious political stage.

The wind picked up and the water around the boat grew restless. He stared at the distorted reflections. He caught glimpses of sky, the broken outline of the boat and his silhouette, shifting in the ripples like the elements of a teasing puzzle. Hegarty had made the most of his hospitality and left, deceiving everyone, disappearing back into his informer's world of shadows and fragments, another mystery to lurk in the margins of border country. He hoped that the spy would not try to make contact with him again. Already, he had allowed himself to be influenced too much by Hegarty's thinking. The spy belonged to that group of men more interested in chaos than symmetry, intent on complicating their untidy pasts, their cover-ups and betrayals, sowing confusion and intrigue rather than understanding and closure.

He thought of his father and his life-long refusal to speak the truth. That had been a cover-up, too. It occurred to Daly that the real reason he had undertaken the investigation was not to solve the riddle of his mother's death, but to understand the mystery of his father's silence. He had resisted concluding the investigation because that meant no longer hiding in his father's reticence, his absent frown, his discreet way of trying to make tragedy disappear, which had been his gifts to his only child, gifts that proved more troublesome than countless family arguments and interrogations.

However, he had listened to that silence long enough. Hegarty was right. If he was going to match his father's strength of character he would have to start speaking about the past. He would have to carry the truth to a bright place, and somehow carry himself there, too.

He looked all around him. He felt conspicuous and exposed standing at the riverside. He pulled the collar of his jacket around his neck and walked back to his car. Before climbing in, he listened to the noise of the wind stirring the new buds in the willow and alder trees. The evening sky seemed very pale after the darkness of winter. Something else occurred to him. An image floated before him without any direction from his consciousness. For a moment, everything seemed clarified in his mind's eye. He saw his mother's face, bright and happy, sinking back into the spring growth. He wanted desperately to hold on to that image, to hear her voice once again. What a blessing that would be, but she was slowly sinking out of sight, flowers and budding leaves growing in a network of lines that enlaced her face, blossom upon blossom overlapping until all that remained were the watchfulness of her eyes and her smile. This was the final symmetry, he thought, the nearness of the dead amid the continuing signs of life.

ABOUT THE AUTHOR

Anthony Quinn is an Irish author and journalist. Born in Northern Ireland's County Tyrone, Quinn majored in English at Queen's University, Belfast. After college, he worked a number of odd jobs—social worker, organic gardener, yoga teacher—before finding work as a journalist. He has written short stories for years, winning critical acclaim and, twice, a place on the short list for the Hennessy Literary Awards for New Irish Writing. His book *Disappeared* was nominated for the Strand Critics Award for Best Debut Novel, and *Kirkus Reviews* named it to their list of 2012's Top 10 Best Crime Novels. Quinn also placed as runner-up in a Sunday Times food writing competition.

Silence is Quinn's third novel featuring Inspector Celcius Daly. Quinn continues his work as a journalist, reporting on his home county for the *Tyrone Times*.

MYSTERIOUSPRESS.COM

Otto Penzler, owner of the Mysterious Bookshop in Manhattan, founded the Mysterious Press in 1975. Penzler quickly became known for his outstanding selection of mystery, crime, and suspense books, both from his imprint and in his store. The imprint was devoted to printing the best books in these genres, using fine paper and top dust-jacket artists, as well as offering many limited, signed editions.

Now the Mysterious Press has gone digital, publishing ebooks through **MysteriousPress.com**.

MysteriousPress.com offers readers essential noir and suspense fiction, hard-boiled crime novels, and the latest thrillers from both debut authors and mystery masters. Discover classics and new voices, all from one legendary source.